CLEMENTINE AND RUDY

SIOBHAN CURHAM

WALKER
BOOKS

First published 2020 by Walker Books Ltd
87 Vauxhall Walk, London SE11 5HJ

2 4 6 8 10 9 7 5 3 1

Text © 2020 Siobhan Curham
Cover illustration © 2020 Grace Lee
Cover typography © 2020 Jan Bielecki

This book has been typeset in Berolina

Printed and bound by CPI Group (UK) Ltd, Croydon CR0 4YY

British Library Cataloguing in Publication Data:
a catalogue record for this book is available from the British Library

ISBN 978-1-4063-9023-0

www.walker.co.uk

This book is inspired by and dedicated to all of the activists, artists and creatives striving to make this world a better place. Keep on blazing your trail. . .

"We never know how high we are
Till we are called to rise;
And then, if we are true to plan,
Our statures touch the skies."

Emily Dickinson

RUDY

Tyler says that if you listen closely enough, everything has a soundtrack. He says that we're so obsessed with what we see we've forgotten how to hear. Tyler says a lot of weird stuff like this and normally, I'm like, *Yeah, whatever...* before drowning him out with a hiss from the coffee machine. But now his words have come back to haunt me; now they *are* my soundtrack, along with the thumping bassline of my pulse.

I can't remember a time when I wasn't dreaming about this moment – or practising for it. Whenever I've dreamed about it I've felt high with excitement. So why, now, do I feel sick with fear? That's the thing about dreams, though. They exist in safe little bubbles inside our heads. They only become scary when we try to make them real.

A distant yell cuts through my thoughts. It's the middle of the night. The middle of a *Sunday* night. But this is Brighton. The city that never sleeps, not even on a Sunday. Not properly anyway. On a Sunday night Brighton's like one of those old people you see dozing off on the bus or park benches. Jolting awake every few seconds.

The sickness in my stomach grows. *What if I get caught? What if I get arrested? What if I end up in jail?* A picture of me languishing in an overcrowded cell flickers into my mind. Me and ten tattooed women, built like fridge-freezers. And a cockroach running up my leg. Sometimes having a warped imagination can be a Very Bad Thing.

I reach the entrance to the alleyway and stare down into the gloom. *I don't have do this. I could just go back home.* But I know that if I back out now I'll spend the rest of the week beating myself up for being a tragic loser. I pull my woolly hat down so far it's almost covering my eyes and step into the darkness.

I know exactly where I'm going – to a wooden door halfway down. I discovered this alleyway weeks ago. It seemed like the perfect place for my first time. Tucked away off the main road, with no passing cars. And hopefully no passing people. I glance up and down at the amber glow from the streetlights at either end. What made it seem like the perfect place in the daylight is now seriously freaking me out. It's like a set from a movie – in the scene where the hooker with a heart of gold gets brutally murdered by her psycho pimp.

I glance up and down one more time. The coast is definitely clear. But the longer I stand here, the more chance there is of someone coming along. I have to do it now or not at all. I slip off my backpack and put it on the floor. I take out the old paint tin and prise off the lid. Then I get the brush, load it with wheat paste and slap it on the door. I'm not exactly sure where the door leads. Someone's backyard maybe? The main thing is, it's clean and smooth. The perfect canvas.

Once I've covered a big enough area with paste I put the brush down. The sick feeling in my stomach turns to excitement. I take the picture from my backpack and unroll it. My fingers are trembling so much I hang it at a slight angle. *Crap!* I try to straighten it but the paper starts to crinkle. I'll have to leave it. I dunk my brush into the paste again and coat the paper all over. Done.

I decided to do a paste-up for my first-ever piece, as it's quicker and lessens the chances of my nightmare jail-cell-cockroach scene coming true. I take a step back and admire my work. For a moment, I'm not Rudy Knight, random teenager standing in a grotty Brighton alleyway; I'm Rudy Knight, internationally renowned urban artist, gazing proudly at one of my masterpieces on the side of some iconic building … in New York maybe. I hear what sounds like a footstep from the end of the alleyway. *Shit!* I shove the lid on the paste and stuff it and the brush into my backpack. I glance in the direction of the sound, preparing to run. A fox is silhouetted scrawny and black against the amber light, its ears pricked, its tail trailing on the ground. I breathe a sigh of relief so deep I swear it takes every last molecule of oxygen from me.

Tyler says we all have an animal guide watching over us, protecting us from harm. Maybe my animal guide is the urban fox. I take a can of black spray paint from my bag and give it a quick shake. The rattle is amplified by the silence – or maybe it's fear that makes it seem so loud. I quickly add my tag to the paste-up. Then I hoick my backpack over my shoulder and jog towards the street. It's only when I'm down by the sea that I realize I forgot to take a photo. I gaze out across the water. It's so dark I can't tell where the sea ends and the sky begins. I breathe out and my breath appears like a cloud in the freezing air. It doesn't matter that I didn't get a photo. What matters is that, tonight, I finally took my dream from my head and made it a reality. Tonight, I officially became a street artist.

CLEMENTINE

INT. KITCHEN – DAY

It's early Monday morning. **CLEMENTINE** *(15 but longing to be 18 so she can escape the hell that is her home life) and her brother,* **DAMON** *(8), sit at the granite-topped breakfast bar in their immaculate kitchen.* **CLEMENTINE**'s *mother* **JULIA** *(40 but in huge denial about that fact) rushes into the room. She looks as perfect and expensive as her kitchen – but don't let that fool you...*

JULIA   Clementine, have you had any breakfast?
                  Damon, why aren't you dressed?

DAMON *ignores his mother and continues creating a sculpture out of soggy breakfast cereal.* **CLEMENTINE** *stares into space, wondering if it's possible to die of longing.*

JULIA   Damon! Stop playing with your food.
                  Clementine, did you hear what I said?

"Yes. Sorry." I snap back to reality. My English homework this weekend was to write a scene from my home life in screenplay form, as if it were a scene from a movie. It's been surprisingly therapeutic – especially when you live in a house like mine, with a family as dysfunctional as mine. It can really help to pretend that it isn't real; that it's all just something that's been imagined up for the silver screen. Certificate DD (for Deeply Disturbing).

Mum opens the fridge and a takes out a bottle of green juice. Then she slams the bottle back into the fridge and takes out a huge block of cheese. I look at the clock on the wall. It's almost seven-thirty.

"Where's Vincent?" I ask. I refuse to call him Vinnie like everyone else does, on principle.

"Vincent isn't here," Mum says curtly, hacking off a chunk of cheese.

Uh-oh. Mum only calls him Vincent when he's been horrible to her. She's been calling him Vincent quite a lot lately.

Damon finally stops playing with his cereal. "Where is he?"

"At work." Mum fills the cafetière with water.

I take a moment to ponder this latest development. Vincent went to London yesterday to go to a football match with his friends. He was supposed to be back in time for dinner but called Mum to say there was a "problem with the trains". There was no problem with the trains that I could see when I checked the Network Rail website. I wonder if Mum checked it too, and if he stayed in London all night. I was up till gone midnight, writing poems for my Instagram and I didn't hear him come in. I don't have many memories from when Mum left Dad for Vincent but one thing I do remember is Dad yelling at Mum, "If he's cheated on his wife, he'll cheat on you too!" I was only five years old at the time so I thought Dad was talking about some kind of game; like Vincent had put a hotel on one of his Monopoly properties when his wife wasn't looking or something.

Mum takes a pack of croissants from the cupboard. "Do you want one?"

I don't. I've already had toast and fruit but Mum is obsessed with what I eat. She's always saying I don't eat enough – even though I eat loads. And when I do eat loads, she gets all up-tight about how I never put any weight on and how unfair it is. Apparently, she just has to look at a bar of chocolate and she puts on a kilo. She's always on some kind of diet or working out like a maniac. According to an article I read in *Cosmopolitan*, I think she might have "projection issues" – as in, she's project-ing her issues all over me.

"OK. Thanks."

She puts a croissant on a plate and hands it to me. Then she takes one for herself, along with a piece of cheese. The worst thing about her obsession with shrinking herself is that it's all to keep Vincent happy. To keep him, full stop. I look at the framed black and white print of him staring down at us from the kitchen wall, taken when he was a big radio presenter back in the nineties. Back when his hair was still naturally brown and he didn't look ridiculous in skinny jeans. Mum had the exact same picture on her bedroom wall when she was a teenager and he was her idol. I try not to think about this if I can help it, as it feels seriously creepy. They didn't actually get together till she was in her twenties and working as a producer on his radio show but still… I look at Vincent's cocky grin and grimace. While Mum's been obsessively trying to lose weight, he's grown a paunch and an extra chin.

"Did Vincent come home last night?" I'm in a constant battle between not wanting to upset Mum and wanting her to wake up and see how unfair her situation is.

"Yes." Mum sits down opposite me but she avoids making eye contact, fiddling with her thick diamond-encrusted wedding band instead. "He – he had to go in early to have a meeting with his producers – about the show."

Vincent is still a radio presenter. He seems to think this makes him Boss of the Universe, even though his glory days are long over. He used to present the breakfast show on the biggest radio station in Britain. Now he presents the early-afternoon show on a local station and he does the voice-over for the most annoying commercial ever, for a beer called Brewer's Dog, catchphrase: "Its bark is worse than its bite, all right! WOOF!" According to Mum, Vincent changed jobs because he wanted to be around for us more when she had Damon but on Wikipedia it says he was fired from the breakfast show after turning up late and drunk for work three times in a row. I know we're not supposed to believe everything we read on Wikipedia but Vincent being more of a drunkard than a family man I *can* believe.

INT. KITCHEN - DAY

JULIA *looks at* **CLEMENTINE**, *then looks pointedly at*
CLEMENTINE's *croissant, as if she's waiting for permission to*
eat her own. **CLEMENTINE** *takes a huge bite, even though her*
anger is making her feel sick.

RUDY

I hate Mondays because I have to work for two hours at the café before going to school. But this morning, when the alarm on my phone goes off, I actually wake up with a grin. And trust me, this *never* happens on a Monday morning. I have a quick shower, shove my school uniform in my bag and put on my café uniform of black T-shirt and skinny jeans. I dab some oil on my hair, then pull it back from my face with my skull-and-crossbones bandana. I'm feeling pirate-style badass today, now that I'm an urban artist and all. Before I head for the door I grab my latest So Dark Fairy from my desk and apply some glue to the back.

I started making my So Dark Fairies a few years ago, when Mum sent me to this crappy art camp in the community centre on our estate over the Easter holidays and the woman running it told us girls to "draw some pretty fairies". In case you haven't figured it out yet, I'm not exactly the pretty-fairy type, so I drew a fairy dressed in black, with a Mohican and the tattoo of a cobweb on its face. This did not go down well at all. The woman running the camp emailed Mum to say she was concerned an eleven-year-old would draw something "so dark" and thought I might have some "unresolved anger issues". This, in turn, ended up triggering Mum's own "unresolved anger issues", AKA her infamous hot-headed temper, and she stormed down to the community centre and accused the woman of being a "*bleep*ing judgmental *bleep* who had no *bleep*ing right to accuse her daughter of having issues." (It's way too early on a Monday morning for all that cursing.) I spent the rest of the holiday hanging out in Tyler's flat, drawing an entire family of "so dark" fairies and I still draw them to this day. They're my comfort art; something I do when I want a quick creative fix but I don't have the time or energy to work on something bigger. My latest So Dark Fairy is inspired by Tyler. Thin, with long hair and rocking out on an electric guitar, his wings covered in musical notes.

I creep down the hallway past Mum's bedroom. Mum works in Russian Roulette, a casino down by Brighton Marina, which means she doesn't get home from work till around three or four in the morning, so she'll have only just gone to sleep. I let myself out of the flat and scour the harshly lit corridor for somewhere to stick my fairy. It needs to be somewhere Tyler will see it so I head to the stairwell. Tyler lives in a flat on the top floor of our block, or as he likes to describe it: the Penthouse Suite. (As well as being a musical genius, Tyler is next level when it comes to irony.) I put the Tyler fairy just above the skirting board by the door inside the stairwell. My So Dark Fairies are only about four centimetres tall but I know Tyler will spot his because he's always on the lookout for them. I started sticking them in random corners around the estate about a year ago, when I realized that I wanted to be a street artist but didn't have the guts to do it properly. I only put up about one a month but people seem to like them. No one's taken them down yet and someone even wrote, *SICK!* in black marker by the one I put up in the corner of the lift. My first-ever art review.

As I head towards the North Laine part of Brighton I think of my picture on the door in the alley. My baby is now out there all alone, unprotected. I hope people like her. *Who cares what people think?* I tell myself as I check my reflection in the guitar shop window. But it's hard not to care. I pour so much of myself into my artwork, it's like my blood is mixed in with the paint. I adjust the collar on my leather jacket and look down at the flashes of brown through the rips in my jeans. Whenever I wear these jeans Mum tells me off for showing too much skin. To which I always say, "Er, hello?" She claims she has to wear short skirts in the casino – it's part of the job description. Knowing that makes me even more determined to only ever work for myself. There's no way I want people telling me what I can and can't wear. I know I have a job at Kale and Hearty but that's only while I'm at school. And anyway, Jenna and Sid aren't like proper bosses – they're all about freedom of expression. Sid even has a tattoo saying *BORN TO BE FREE* on the inside of his arm. I turn right down Sydney Street. It's only half past six but it's already starting to bustle with the first of the commuters heading to the station. Trev, the fruit and veg man, is standing outside the café by a pile of crates. Tyler and I have this theory that Trev is half man, half vegetable, as his cheeks are as shiny and red as a pair of tomatoes and his body is as lumpy and round as a giant potato.

"Morning," I say as I walk past him.

"All right, Rudy, love," he says. "I've got some right tasty spinach for you lot today."

"Yay!" I immediately feel bad for sounding sarcastic. I became a vegetarian after I got the job here because Jenna made me watch this really gross movie about thousands of cows being crammed into a shed like sardines in a tin and after that I was like, *OK, pass the plants*, but even so, I'm just not that fussed about food. I can't get excited by a vegetable, no matter how organic it might be. I let myself into the café. Nirvana is playing through the speakers in the ceiling, because Tyler begins even earlier than me on a Monday, but for once I don't care that he's got his grungy rock playing. I'm way too excited about what I've got to tell him.

"Hey, Rudy!" Jenna calls from one of the tables at the back, where she's putting out the breakfast menus. Her short bob, which was scarlet the last time I saw her, two days ago, is now bright turquoise. "How are you?"

"Great, thanks. Like the hair."

Jenna smiles. "Thank you. I wanted to try and brighten up February."

I grin. "Mission accomplished. Where's Tyler?"

"In the kitchen, helping Sid make banana bread."

"Cool." I let myself behind the counter and enter the kitchen.

The warm air smells of a delicious mixture of banana and cinnamon. Sid's peeling potatoes at the counter and Tyler's washing dishes at the sink, his long dark hair pulled up into a man bun, showing off his fresh undercut. Three freshly baked loaves of banana bread are cooling on a rack on the table. I take off my coat and put on a clean apron.

"Hey, Rudy!" Tyler calls when he sees me.

"Morning!" Sid says. "Any sign of Trev out there?"

I nod. "Yep. He's just arrived, with some killer spinach apparently."

"Ace!" Sid's eyes light up like I just told him Santa's outside with a sack full of presents. As Kale and Hearty's head chef and vegetarian-in-chief, he gets stupidly excited about fruit and veg. "Better go and pay him." Sid puts down his peeler and heads outside.

"Well?" Tyler's brown eyes are wide with expectation.

"Well, what?" I say, even though I know exactly what he's asking.

"Did you do it?"

I nod before going over to the counter by the industrial-sized fridge. On Monday morning it's my job to prep the salads.

"No way!" Tyler comes over and high-fives me. I notice that he's added even more leather bracelets to his thin wrist. "Did you take a picture?"

"I forgot. A fox made a noise in the alleyway and scared the crap out of me. But don't worry. I'm going to go back this evening and take one."

"What was it like, doing it?"

"Awesome. And you know I don't use that word lightly."

Tyler grins. "I didn't think you used it at all."

"Exactly."

He flings his arms round my shoulders and hugs me. "I'm so proud of you, Jedi sis."

"Thanks, Jedi bruv."

Tyler and I became each other's honorary bruv and sis years ago, to make up for the fact that we don't have any actual siblings. We became *Jedi* bruv and sis when Tyler got all obsessed with the Star Wars movies – and passed his obsession on to me. In every other way, though, we're like chalk and cheese. I'm black, he's white. I like hip-hop, he likes nineties rock. I like real world entertainment, he's obsessed with video games. I like thriller movies, he likes sci-fi. I love art, he loves all things sound. But the one thing we have in common is our dream of making a living from our passions. In my case, making art; and in his, being a sound designer on movies. We're constantly pushing each other to find the courage to fulfil our dreams, or "feel the force", as Ty likes to put it.

Tyler takes off his apron and hangs it on the back of the door. As always, he's wearing black jeans and a vintage rock T-shirt. Today's choice, faded Guns N' Roses. "Right, better get ready to feed the starving millions," he says with a grin. Tyler's worked full-time in the café on an apprenticeship since leaving school last year at sixteen. He said he didn't want to stay on at sixth form because the education system is obsessed with "turning us all into robots and killing our creativity". But even though I agree with him, I know that there's more to it. Tyler's mum has MS and his dad lost his job last year. I think he had to leave school for the money.

"OK, Jedi bruv," I call back as he heads into the café. "May the force be with you."

CLEMENTINE

In my favourite Emily Dickinson poem, she talks about hope being like a bird, perching inside our soul, singing endlessly. As I hurry out of school at lunchtime I try to conjure up the image of a hummingbird hovering inside me. But although it's opening its beak, it's making no sound. I'd hoped that things would be better after the Christmas break. But, a month in, they feel even worse. Everything about school seems old and tired. Especially my friendships. I'm not sure if I've outgrown my friends or they've outgrown me but one way or another, we just don't fit together any more. All they want to do is talk about their boyfriends – when they're not hanging out with their boyfriends. I don't have a boyfriend. I like to tell myself that this is totally out of choice but the truth is, no boy has ever asked me out. On the positive side, I've never met a boy I wanted to go out with. None of them match up to my dream boyfriend.

My dream boyfriend is called Luc. He has dark floppy hair and big soulful eyes and he writes poems and lives in an attic apartment in Paris, above a bakery. He spends his weekends browsing secondhand bookshops, eating cheese and freshly baked bread and *flâneuring*. *Flâneuring* is one of my favourite words and pastimes. It originated in Paris and it means strolling around with no particular place to go, simply watching the world go by. I love watching the world go by. And so does Luc. When I finally meet him, we will spend entire days flâneuring – when we're not browsing secondhand bookshops. The thing I love most about my dream boyfriend is that he's genuinely interested in me and he encourages me in my passions for dance and poetry. I so hope a boy like this actually exists because it seems to me that as soon as a woman enters a relationship, she has to shove her true self away in a closet like an embarrassing dress. My so-called best friend, Becky, is a classic example. I say "so-called" because I hardly ever see her now that she's going out with Justin. She's always watching him play rugby, or round at his house playing *Call of Duty* on the PlayStation. Becky always hated rugby. She said it was just an excuse for guys to grope each other and they ought to go get a room. And as for *Call of Duty*... Becky's family are Buddhists and she won't even tread on an ant because of karma issues. Now she's shooting up Nazis and terrorists online just to keep Justin happy. She used to spend all her spare time going to the cinema or plays or musicals with me. Has Justin ever once gone to something like that with her? No. Because it's all about him, just like Mum's marriage is all about Vincent.

I hurry up the hill, heading for the alleyway that cuts from Hove to Brighton. I need an injection of Brighton buzz to keep me going through the afternoon's lessons. It's only when I'm halfway down the alley that something stops me dead. A picture has been stuck on one of the doors. It's of a black girl with a huge Afro, dressed in an emerald-green catsuit, gazing into a gilt-framed mirror. Although she's been drawn by hand, the mirror is a black and white photo, its frame painted over in gold. I vaguely remember doing something like this in art class. I think it's called mixed media. Although the girl looking into the mirror is muscular and slim, her reflection is so bloated it almost takes up the entire frame. It's like one of those distorted mirrors you get in a fairground that make you look crazily fat or short or tall or thin. But I don't think this woman's in a fairground. I think the distortion is coming from her mind. I grab my phone from my bag and take a couple of photos. Already, words are sparking to life in my mind. Once I've got a photo I'm happy with, I hurry from the alleyway and head down to the sea. I sit on the first empty bench I find and open Instagram on my phone. I find a filter that most clearly defines the lines of the drawing and makes the gold of the mirror-frame shine, then I click into the description box. Sometimes I'll have a piece of street art on my phone for weeks before I can find the right words to accompany it. Others come straight away, as if they were just waiting for me to find their picture. This is one of those times. I type the poem into the box, make a few tweaks, then add the usual hashtags: **#brightonstreetart #urbanart #streetarteverywhere #micropoetry #poetsofig**. I'm about to upload the post when I realize I haven't credited the artist. I study the photo and see a tag sprayed in black at the bottom. It says, FIERCE. I add a couple more hash-tags — **#fierce #fiercestreetart #fiercestreetartbrighton**. I don't know if the artist is from Brighton. I definitely haven't seen any of their work before. I make a mental note to look out for more, then I press SHARE.

I feel the same release I always do when I've published a post. Like the tension inside me has been turned down a notch or two. I lean back on the bench and stare out at the sea. I love the beach in winter and how the icy wind strips it clean of tourists and I can pretend it's all mine. I watch as the slate-grey waves slide in and out, in and out. Things may seem as if they're never changing but they are. Time keeps ticking and a larger, invisible tide is pulling me towards the life I'm meant to be living. The hummingbird inside me starts to sing.

RUDY

"Hey, baby girl!" Mum calls from the kitchen as soon as I walk through the front door.

I read my mum's greetings the way other people read tarot cards. From every greeting I can tell what has happened in the recent past and what is about to go down in my future. "Hey, baby girl" means that Mum's had at least one glass of wine, she's spent the day with her Idiot Boyfriend Dave, and I'm about to get a hug and probably a kiss.

"Hey, Mum." I come into the kitchen and drop my backpack on the floor.

On the iPod dock Ray Charles is singing about taking these chains from his heart; two empty frozen pizza boxes are sitting on the counter, along with the usual chaotic jumble of Mum's books and make-up and magazines. The air smells of burned cheese. I make a mental note that "Hey, baby girl" might also mean ruined dinner. Mum comes over and gives me a hug and kisses me on the cheek. Her hair smells of Dave's aftershave and her breath smells of wine. Just call me Psychic Suzy.

"How was school?" Mum sits back down at the table and

starts fixing her make-up. She always wears loads of make-up to work – extra-long eyelashes and glossy red lips. She says it's her mask, so the customers don't get to see the real her. She says only God and Jesus and I get to see the real her, which is probably the only time I'll get to be part of a holy trinity.

"It was OK." I go over to the oven and open the door. Once the cloud of smoke has cleared, I see two blackened pizzas smouldering on the shelves. I quickly take them out and plonk them onto plates. A piece of charred cheese hangs mournfully from one of them like a teardrop. I mentally sketch a black teardrop in my mind. Nice. Something to try later, maybe. "Dinner is served – or should that be *cremated*?" I say as I place the pizzas on the table.

"Oh, whoops!" Mum giggles as she applies a coat of cherry-coloured lip gloss. "I wasn't that hungry anyway. Dave and I had kebabs at lunchtime."

Can't beat a kebab for romance. Mum might think that the sun shines out of Dave's butt and he's *quote* "the kindest man I ever met" but I'm pretty sure he's a kebab-munching loser. And when it comes to being a poor judge of the opposite sex, Mum has most definitely got previous.

Mum clicks open her purse and hands me a five-pound note. "Here, take this. Go and get a burger or something."

I shake my head. "It's OK. I ate at Kale and Hearty."

Mum gives a sarcastic snort. She doesn't really get the whole vegetarian thing. When I told her I'd stopped eating meat she gawped at me like I'd told her I'd started eating human babies. "Well, keep it in case you get hungry later."

"OK. Thanks."

Mum's phone bleeps. She picks it up and giggles. "Dave's so funny," she sighs, like a love-struck kid.

Yeah, he's so funny till he dumps you like all the others did. "I think I'll go to my room," I say. "I've got some homework to do."

"OK," Mum replies, tapping away on her phone.

I don't actually have any homework, but I'm dying to get stuck into some of my own work. It's weird because although I'm taking art at school we're always told exactly what to do and my work doesn't feel like my own. I feel like I have to hold back, like I need to do the right thing to get the right marks so I can eventually go to university. *If* I go to university. I'm not even sure about that any more. Sometimes I think the only reason I want to go is so I can get away from here. I follow the narrow hallway down to my bedroom at the end of the flat. As soon as I enter the room I hear the thumping beat of the upstairs neighbour's music pounding through the ceiling. I feel so trapped here, in this block of flats, in this life. I dump my bag on my bed and kick off my trainers. I lay my sketch pad on the floor and turn to my work-in-progress. Unlike my last one, this one's a self-portrait. Self-portraits are my form of therapy. So far I've sketched a picture of me tied to a chair. When I create the final piece I'm going to use a photo I took of this really cool antique dining chair I found in Snooper's Paradise and I'm going to stick a cross of black tape over my mouth. I think of the idea I had earlier, inspired by the burned pizza, and add a black tear to my face. It looks great.

"I'm off to work, sweetheart," Mum calls from the hall.

"OK. Have fun." I used to hate the fact that Mum worked at night, but that was when I was younger and I didn't realize that I could turn it to my benefit. That was when I still got creeped out by random noises around the flat, convincing myself that there was a psycho killer hiding under my bed.

I wait until I hear the front door close. Then I go to the window and listen for the *click-click* of Mum's heels on the pavement. She walks through the glow of the streetlight, spine straight and hips swaying, as if she's on a catwalk. "Never forget that you're a queen," she always used to say to me, when we had girls' nights on the sofa doing our make-up or nails. It used to make me feel great when she said this, like she and I were some kind of superheroes and could do anything. But now I'm older, and I've seen the crap she's put up with from her boyfriends, it makes me sad. It's like she didn't quite believe the words she was telling me were true for her too. I watch until she disappears round the corner then I go over to my wardrobe. It's big and ugly and made of dark, scuffed wood that doesn't even look good in an ironic or "vintage" way. Mum got it from a clearance sale. She got most of our furniture from a clearance sale. She had next to no money when Dad left and less than no money when the guy after Dad left, as he disappeared with the widescreen TV and all of Mum's savings. I grab hold of one side of the wardrobe and start shuffling it into the room. The wall behind is covered in a rainbow spectrum of paint. Mum would go nuts if she knew but I need somewhere to practise and I'll just paint it magnolia again before I move out. I take my paints from my wardrobe and put on my oldest tracksuit bottoms and hoodie. Then I flick through the playlist for *Jazzmatazz* by Guru, pop a stick of gum in my mouth, put on my headphones and smile. Finally, I'm in the zone.

CLEMENTINE

My bird of hope ended up carrying me all the way through the rest of the day at school – even when Becky turned down my suggestion of a hot chocolate on the beach because she had to go and help Justin buy some new trainers. It's only when I sit down for dinner that hope's song starts to fade – drowned out by Vincent's annoying voice.

"Did you hear that new feature I did on the show today, babe?" he asks Mum as he shovels a load of pasta onto his plate. "The one about the worst dates."

Mum shakes her head. "No, I didn't listen to the show. I was too busy."

Vincent snorts. "Busy? Doing what?"

Lately, Vincent keeps making digs about Mum not working. Even though he was the one who insisted she give up her job when she had Damon.

"I was busy cleaning this place," Mum replies, her face flushing beneath her immaculately applied make-up.

I glance around the dining room, at the perfectly arranged flowers on the side and the sparkling chandelier creating pools of gold in the sheen of the polished table. The more time Mum spends polishing this place to perfection, the more her personality seems to disappear, as if she's rubbing it away too with her cloth.

"Right," Vincent replies. "Well, some bird rang up and said that this geezer asked her to smell his earwax – on their first date!" He snorts with laughter and Damon starts to giggle. I feel sick. I've always got on well with Damon but what if Vincent brainwashes him into becoming a miniature version of him? Surely it's my big sisterly duty to try and save Damon from the evils of misogyny.

"Hey, Vincent. The 1970s just texted. They want their sexist language back."

Vincent looks at me blankly. The bags beneath his eyes and wrinkles on his forehead make his dyed brown hair look even more ridiculous. Ditto the leather string with a pendant saying DUDE around his neck. "What do you mean?"

"I mean, calling women birds."

"That's not sexist. How is that sexist? Calling someone a bird isn't a bad thing. It's an affectionate thing." Another annoying thing about Vincent is that he speaks with the twang of an East London gangster, even though he was born in Berkshire and went to private school.

This is why you shouldn't have bothered saying anything, my inner voice of reason says. *There's no way you'll ever get him to change.* I decide to ignore reason, which I'm aware is never the advisable thing to do, but I'm too angry now to wind myself in.

"I can honestly say I don't know any woman or girl who likes being called a bird."

"Oh, for God's sake," Vincent snaps. "This is exactly what's wrong with this country. All this PC bullshit."

"Vincent!" Mum looks pointedly at Damon.

"What? Oh, come on, Julia. Don't you go all militant on me too. It's like living with a bunch of feminazis."

"What's a feminazi?" Damon asks.

"A woman with no sense of humour, son."

"I've got a sense of humour," I say.

"Do you know what, I really don't need this." Vincent pushes his plate away.

"It's OK, darling. Clementine didn't mean to be rude, did you?" Mum looks at me.

What the hell? "I'm not the one being rude."

Vincent gives a sarcastic snort.

"Now, Clem, let's just all have a nice dinner together." Mum's voice is shrill. She turns to Vincent. "So, did the new feature go down well?"

The frown on Vincent's face fades. "Yeah. Very well. The listeners loved it." He looks straight at me.

I stand up. "I'm going to my room. I've got loads of homework to do."

"But you've hardly eaten a thing." Mum studies my plate.

"I'm not hungry."

Vincent gives a theatrical sigh and shakes his head.

"Oh, come on—" Mum starts.

"Let her go," Vincent cuts in. "At least the atmosphere will improve."

I look at Mum. Is she seriously going to let him get away with this?

"OK," she says quietly, prodding at a pasta shell with her fork.

I'm so angry I can barely see as I stumble from the room and upstairs. It's so unfair. Even though he's the one who treats her like crap, I'm the one who gets the blame. As I march into my bedroom it takes everything I've got not to slam the door. I'm not playing into his stupid "feminazi" theory. I lie on my bed and push my fists into my eyes to fight the annoying urge to cry. Once it's passed I take my phone from my pocket. I think about WhatsApping Dad but there's no point. It's not as if he can do anything to help. Dad moved to Berlin three years ago, after marrying Ada, a German woman he met through work. Now I only get to see him on school holidays. Ada is expecting a baby in June. I try not to think about what this might mean for Dad and me.

An Instagram notification flashes up on the screen. I click on it and see that my earlier photo-poem has got a load of new likes. I know that being obsessed with social media is like being some kind of crack addict, hooked on dopamine hits, but right now I need this. I need the validation that I *am* good at something. That my words mean something. That maybe, just maybe, they'll help me to escape.

RUDY

The thing I love most about art is how I lose myself in it. When I start to paint or draw it's like I've wandered deep inside a labyrinth, where nothing else matters and anything that's been stressing me out fades away and all that's left is the picture; all that *counts* is the picture. It's gone midnight when I finally stop working. I've pretty much got all of the separate pieces done. Now it's just a case of layering them together, but I'll do that tomorrow when tiredness isn't making me feel dizzy. I move the wardrobe back and put my paints away. Suddenly I'm starving. I go to the kitchen and make myself a mug of ginger tea and hunt around the cupboards. Unfortunately, Mum doesn't like shopping. OK, scrap that. Mum *loves* shopping, if it's for make-up or clothes or accessories so sparkly they blind you when they catch the light, but shopping for food? Forget it. I find a box of mince pies left over from Christmas that are just inside their sell-by date and a solitary satsuma.

I take my festive midnight feast back to my room and start scrolling around on my phone. Tyler says that social media is dumbing us down, hashtag by hashtag, but I say that it's all in the curation. If you only follow who and what you want to see, it's all good. I use my private Instagram account to follow urban artists, so for me social media is all about inspiration. Case in point: my hero, a French urban artist named Miss.Tic, has just posted a new photo. It's of one of her famous stencilled women, standing beside a black cat. The words *"Je ne gris pas que les cœurs"* are stencilled in Miss.Tic's distinctive red script at the side of the picture. French is one of the classes where my brain goes missing in action so I put the words into Google Translate. It comes up as *"I do not gray that hearts"*. Hmm. Maybe I should pay more attention in French, as I'm pretty certain that can't be right.

I wish Miss.Tic would one day do a piece with the words in English. So often the meaning of her pieces get lost in Google-translation. I scroll on down and a photo comes up under the hashtag **#streetartbrighton** that makes my hackles rise. It's of a huge woman's backside, and the woman is wearing the tiniest G-string. The artist has sprayed his tag across one of the butt cheeks like a tattoo: LADZ. Looking at the picture makes me feel sick. It makes me want to grab one of my cans and head into Brighton and spray *DEATH TO THE PATRIARCHY* on the other butt cheek. But I'm way too tired so I keep on scrolling. Then I see something that makes my heart practically beat its way out of my ribcage. Someone has posted a photo of my picture! I blink hard to make sure I'm not seeing things. But it really is my picture on Instagram. It's been posted by a profile called **@SpilledInk** and they've written something in the description box alongside it.

In the hall of mirrors made by the media
In the lens of lies created by your fear
Your reflection is bloated beyond recognition
While the real you shrinks and your dreams disappear.

What the hell? Not only have they posted my picture, but they've really understood it. I'm not sure what to do with this information. I call Tyler. He's always up until at least 3 a.m. playing video games but the call tone rings and rings. Finally, he answers. Thankfully, I can hear music playing softly in the background so I know he can't have been asleep.

"Hey, Jedi sis. You OK?"

"Yeah. Something really cool just happened."

"What, cooler than me just winning *Fortnite Battle Royale*?"

"Er, yeah, if that's a good thing?" Tyler's gaming-speak is like French to me. "Someone's posted a photo of my street art on Instagram."

"What?" Tyler turns off his music.

"I found it just now on my feed."

"But how…?"

"They used the Brighton street art hashtag. It's one of the ones I follow."

"You're kidding? Oh my God, you're Insta-famous. Like that family of eejits who all begin with 'K'."

"Hardly." I laugh. "But whoever did it has written a poem to go with it."

"OK, now that is cool."

"I know, right. I'll show it to you tomorrow in the café."
I get into bed and pull the duvet up over me.

"Great. So, how was school?"

"Like being in prison. It's so crap now you're not there."
Although Tyler was two years above me, we always hung out
together at break times. Not having him there any more has
introduced me to a new brand of lonely.

"I wish I could say the same but…" Tyler laughs.

"How was it at the café?"

"We did a roaring trade in green juice and smoothies. I guess
everyone's still on their post-Christmas detox."

I look at my pack of mince pies. "Ha! Not me."

"Me neither. It's February, the month of the year where joy
goes to die. Now is not the time to starve ourselves of comfort.
So, what are you going to do about this Insta-poet then? Are you
going to contact them?"

"What? No! What would I say?"

"You could tell them that it's your picture, thank them for
writing the poem."

"Oh, no, I don't think so."

"Why not?"

"It feels a bit cringe."

"Ah, I see. You're going for the enigmatic urban artist look."

"Something like that." I yawn. "I suppose I'd better get some
sleep."

"Lightweight."

"Yeah, well, we can't all survive on four hours' sleep a night."

"I don't just survive. I thrive."

"Yeah, yeah. I'll remind you of that in the morning."

Tyler laughs. "Night, Jedi sis."

"Night, Jedi bruv."

I put my phone on my bedside table and close my eyes. But my thoughts keep sparking like matches in the darkness. Somebody posted a photo of my work under the **#streetart-brighton**. Now it really is official – I'm an urban artist.

CLEMENTINE

After a night of stress dreams about Mum and Vincent I wake up feeling more tense than I did before I went to sleep. But I'm determined not to have another day like yesterday. I get out of bed and put on my Spotify "Dance the Crap Away" playlist. I close my eyes and take a deep breath, as if I'm inhaling the melody. Then I stretch my arms. As the beat gets faster and I start to loosen and shake out my limbs, I shake out the tension and the grogginess of sleep. Then I move my attention to my feet as they start tracing the rhythm. None of it matters, I tell myself. Not Vincent. Not Mum. Not school and the fact that I appear to have outgrown my friends. One day I'll be out of here and free from it all. I start dancing my way into my dreams. An attic flat in Brighton, with a view of the sea. A room full of old books and vintage typewriters and antique furniture, every object containing its own story, instead of the soulless new furniture that Mum insists on filling the house with.

I open my eyes, take in the immaculate white walls and the immaculate white furnishings, all carefully arranged for symmetry. Mum says this house is her full-time job. She pours all her energy into creating a living space that's flawless, but I can't help thinking it's her way of trying to hide the mess that lies beneath. I close my eyes again. Spin in a pirouette, trying to spin my way back to my dream…

I'll live on my own in my attic flat but it will always be full of a colourful cast of characters, creative friends who really understand me. And my loving and totally supportive boyfriend, Luc, of course. They'll always be welcome and they'll never have to take their shoes off for fear of ruining the carpet. I won't have a bland cream carpet for a start. I'll have an antique carpet in deep, rich colours and an assortment of cosy rugs. I'll have a black chandelier hanging from the ceiling and red candles dotted around the room in old wine bottles, the wax trickling down the sides and—

"Clementine, what are you doing?"

I halt, statue-still, at the sound of Mum's voice. She's standing in my doorway, wearing her pink satin dressing gown, not a perfectly straightened hair out of place. Sometimes I wonder if she even sleeps at all, for fear that rolling over in the night might make her messy.

"Just practising," I say, quickly turning off the music. "For the auditions at dance class this evening." This is only partly a lie – we do actually have auditions for the summer show this evening.

"Oh yes." Mum nods thoughtfully. "Can I come in?"

I frown. Mum never normally asks. She normally just barges. It's been the source of many an argument recently. "OK."

I sit down on the bed and Mum sits next to me.

"I'm sorry – about last night."

She never normally apologizes either. Maybe I'm still in bed and dreaming. "Oh, uh, that's OK."

"Things are a little difficult at the moment – with Vincent."

"Right." The tiniest nib of hope pokes its way into my mind. Mum is never normally this forthcoming about things with Vincent.

"Anyway, I'm sorry I snapped at you."

"That's OK."

Mum starts fiddling with the belt on her robe. "It's just that he's under a lot of pressure at the moment."

"Why?"

"The figures for his show are down. Way down. He had a meeting with his bosses last week and they've told him he has until March to turn things around."

"I see." I know it's wrong to take pleasure in another's pain but I can't help feeling a twinge of satisfaction at this news.

"So, if you could be extra patient with him I'd really appreciate it."

I want to yell at Mum for always putting his feelings before everything but then I see how tired she looks; how the lines around her eyes look so deeply etched without her usual mask of make-up. "Of course."

"Thank you." She hugs me. As always she smells amazing. Expensive. Her lotions and potions bought, like everything else in this house, by Vincent. I wonder if this is why Mum puts up with his crap – because she's reliant on his money. "I'll go and make you some breakfast. Do you fancy a bagel?"

"Sure."

As soon as she's gone I pick up my phone. I need my early morning dopamine fix. There's an Instagram notification. I click on it: "**@FierceUrban** and **27 other people** liked your photo." **@FierceUrban**. Could it be? A shiver of excitement runs up my spine. I click on the link but the profile is set to private and there's no profile pic. They have no followers so I click on the list of people they're following. They all seem to be street artists. Hmm. So **@FierceUrban** could be a street artist themselves, or they could just be a fan of street art and it's a coincidence. Let's face it, Fierce isn't exactly an unusual word, there's no proof it's the artist. But what if…?

RUDY

One time, when I got caught trying a cigarette with a couple of other kids behind the bins, Mum sat me down and gave me a talk about the importance of not just *knowing* the difference between right and wrong but making sure I *did* the right thing – no matter how tempting doing the wrong thing might be. *But what if you genuinely don't know what the right thing to do is?* This question hangs above my head like a comic-style thought bubble as I stare up at the picture by LADZ. Objectifying women like this is definitely wrong. But does that make what I'm about to do right?

"*Two wrongs don't make a right,*" Mum's voice echoes round my head. But surely a wrong left unchallenged is even more of a wrong? Before I can get myself any more confused I quickly glance up and down the street. LADZ had added the location to his picture so it was easy to find – a narrow back street full of lock-up garages, tucked away behind a warehouse. Thankfully it's deserted, the only sound the screech of seagulls and the distant hum of Brighton traffic. I take my can from my bag and give it a shake. Check the street once again – left and right – take

47

off the lid and start to spray. Even though the butt cheeks are enormous, there's not quite enough room to paint DEATH TO THE PATRIARCHY, so I spray on a pair of shorts instead, in denim blue. I check the street once again. It's still deserted, so I get my can of black paint from my bag and spray a back pocket on the shorts, with my FIERCE tag like a brand logo. Then, just to make sure that LADZ gets the point, I spray DON'T OBJECTIFY WOMEN beneath the butt cheeks. I take a step back and grin. Even though I've probably just broken all kinds of unwritten street art rules, it definitely feels like I've done the right thing. I hurry off to catch the bus to school.

Here's an interesting observation I've made about school … when you genuinely don't care any more about the cliques and the bullies and the rules about what's cool and what's not and who's got a crush on who, they stop caring about you too. You have to genuinely not care though, it's no good talking the talk if you're still crying yourself to sleep every night.

When I first started at Kemptown High I really cared who liked me. I'd watched so many high-school movies and had such high hopes of finding a friendship group who really got me. But all I found were girls I had nothing in common with and boys who were seriously immature. So I ended up hanging around with Tyler, even though he was two years above me. My refusal to hang out with kids my own age got me labelled as one of the "weirdos" and I'd be lying if I said that didn't hurt at first. But then, about a year ago, I genuinely stopped caring and decided to see my so-called "weirdness" as a superpower.

Just like Beyoncé did with her alter ego, Sasha Fierce, I created a butt-kicking alter ego, Lightning Girl. I started out by drawing pictures of her, then slowly, I changed myself to match, growing my Afro and getting my piercings, painting a silver skull and crossbones on my DM boots. And as soon as I'm old enough I'm going to get a lightning bolt tattooed on my wrist.

The funny thing is, it turns out there's an interesting kink in the school "weirdo spectrum", when you become so different from the norm you're actually deemed cool. Now, people talk to me like they want *me* to like *them*. Now, as I walk in late to my art class, my fellow students look up at me and smile. And not in a mocking way but in a *Oh, hey. Late again? What are you like?* kind of way. The trouble is, I still feel like a jigsaw piece that's been shoved back in the wrong box. I don't fit in here and I never will.

"Thank you so much for being kind enough to join us, Rudy," my art teacher, Ms O'Toole, says, but there's a twinkle in her eye as she says it. Ms O'Toole is one of the nice teachers, one of the ones who genuinely seem to care about their students. She's really old, like at least fifty, but she's not judgy at all.

"You're welcome," I reply.

"Today, we're doing still-life drawing," she says, pointing to an apple that's been placed on the table in front of me.

An apple-shaped piece of me dies inside.

"I'd like you to focus particularly on the light and shade."

I nod but already I'm falling into a stupor.

I take the sketchpad from my bag and open my pencil case.

I look at the apple. It's not even red and shiny like the poisoned apple in *Snow White*. It's an insipid pale yellow. I imagine taking a photo of it and painting a maggot crawling out. A zombie maggot with a skeletal head. I start sketching the outline of the fruit. It looks exactly how I feel, dull and uninspired.

"Is everything OK, Rudy?" Ms O'Toole asks as she comes to stand beside me. She's wearing a pair of her trademark dungarees and her glasses are perched on top of her cropped grey hair.

"Yes, why?"

"You're late again. Remember what we said about your lateness last month?"

I have a flashback to Ms O'Toole warning me that my grades were going to suffer if I didn't start making it in on time for my lessons.

I nod. The truth is, it isn't my time-keeping that's the problem, it's being made to draw boring pictures of boring fruit all the time. As if I don't get enough fruit and veg at Kale and Hearty.

Ms O'Toole looks over my shoulder at my pad. I know what I've drawn is bad. And I know it's not her fault, she's just teaching us what she's told to. Like Tyler says, we're all part of the giant sausage machine, even the teachers.

"Is there any way I can make a mixed-media piece featuring the apple?" I ask her hopefully.

She shakes her head.

I sigh.

"You have to learn the rules first if you want to break them well," she says.

"Why?" I become aware of the other students around me prickling to attention.

"It's all about honing your technique. When you've mastered the basics you're able to challenge them far more powerfully."

I look at the apple. I truly don't get how drawing it is going to help me with the art I want to make. I want to draw people not fruit.

"Stop thinking of it as an apple," Ms O'Toole says, as if reading my mind. "Focus on the light and shade."

"OK." I lean back on my stool and stare at the apple, chewing on the end of my pencil. The harsh glare of the strip light above is shining right on it. I take my science textbook from my bag and prop it beside the apple, partially blocking the light and causing the apple to cast a weird elongated shadow on the table. Now, it's starting to look interesting. I start tapping my foot to an imaginary hip-hop beat and all of a sudden the entrance to the labyrinth comes rushing up to meet me.

CLEMENTINE

Every Tuesday after school, I go to performing arts school.
I know it's probably most people's idea of hell attending after
school – but I love it. Or at least, I used to. Over the past few
months the emphasis has shifted away from enjoyment to getting us all "exam- and audition-ready", which has made things
slightly more stressful. Even so, the two afternoons a week
I spend at the Dana Roberts Performing Arts Academy are the
closest thing I've got at the moment to living my dancing dream.
As I make my way along the seafront I inhale lungfuls of cold,
salty air and exhale the boredom and frustration from my day.

The Academy is in what was once a grand old hotel between
Palace Pier and Brighton Marina. The main building is on the
promenade overlooking the sea but last year they built a dance
studio on the beach. The wall of the studio facing the sea is
entirely made of glass. The first time I danced there, looking at
my beloved sea, I thought I might burst I was so happy. I hurry
along the narrow path from the promenade to the studio entrance. Twilight is rolling in and the beach is deserted. I go into
the reception area and poke my head round the studio door. As

usual, I'm the first to arrive. My teacher, Bailey, is playing some of her favourite trance music while she sets up and the studio smells of geranium and patchouli. Bailey is a great believer in the power of aromatherapy and she likes to "cleanse the space before we dance". She's from California.

"Hey, Clem," she calls when she sees me. "You all set for the audition?"

"Absolutely," I say but as soon as I do, fear begins nipping at me. I've tried to tell myself that this show isn't a big deal, that it doesn't really matter if I get cast or not but I was lying. Actually, having a show to focus on and rehearsals to lose myself in over the next few months will be a sanity-saver.

"Remember what I said to you before the Christmas break," Bailey says. "Lose the stiffness, let your true self shine."

"OK. I will. Thank you."

I go to the toilets and into a cubicle. I pull off my school uniform and get into my vest top and lucky leggings. They're my lucky leggings because I wore them in my street dance exam last year and passed with distinction. Just as I'm coming out of the cubicle the toilet door crashes open and Jody and Abby come in. Jody and Abby go to a high school in Kemptown. I feel like maybe they think I'm stuck-up because I go to a private school. Scrap that. I *know* they think I'm stuck-up because I overheard them talking about me one day in the toilets. "That Clementine so thinks she's better than us," Jody had said. "Yeah, it's like she can't even lower herself to talk to us," Abby chimed in. I'd sat frozen and mortified in my cubicle, wishing there was some way I could flush myself down the U-bend. The truth is, I'm not stuck-up, not at all, I just find it hard to make conversation with people I don't know. I wish shyness didn't so often seem so close to arrogance.

"Hey," I say cheerily as they walk in. One of my New Year's resolutions was to try and prove them wrong and get them to be friends with me. Or be friendlier to me, at least. One month in, and I'm still trying.

"All right," Jody says, but her voice is full of suspicion.

Abby meets my gaze in the mirror above the sinks and nods almost imperceptibly.

"All set for the audition?" I say, determined not to be beaten.

"Yeah," Abby says, but her voice is full of defiance, like I'm asking a trick question.

"That's great," I say, dropping the final "t" in *that's* to try and make me sound more street, which I'm aware probably only makes me sound more pathetic.

Jody turns to Abby. "Can I borrow your lip balm, babe? I left mine in my locker."

My body smarts from the rejection. *I told you you shouldn't have bothered*, my inner voice goads. *Now you just look more stupid.* I go back into the cubicle and lock the door. I press my burning cheek to the cold wall. Why does life have to be so difficult?

"Oh my God, look at my left eyebrow!" Jody shrieks. "It's got a mutant hair growing out of it."

"Oh my God, it's, like, three centimetres long!" Abby gasps.

I flush the toilet and visualize it taking all of my stress with it. I need to relax. I need to get in the right mindset for the audition.

I go over to the sinks, where Jody and Abby are now in a collective meltdown about the mutant eyebrow hair. As I wash my hands they look through me as if I'm invisible.

When I go back into the studio most of the class have arrived and it's buzzing with laughter and chatter. I find a spot by the glass wall overlooking the sea and I do a couple of stretches to ground me. *Don't let anyone silence you / speak speak speak / through your lungs and your heart and your feet.* The words start dropping into my mind as soon as I start warming up. This always happens at dance class. There's something about moving my body that frees my mind. I can't be thinking about poems now, though, I have to focus on the dance.

A hush falls as Dana Roberts walks in. Her shiny raven hair is pulled back into a tight bun and she's wearing a scarlet leotard and a long black skirt. Dana Roberts is the founder of the Academy and a former dancer with the Royal Ballet. She's inspiring and terrifying in equal measure.

"OK, people," Bailey calls. "Let's begin."

RUDY

It's 12:27 at night and I'm in Tyler's bedroom. I've been obsessively watching his digital alarm clock ever since I got here about three hours ago.

"I reckon we should go now," I say.

"Are you sure? Is it late enough?" Tyler pauses the movie we've been watching, *Return of the Jedi*. An image of Princess Leia looking nervous but determined freezes on the screen. I know exactly how she feels.

"I think so. If it's still too busy out we can wander around till it quietens down."

"Are you sure you don't want to watch the Sarlacc battle one more time for motivation?"

"Seriously, Ty, if I watch that scene one more time I'll be strangling Jabba the Hutt in my sleep!"

Tyler laughs and gets up from the bed, checking himself in the mirror on his wardrobe door. As usual, he's wearing black skinny jeans and a vintage rock T-shirt, The Clash this time. He pulls on a black hoodie. "Do I look OK? Should I be wearing a balaclava or something?"

"We're only going to make some art, bruv, not rob a bank."

Tyler shrugs. "All right, all right. Just wanted to check the urban art etiquette. This is all new to me."

"Yeah, well, it's all new to me too." I get up and put on my jacket. I notice Tyler's brainstorming notepad open on his desk. REASONS TO KEEP BELIEVING is written in his spidery scrawl across the top of the page.

"What's this about, Ty? Don't tell me you're losing your faith in the force."

He shakes his head and his cheeks flush. "No. It was from this YouTube video I was watching. One of those motivational ones, you know, where a dude's vlogging from his garage in LA just so he can get his bright yellow Ferrari in the back of the shot."

"I thought we vowed never to watch those kinds of videos."

Tyler gives a sheepish grin. "I know but I was desperate."

"What? Why?" I feel a stab of concern. I hate the thought of Tyler feeling anything other than his normal super funny and positive self.

He sighs. "I don't know, it's just that sometimes my dream life feels so far away from my real life, you know. Even with doing all my shifts at the café, I don't know if I'll ever be able to afford a proper mixing console."

"You will." I take hold of his arm and give it a squeeze. "Trust me, you're so talented. You just have to believe."

"Thank you. That's exactly what Trey Masters said."

"Trey Masters?" I look at him quizzically.

"The YouTube guy with the bright yellow Ferrari."

"Oh my days! Come on, let's get out of here."

We head down to the seafront, then I lead Tyler up a darkened side street just past the new pier. The street is full of restaurants but they all closed hours ago. The only sign of life is a homeless person curled up beneath a duvet in one of the doorways. I feel a sharp twinge of sorrow as I think of how cold he must be.

"Where were you thinking of doing it?" Tyler whispers.

"Just up here, on this wall." I lead him over to a large wall at the end of the street. It's the back of a theatre and, with no windows or doors, it makes a great canvas. One half is covered in paste-ups by one of my favourite Brighton street artists, Dynamite. As I look at his work I feel a stab of nerves. Should I be pasting on the same wall as him? This is another aspect of urban art etiquette I'm not sure about. Would it be like some upstart pub band crashing the stage at the O2 when Jay-Z's playing?

"You OK?" Tyler says, able as always to read my every mood with his spooky Jedi mind powers.

"Yeah, I'm just not sure if I should do it here."

"Why not? It's perfect."

"Yeah, but it's right by that." I point to Dynamite's work.

"So? I think yours will look great next to it."

"Are you sure?"

"Yeah." He takes hold of my arm. "Come on, sis, it's time to feel the force."

I give a nervous laugh. "OK then." I glance quickly up and down the street. It's still completely deserted. "You keep watch. Let me know the second you see or hear someone."

I take my picture from my backpack and carefully unroll it and hand it to Tyler. Then I prise the lid from my pot and start slapping paste all over a patch of the wall. Laughter echoes up from the seafront and my stomach does some weird kind of backflip.

"Someone's coming," Tyler whispers.

"Give me the picture, quick." I grab it from him and stick it to the wall. Once again, in my rush, it goes on slightly uneven. The voices and laughter get closer. *Crap!* "Quick." I grab Tyler by the hand and pull him into a darkened doorway. "Let's wait here till they've gone past. I still need to do my tag."

"And we need to get a photo of it, remember?" Tyler whispers.

The voices get even louder and Tyler holds me.

"What are you doing?" I hiss.

"Making it look like we're making out," he hisses back. "We don't want to arouse suspicion."

"We don't want to arouse *anything*," I say and we both crack up laughing. Tyler and I are so like brother and sister the thought of anything happening between us is truly gross. He's right, though: kissing couples in Brighton doorways totally blend in.

The people walk past and their voices fade away to nothing.

"Right, quick," I say, barging past Tyler with my paste can. I quickly coat the picture, then I take my spray paint from my bag and start stencilling the final touches, being careful not to spray over the edges of the card. When that's finished, I do my tag.

"Awesome!" Tyler exclaims behind me. I turn and see that he's taking photos on his phone.

"None of me," I say.

"I only got your back. It looks really cool. You're just this shadowy figure."

I check his phone. He's right. It does look really cool. The light from the top of the building is spilling down on the picture, illuminating it perfectly, but I'm in the shadows, a darkened silhouette. It makes me think of the apple in art class earlier and the really cool shadow it created on the table.

We stand there for a second looking up at the picture.

"I just got a funny feeling," Tyler says, "in the pit of my stomach."

"What did I say about getting aroused?" I joke.

Tyler laughs, then he turns to me. "It's this," he says softly, casting his arm around at the picture and me and the darkened street. "It's like you've finally made it. You've actually started to live your dream."

I link my arm through his and pull him close to me. "Don't worry, bruv. It'll be your turn next."

CLEMENTINE

I wake to the sound of Mum and Vincent having an argument. Annoyingly, they're arguing just loud enough to wake me but not loud enough for me to be able to hear what they're saying. I creep over to the door.

"Kids ... time ... unfair..." I hear Mum say.

"Yeah well, one of us has to earn a living," Vincent's voice gets clearer as he passes right by my door.

My skin prickles with anger. Why does he keep picking on Mum for something he made her do?

"I ... children ... agreement." Even in an argument Mum remains contained. She somehow manages to raise her voice without actually raising it. I wonder what would happen if all of her pent-up tension erupted one day. I hope it doesn't happen inside our perfect show home, as I have a feeling it would be seriously messy.

I hear the front door slam and leap over to my window. Vincent is pacing down the street towards the seafront. He's wearing a brand-new tracksuit and trainers. He started running recently, which I'm using as further evidence that he's having a midlife crisis. Previous evidence includes his buying a two-seater sports car and dyeing his greying hair with something called Man Up.

I go back over to my bed. I wonder if it's possible to have a pre-life crisis. It definitely feels as if I might be having one. My life hasn't even really begun and I have no clue what to do. I sit cross-legged and rub my aching feet. After my initial nerves faded last night I took Bailey's advice and really let go and lost myself in the music. It was so cool dancing so close to the sea. Even though it was pitch black outside, just knowing it was out there was enough to calm me. I know I gave the audition my best shot. Now I just have to wait and hope that I'm cast in the show. *But what if you're not? What if you're not good enough?* my inner voice whispers, like some kind of cartoon bad guy.

I pick up my phone, in need of a distraction. As soon as I check my Instagram I feel a flutter of excitement. "**@Fierce Urban wants to send you a message**" one of my notifications reads. I click ACCEPT and open the message. It's a photo. In it, a shadowy figure is standing in front of a wall displaying a piece of street art. The picture is slightly obscured but I can make out the face of a young black woman in the painting. I zoom in on the photo. There's what looks like tape in a cross-shape over her mouth and a jet-black teardrop on her cheek. Although the woman in the picture is different from the one in the piece of art I saw yesterday, there's no doubt that it's by the same artist. I zoom back out. It's impossible to tell if the figure standing in front of the picture is male or female. All I can see is that they're dressed in black, with their hood up. They're holding something in their left hand. It looks like a spray can. A shiver of excitement runs up my spine. It must be the artist. And **@FierceUrban** must be their Instagram account. Then I see that they've written something beneath the photo in the message: Over to you...

Over to me? Now I'm properly excited. Is this some kind of challenge? Do they want me to write another poem? But I'd need to get a clear photo of the artwork to do that. I'd need to see the whole thing. I scan the message for any mention of a location but there's nothing. Then I notice a splash of colour in the corner of the photo, the edge of another piece of street art that looks really familiar. I click onto my profile and start scrolling through my pictures until I find it. It's a piece by a Brighton street artist called Dynamite, a picture of a refugee kid blowing bubbles in the shape of peace signs. My skin tingles as I wrack my brains trying to remember where I saw it. I have a feeling it was when I was on my way home from dance class one night, down one of the side streets that cut up from the sea. I check the time on my phone. Thanks to Mum and Vincent's argument it's still really early. But I'd never have time to get down to that end of the seafront and back unless...

I quickly pull on some jogging bottoms, a hoodie and trainers. As I race out of my room I almost crash into Mum on the landing.

"Oh, Clem, you're up early." There are dark rings under her eyes.

"Yes, I, uh, thought I'd go for a jog."

"A jog?" She stares at me like I just announced I was off on an expedition to the moon.

"Yeah, I won't be long, I just fancy getting a bit of exercise. My legs are really stiff after yesterday."

"OK then. Vincent's gone for a run too." Mum gazes numbly into space. "I'll start getting breakfast ready then. Do you fancy a sausage sandwich?"

"Sure." I hurry past her and down the stairs.

RUDY

Wednesday is "Breakfast with Mum Day". I don't mean it's one of those official days that comes with its own hashtag, like **#TakeYourDogtoWorkDay**, but in our flat at least, it's official. Last year, Mum started stressing that we weren't getting enough quality time together, what with my school and café job and her shifts at the casino. So, having breakfast together on a Wednesday has become a non-negotiable. The trouble is, we're always both so tired on a Wednesday morning that to call it "quality" time is definitely questionable.

While Mum makes the coffee I slump over the table. I didn't get back home last night until two and then Tyler ended staying for about half an hour, nagging at me to contact the poet. Mum will be even more tired than me though, as she didn't get in till almost four in the morning and hasn't even been to bed yet.

"So, what's new, baby girl?" she asks, sitting down opposite me.

"Not much really. In art yesterday we had to draw an apple."

"An apple?" She raises one of her perfectly sculpted eyebrows.

"Yeah. I asked if I could paint a zombie maggot coming out of it but my teacher said no."

Mum lets rip with one of her belly laughs and pats me on the shoulder. "Oh, Rudy, I don't know where you get your dark sense of humour."

There's a beat of silence — a beat too long, as we both think of the most likely suspect: my dad. Walking out on us on my first day of reception class certainly took a warped sense of humour. As if I hadn't been traumatized enough, left alone in a classroom full of noisy kids for the day, coming home to find my dad gone definitely made it a day to remember. Maybe that's why I've always had a problem with school. Maybe deep in my subconscious it's forever linked to parents going missing.

"Is everything else OK?" Mum asks.

"Sure." And for once, I almost mean it. Everything isn't OK but it feels as if maybe it could be. I think of what Tyler said last night, about me finally living my dream. That's how it felt to me too. Even though I'm such a newbie when it comes to my street art, and even though I'm still making rookie errors because of my nerves, like not hanging my pictures straight and spraying over the edge of the stencil, at least I'm on the right track, at least I've started. I only wish Tyler could find a way to get properly started on his sound-design dreams too.

"That's great." Mum taps her diamanté-studded nails on the table and I realize there's something she wants to tell me. Something she's too nervous to. This does not usually bode well.

"Is everything OK with you?" I raise myself from my slump and study her face.

"Yes, yes, everything's fine!" she exclaims, a little too brightly.

"Cool."

The kettle stops boiling and Mum leaps up. "I was wondering..." she says, with her back to me.

"Yes...?"

"How would you feel if Dave moved in?" She stands motionless, waiting for my response.

But my brain seems to have frozen too. I can't think of a single thing to say to this very worst of all questions.

"We've been together almost six months now, it feels like the right time, the right thing to do." Mum remains facing the kettle.

My brain kicks back into life with a flurry of "but"s. *But you and I have been together fifteen years... But he's an idiot and he's bound to leave you.*

"And it would really help us out financially." Finally, Mum turns to look at me.

"I can work more shifts at the café if we need more money."

"No!" Mum frowns. "I don't want you working any more than you already do. You've got your GCSEs to think about."

"I don't care about them." I shrug.

Mum comes over to the table. "Well, you should. Don't you understand, Rudy? Those exams are your ticket out of here. If you pass them you can do your A levels and then you can go to university." She says all this like it's a good thing. She has no clue that what she's just described sounds like a death sentence to me.

"I want to be an artist," I tell her.

Mum sighs. "You'll never make a living as an artist."

"Why not? Loads of people do. Look at Banksy."

"What, Banksy the street artist?"

"Yes. His artwork goes for millions."

Mum puts her hands on her hips. "And how many other artists do you know who are making that kind of money? Rudy, honey, you need to start living in the real world."

"You think I'm not living in the real world?" I clench my hands into fists beneath the table. The countdown to one of Mum and my almighty arguments has begun.

Ten . . . nine . . . eight . . .

"Not if you think you're going to make a living from some kind of pipe dream."

Seven . . . six . . . five . . .

"It's not a pipe dream!" I'm yelling now but I can't help it. It's like Mum's saying everything that's guaranteed to make me freak out.

"OK, OK, honey. I'm sorry." She sits down. "But at least if you got an art degree you'd be able to teach."

I have a horrific flash-forward to myself trudging around a dreary classroom placing an assortment of fruit on tables and droning on to my students about the importance of light and shade. "I don't want to teach."

"Oh, really?" Mum purses her lips.

Four . . . three . . .

"Yes, really."

Two . . . one. . .

"I think you need a bit of a reality check, Missy." Mum marches over to the fridge-freezer and pulls a bundle of brown envelopes down from the top. "See these?"

I nod.

"They're all bills. Bills I have to pay. And because I thought I knew it all when I was your age, I don't have a single qualification to my name, so I have to work my butt off every night in that crappy casino."

"I thought you liked your job…"

"Yeah, well, you thought wrong."

If Mum and I were playing chess she'd have just got me in checkmate. "I'm sorry."

"Oh, honey, I'm sorry too." Mum puts her arm round my shoulders. "It would just really help if Dave lived here. It would cut my outgoings in half."

"But…" I want to ask her if she'd still want Dave to live with us if she had a million pounds in the bank; if she wants to live with him because she loves him … but she's looking at me so hopefully I don't have the heart to. "OK."

"Really?" Her face lights up.

"Yeah, sure."

As Mum goes back over to the kettle all of my earlier excitement dims. Everything is nowhere near OK. Same as it's always been.

CLEMENTINE

As my feet pound the path along the seafront the aching in my legs starts to ease a little and I find my rhythm. The sky is that unforgiving shade of milk-white you only get in February and the sea is so dark it's almost black. Everyone moans about this time of year but I quite like it, or at least I will when I'm living my dream. I add a large antique fireplace to my mental vision board of my flat in Brighton. I picture myself lying in front of a roaring fire on a furry rug, my nose stuck inside a book of poetry taken from one of the many teetering piles of books on the floor all around me because my dream flat will not be governed by Mum's obsession with perfect symmetry. As I run past the skeletal remains of the old pier, I picture myself running away from the tension at home, literally and metaphorically, and excitement rolls in like a tide to replace it. I can't believe the artist contacted me!

When I get to Palace Pier music is already pounding from the speakers outside but the weather is so bleak even the flashing light bulbs in the sign look mournful and dowdy. The road that runs parallel to the front is filling with the first of the rush-hour traffic. I wait at the crossing for the lights to change and catch my breath. Then I head over to the side street where I think Fierce's new art might be. My excitement fades. The only urban art I can see is a faded paste-up of a cartoon dog and some graffiti. I take my phone from my pocket and check the photo for clues. Maybe it's in the next street along. I spot a narrow alleyway between two of the buildings and cut through. I'm reaching the end when a man comes stumbling towards me. His hair is tangled and greasy and his clothes are grimy.

"All right, love. Don't suppose you've got any change?" He smiles, showing dark gaps between his teeth.

I shake my head. "No, I'm sorry, I don't have any on me." Seeing his thin face and threadbare clothes really makes me wish that I did.

"No worries, love. You have a good day."

"You too."

I emerge onto the street and glance up and down. A splash of red on the wall opposite pierces the gloom, sending a bolt of recognition through me. It's the piece by Dynamite. And there, next to it, is the picture Fierce Urban sent me. I hurry across to it. Now that there's no one obscuring it I can see that the girl in the picture is tied to a chair as well as having her mouth sealed by a cross of black tape. As before, it's a mixed-media piece. The girl has been drawn but the chair is a black and white photograph and all around the picture are lightning bolts in silver and gold. I stand still and drink it all in. There's so much pain on her face. Not just the black tear on her cheek but her tortured expression. The rumble of a delivery van making its way up the narrow street breaks me from my daze. I quickly take some photos of the picture, trying to get the best angle and making sure I get the FIERCE tag in.

"I saw them doing it, you know." I turn and see the man from the alleyway standing behind me.

"Sorry?"

"The picture. I saw them doing it. Last night. I was kipping in that doorway." He nods to a restaurant doorway across the street. An old duvet is heaped on top of a flattened cardboard box in the corner.

"Oh, I see. Did you say 'them'?"

He nods. "There was two of them. One of them put it up and did the painting. The other one took photos, like you."

"What did they look like? The one who put it up?"

He shrugs. "Hard to tell, really. It was dark, you know, and she was wrapped up well."

"She? It was a woman?"

"Yeah – well, a girl, really. 'Bout your age, I'd say."

My excitement builds. "Thank you. Thank you so much."

"No problem." He shuffles back over to the restaurant doorway and picks up the old duvet.

Sorrow slices through my excitement at the thought of him having to sleep out in the icy cold on the street.

As I jog back along the seafront, I process this latest development. **@FierceUrban** is the artist – or at least they were with the artist. I should have asked the man about the other person, the one taking the photos. But the main thing is, the artist did a new picture and messaged me immediately, saying, *Over to you...* They must want me to write another poem. The girl bound to the chair is kind of like the girl in the other picture, the one with the distorted reflection. Both of them are trapped but in different ways. I start mulling over ideas as I run. I think about what I'd say to the girl in the picture if I was standing in front of her. I'd want to tell her to break free. To stand up. No, to *rise* up. To speak up. To... I glance down at the beach and see a sight that makes my thoughts come screeching to a halt. Vincent in his shiny new tracksuit, standing outside one of the cafés, talking and laughing into his phone. Through the sudden silence caused by a gap in the traffic a few of his words drift up to me. "Miss you too, darling..."

RUDY

I'm so angry about the whole Idiot Dave Moving In thing that I make an executive decision to pull a sickie. The truth is, I genuinely am sick – sick of adults ruining everything. As soon as I've faked a call from Mum telling the school office that "My Rudy's got a stomach bug..." I decide to go and check out my art, and get some photos of it. It's funny how different the street looks in the daylight, and how much more chilled it feels when I'm not about to do something illegal. There's no sign of the homeless man from the night before, or his duvet in the restaurant doorway. I guess he has to move on before the staff show up for work.

As soon as I see my picture my disappointment at what happened this morning with Mum is replaced with defiance. It looks OK. Better than OK. Even next to Dynamite's amazing piece it seems to fit in. The tortured expression on the girl's face is powerful and the lightning bolts around her glimmer in the pale morning sunshine. Mum was wrong. I can be an artist. I *am* an artist. *Yeah, but how are you going to make any money?* a voice in my head says. A voice that sounds annoyingly like

Mum's. And then a load of other crappy thoughts start crowding in. *You're going to be living with Dave. The only way to escape will be to go to university and stay in education for an eternity. You're never going to be free.* I look back at my self-portrait. I should have added shouty thought bubbles above my head, full of my fears. I wonder if other urban artists ever feel like this – like, as soon as their work is up on the wall, they can see about a million different ways to improve on it.

"I saw them doing it, you know," a man's voice says behind me.

I turn and see a young guy with dark, matted hair and dirty, over-sized clothes, standing by an alleyway on the other side of the street. "Saw who doing what?"

"That," he points to my picture. "They did it last night. You're the second person this morning to stop and look at it."

"Really?"

"Yeah. The other girl even took a photo of it."

"Oh, did she?" Now I'm properly interested.

"Yeah. She wanted to know all about who did it too."

"Oh, did she? What did you tell her?"

"Don't suppose you've got any spare change, have you?"

"Sure," I say as I fumble in my pocket for some money.

"Bless you." He gives me a warm smile and I get a brief snapshot of the person he truly is, beneath the grimy mask of homelessness. I file the idea away in my mind as a potential art piece. "Not a lot I could tell her, seeing as it was so dark. I was kipping over there, in that doorway."

He's the homeless guy from last night. Could the girl he's talking about have been the poet **@SpilledInk**? Would she really have come down here so soon after accepting my message request on Instagram? "I don't suppose… Did you see her write anything?"

"Nah, she just took a couple of pictures and left. She was running."

"What?"

"You know, like out for a run."

"Ah, OK. Thank you." So it could have just been a passing jogger. But why did she ask this guy all the questions? This sounds like a case for my Jedi brother. I say goodbye and start heading up the road to Kale and Hearty.

CLEMENTINE

I watch Vincent for a few seconds until my teeth start chattering. Although I'm not able to hear any more of his conversation due to the traffic and the seagulls I can tell from his body language and the way he keeps laughing that he's definitely on a personal call – but to who? I start jogging back home, my brain knotted in confusion. Should I tell Mum? But what would I say? It's not a crime for Vincent to make a phone call. And even if I did tell Mum and she confronted him, he'd be bound to come up with some kind of excuse, like he was speaking to a work colleague. I have to play this super vigilantly, look out for other evidence that he might be cheating. Right now, I have the upper hand because he doesn't know I saw him. As I let myself into the house I feel really uneasy. I head straight for my ensuite bathroom and into the shower, where I turn the water on full force to try and wash away the uncomfortable feelings.

"Clem, breakfast's ready," Mum calls up the stairs as I'm getting dressed.

"I'll be down in a minute," I call back. The thought of having to play happy families over breakfast with Vincent makes me feel sick. I flick through the photos of Fierce's latest picture on my phone. As soon as I see them I feel slightly better. I have a poem to write. I can focus on that during breakfast as a distraction.

By the time I get dressed and go downstairs Mum is bustling between the fridge and the hob and Vincent and Damon are both sitting at the table.

"And that's why you should never trust a Gooners fan, son," Vincent is saying to Damon.

"Hey," I mutter as I sit down.

"What about Chelsea fans?" Damon says, neither of them acknowledging me. I feel like I do when I visit Dad and he and Ada start talking in German. Football-speak is a foreign language to me.

"Nah," Vincent says, "they're all plastics."

He and Damon start laughing.

"Do you want a hand, Mum?" I ask, even though it really bugs me that the division of labour in this house is a textbook illustration of the evils of the patriarchy.

"No, it's OK," Mum replies in her sing-song voice as she brings a plate of sausage sandwiches over.

"Cheers, love," Vincent says, grabbing one and demolishing most of it in a single bite.

"Sausages!" Damon exclaims.

"Yes, well, your dad and Clem have both been running. I thought you'd need something filling."

"You've been running?" Vincent finally acknowledges me.

"Yes." I stare back at him.

"Where did you run to?"

"Just along the seafront." I study his face for any sign of a reaction.

"Oh – er – that's great." From the way he's stammering he definitely seems rattled.

"You should go together next time," Mum says.

My stomach tightens with dread at the prospect but I force myself to grin. "That's a great idea." If he is using his morning jogs as a cover to call another woman this will really get to him.

"Yeah," he mutters. "Maybe. Any more coffee going?"

As Mum hurries over to get the coffee I want to scream. Why does she do everything for him? Is that why he's been putting her on such a guilt trip for not working? So she'll run around after him like a servant? As Vincent and Damon start talking football again I look at **@Fierce**'s picture on my phone and a line pops, perfectly formed, into my head: *When did you forget that you were born to rise?*

It's a question I want to ask Mum as well as the girl on the chair.

> *When did you forget that you were born to rise –*
> *Born to blaze a trail, like a star across the skies?*

I quickly tap the lines into the notepad on my phone.

"No phones at the table, Clementine," Mum says sternly, bringing Vincent's coffee over.

"Sorry, I was just writing a note to myself about my homework."

"Yeah, right," Vincent sneers. He turns to Damon and grins. "I bet she's texting her boyfriend."

"I don't have a boyfriend," I snap as they start sniggering.

"Now why doesn't that surprise me?" Vincent mutters.

My face flushes red. *I hate him. I hate him. I hate him.* "What's that supposed to mean?"

"Well, all you feminists hate men, don't you?"

"Not at all. We only hate the dickheads."

Damon sniggers.

"Clementine!" Mum looks at me, horrified.

"What?"

"No swearing."

"Oh my God."

"What?" Mum stares at me.

"Trust me, me saying dickheads should be the least of your worries." I stare pointedly at Vincent. "I'm going to school." I stand up.

Mum looks confused. "But you haven't had any breakfast."

"I'll get something from the canteen."

"But—"

"Let her go," Vincent interrupts Mum. He doesn't look at me when he says it, but his tone has softened – he definitely wants me to leave.

I race into Kale and Hearty and over to the counter. Tyler is standing with his back to me, putting a load of berries into the juicer.

"Someone was asking about my picture," I say excitedly, as I pull up a stool and sit down.

"What? Who? Hello!" Tyler turns to greet me. He's wearing his favourite Pink Floyd T-shirt and his hair's tied up, making his cheekbones look even more pronounced. They're so striking I instantly want to draw him.

"Hello. I don't know. A girl."

"OK, rewind." Tyler puts down the fruit and comes over.

"I went to see it just now, to check out what it looked like in the daylight, and that guy was there – the one who was sleeping in the doorway last night."

"Right." Tyler nods.

"So, he came over and said that I wasn't the first person who'd looked at the picture today; a girl had been there earlier and she'd taken a photo."

"That's awesome." Tyler grins. "But I'm not surprised. It's a great piece of art, sis."

"She was asking him questions too, about who did it."

Tyler frowns, causing his thin eyebrows to meet. "Really? What did he tell her?"

"Nothing much. He said he couldn't see who did it because it was so dark and we were covered up. He didn't realize it was me." I grin at him. "I think it might have been her – the poet. She accepted my message request so I know she's read it."

"Wow."

"I know!"

"Has she posted a picture of it on her account?"

"Not the last time I looked." I take my phone from my pocket. I've got a message from Mum: I love you, baby. xxxx. *Yeah, whatever.* I click onto Instagram and **@SpilledInk**'s profile. There have been no new photos since yesterday, when she posted a photo of the sea and a quote about hope by someone called Emily Dickinson.

"I guess she'll need some time to write her poem." Tyler goes over to the coffee machine. "Drink?"

"Please."

Tyler looks at his watch. "Shouldn't you be in school?"

I shake my head. "I'm off sick."

"Why? What's up?" Tyler looks so concerned it makes me feel warm inside. At least someone genuinely cares about me.

"Idiot Dave's moving in."

"What?" The fact that Tyler looks so horrified at this news makes the warmth inside me grow.

"Yep. Mum told me this morning and I've been feeling sick ever since."

"Oh, sis. I'm sorry."

"The thing is, Mum needs the money. I offered to do more shifts here but then she got all militant about me needing to study so I could go to uni. I don't even want to go to uni."

Tyler nods. "I hear you."

"Hey, Rudy. No school today?" Sid calls as he comes out from the kitchen.

I shake my head.

"She's had some bad news," Tyler says.

"Oh no." Sid comes over. "No one's died, have they?"

"Only all the hope inside me," I reply.

Sid gives a relieved laugh. "Oh dear. Sounds like a definite case for banana bread." He goes over to one of the freshly baked loaves on the counter and cuts me a huge chunk. I go to get my purse out to pay but he shakes his head. "On the house, hun. Sounds like you could do with some comfort food."

"Thank you." As I take a bite of the warm banana bread and the sweet taste of cinnamon melts on my tongue I feel the tiniest flicker of hope splutter back to life. Things might be about to get tragic on the home front but at least I have the café and at least I have Tyler, Jenna and Sid. At least I feel at home in my workplace. I try to ignore how desperate this sounds and take another bite of banana bread.

CLEMENTINE

When did you forget that you were born to rise –
Born to blaze a trail, like a star across the skies?
When did you decide that you were meant to crawl –
Crawl and shrink and fade, instead of walking tall?
When will you remember who you were supposed to be?
When will you wake up and finally be free?

As I type the poem into an Instagram post I feel a weird jolt
of recognition deep inside. I'd started writing about the girl
in **@FierceUrban**'s picture and Mum, but now I realize that I'm
writing this for me too. I'm so sick of feeling like I'm an extra
in someone else's movie: someone's difficult daughter, or annoying big sister, or inconvenient stepdaughter, or the boring
wallflower in a high-school drama. Mum isn't the only one
who's been shrinking and fading away, I have too, trying to fit
in at home and at school. School today was really harsh. There
was a moment in English when everyone seemed to be in on
a joke apart from me and I had to pretend that I didn't care,
fake that I was really engrossed in my book. But what if I'm not
supposed to fit in there? What if, instead of trying to fit into the

wrong places, I search for the right place, a place where fitting in comes so naturally it's not even a thing? Does such a place exist? And how will I find it?

I double-check that I'm happy with the photo and the filter I've chosen. Then I take a deep breath and tag **@FierceUrban**. It's the first time I've ever tagged an artist directly. As I press SHARE my heart skips a beat. Then I go to my messages and send **@FierceUrban** a reply: Hope you like it! Over to you…

RUDY

"Rudy, I'm in the kitchen," Mum calls as I shut the front door behind me.

My heart sinks. No "baby girl" or "honey" or "darling" in her greeting usually means that I'm in trouble or something bad's happened – or both.

I check the time on my phone. I was really careful to make sure that I got home at my normal time, even though I haven't been to school. After breakfast in Kale and Hearty I spent the day trawling Brighton's backstreets for urban art inspiration. I even went back to the picture of the butt cheeks by LADZ, to see if he'd seen what I'd done and responded in some way but my FIERCE denim shorts were still on full display. Then I sat for hours on a bench on the pier sketching new ideas in my pad. In truth, I was sketching out all of my anger about Idiot Dave moving in and Mum insisting I go to uni; drawing pictures of dumb-looking men and students being churned out of giant sausage machines.

"Hey, what's up?" I say as I go into the kitchen. "Oh." Idiot Dave is what's up. He's halfway up a stepladder, fixing our broken cupboard door, to be precise.

"All right, Rudy?" he says in his South London twang. "Good day at school?"

For a second I wonder if this is a trick question; if he and Mum know I skived off. I glance at Mum. She's grinning at Dave like an adoring puppy.

"Yeah, it was OK."

"Dave's fixing the cupboard door," Mum says, stating the obvious.

"Really? I thought he was practising ballet." *Don't be sarcastic, Rudy.*

"Don't be sarcastic, Rudy," Mum says, but she keeps grinning. "We were thinking, maybe we could all go out for something to eat, before I go to work."

Two things hit me like a double punch to the gut: Mum and Dave will be "we" now, instead of Mum and me and, when Dave moves in, I'll no longer have the flat to myself when Mum's at work.

"I'm not really that hungry," I say, in a dramatic understatement. I feel totally sick.

"Please, Rudy." Mum turns her puppy-dog eyes on me.

"Go on, you must fancy something," Dave says, coming back down the ladder. The sleeves of his checked shirt are rolled up, revealing the silhouettes of tattoos, barely visible on his dark skin. "You pick."

"Really?"

"Yeah." He grins at me and a pair of dimples appear on either side of his mouth like a set of speech marks. *Yeah, well, your dimples don't fool me, mister. Your twinkly eyes don't either.*

"How about Mexican?" I suggest. Ever since Tyler introduced me to the joys of fajitas I've been a huge fan of Mexican food. Dave probably hasn't got a clue what they even eat in Mexico; he was probably hoping I'd say fish and chips or a doner kebab.

"Mexican would be great," Dave replies. "We can go to Dos Sombreros."

"Cool," Mum says, like an excited kid.

I'm not sure what to make of this latest development. "OK, I'll get changed then."

"Sure." Dave grins. *Dimple, dimple. Twinkle, twinkle.* I fight the instinct to smile back. I mustn't let his cheeriness fool me. One of us needs to stay on our guard around here.

As soon as I get to my bedroom I fling my bag on the floor and myself on the bed. I know what's going on. Dave is embarking on a charm offensive so I'll be chill about him moving in. But what he doesn't realize is that I'm not stupid. I learned long ago that you can't trust anyone – especially men. With the exception of Tyler of course. And Sid.

I take my phone from my bag to text Tyler this latest development and I see that I have a notification from Instagram. I hardly ever get notifications from Instagram, due to the whole carefully-curated-social-media thing. A shiver runs up my spine. **@SpilledInk** has sent me a message.

Hope you like it. Over to you…

Like what? I see from my notifications that she's also tagged me in a post so I click on the link. I see a photo of my picture and next to it the first line of the description reads: *When did you forget that...?* I click through to read the full post. As the words work their way from the screen into my brain my body fizzes with excitement. It's like she's written a rallying call just for me.

I quickly text Tyler. **Spilled Ink has posted my picture and written a poem!**

Almost instantly my phone starts to ring: Tyler.

"What does it say?" he asks breathlessly.

"You all right, mate? You sound like you're having trouble breathing."

"Yeah. Just had to lug all the shopping up the stairs. Lift's broken again. But there was one silver lining..."

"Oh yeah? What's that?"

"I saw your latest So Dark Fairy in the stairwell. Is it me?"

"Yep."

"Sis, you have no idea how much this means to me." Tyler's been begging me for ages to make a So Dark Fairy in his image, it's great to hear the genuine excitement in his voice. "I even took a photo of it to have as my screensaver. I love it! But never mind that, read me the poem."

I read it to him. There's a moment's silence and then...

"Wow!"

"I know, right? She really seems to get what I'm trying to say."

"Absolutely. It makes me think..."

"What?"

"Well, maybe you guys should do some kind of collaboration."

"How do you mean?"

"What if you did a piece of art and included one of her poems, like a poem she'd written about your picture?"

I think of my hero Miss.Tic and how she combines art with words and how I'd recently been wishing I could do the same. "But I don't even know her."

"Yet," Tyler replies, all enigmatically. "Why don't you message her? Suggest meeting."

"Hmm. I'll think about it."

"Do it." I hear Tyler taking a swig of his drink. "You OK, sis, about Dave moving in?"

"Yeah. He's here now. We're going out for dinner. Some kind of cheesy Mexican bonding thing – although the only thing I'm going to be bonding with is my fajita."

"You're going for a Mexican?" I can practically hear Tyler drooling.

"Yeah. Idiot Dave let me choose where to go. That's how cheesy he's being."

"Being taken for a Mexican is a pretty cool silver lining though."

"I suppose."

"Good luck!"

"Thanks, bruv."

I end the call and, before I have time to talk myself out of it, I type a reply to **@SpilledInk**'s message. Love it. Thank you. Do you want to meet?

CLEMENTINE

Apparently, my favourite poet, Emily Dickinson, became a recluse in her later life, to the point where she refused even to leave her bedroom. I stare at my bedroom ceiling, seriously considering this option. After the day I've had, I can see how a person might give up on the outside world but I'm not sure I'm quite that desperate yet. Maybe ... if my bedroom was more to my taste – but the thought of staying trapped in this bland white cube is even more depressing. I sit up. I am going to take the advice of my poem and I'm going to rise out of my bed, out of this room and out of this house. But where am I going to rise to? I decide to go flâneuring.

Thankfully, Vincent has taken Damon to football training, so I only have to get past Mum. I find her in the bathroom of the guestroom, cleaning the already sparkling tiles.

"Hey, Mum, I'm just going to pop round to Becky's for a bit." I hold my breath, hoping that Mum won't find this suspicious, as I haven't been round to Becky's since Christmas. But thankfully she's way too engrossed in her cleaning, rubbing the tiles like her life depends on it.

"OK. Don't be too late, though. You've got school in the morning."

She seems so weird and distracted. A horrible thought occurs to me. What if the "darling" Vincent was talking to this morning on the phone *is* someone he's having an affair with? And what if Mum knows, or suspects at least? Is that why she's been acting so strange lately?

"Are you OK?" I ask.

"Yes, of course." She carries on cleaning.

"All right. I'll see you later then."

"Yes, see you later."

I head downstairs feeling so helpless. I wish there was something I could do. I wish I knew what was going on inside Mum's head.

It's not until I'm outside and heading along the main road into Brighton that I start to relax. It's impossible for me not to feel happy in this city, its energy seeps into me like some kind of weird osmosis. Even though flâneuring was invented in Paris, I feel pretty certain that Brighton has to be the second-best place in the world to wander with no purpose other than to drink it all in. I soak in the sounds – the pounding music from a pub, the laughter from a group of skater boys, the hiss of a passing bus, the call of a *Big Issue* seller. I breathe in the smells – petrol, fruity vape fumes, perfume and pizza. And I allow my imagination to add to the sights – my imaginary boyfriend Luc meandering along beside me, his dark hair flopping down over his eyes. I picture him holding my hand, squeezing it tightly, whispering in my ear, "Shall we go down to the sea?" My phone vibrates in my pocket, interrupting me from my daydream. I stop in the doorway of the Pound Shop and check my messages. There's one from Becky. My heart pounds. Why is she messaging me? Did Mum call her?

Hey, Clem. Hope you're good. I was just wondering if you had time for a chat? Justin's away at cadet camp and I'm SO BORED. xxx

There would have been a time, a couple of months ago, when I would have been so happy to have received this message, but not any more. Now all it makes me feel is angry. The only reason Becky's messaging me is because Justin's away – and because she's *SO BORED*. Clearly I'm just her good old reliable back-up friend. Or at least that's what she thinks. I click out of my messages, and see an Instagram notification. My anger instantly turns to excitement when I see that **@FierceUrban** has contacted me. I practically drop the phone in surprise when I read her message. Not only did she "love" my poem but she wants to meet!

RUDY

There are many things in life that are guaranteed to kill your appetite stone dead. Fungus. The smell of rotten eggs. Slimy seaweed. And high up on the list is the sight of your mum and her idiot boyfriend smooching ACROSS THE TABLE FROM YOU. I hold up my menu like it's a shield and pretend to read. If only they served a dish called Parental Passion Killer. I'd order it for Mum and Dave with an extra side helping. Their PDAs are seriously unnecessary. They're both way too old to be carrying on like this. Mum is going to be forty in a couple of months and Dave is almost fifty. That's, like, half a century! I sneak a peek over the menu. Thankfully they've stopped kissing, but Dave's now stroking Mum's hand and gazing at her in a seriously sappy way.

"Do you know what you want, Rudy?" Dave asks, nodding at my menu.

Yeah, I want you to put my mum down, I think. "The vegetable fajita please," I say.

"Good choice," Dave says. Like I need his approval.

"So, what did you do in school today?" Mum asks.

"Just the usual," I mutter.

"Did you have art?" Dave asks.

"Yeah, why?"

"I know how much you like art," he says. "So it can't have been that bad."

Ha! If only he knew. But the mention of art makes my fingers itch to be drawing.

"Oh, trust me, it was bad," I mutter, mentally composing a comic-style picture of Dave being swallowed whole by a giant taco shell.

Mum gives me one of her stares. When I was little these stares had the power to silence me instantly. But I'm not little any more.

"Don't you enjoy your art classes?" Dave asks.

"No, not really."

"I used to feel like that about English lessons," Dave says.

"What do you mean?"

"I loved reading and writing as a kid but after my English degree I couldn't read a novel for about two years. They got us to analyse writing to death and it killed my love of books. I couldn't read anything without hearing my tutor's voice saying, '*What do you think the author really means by this? What's the underlying theme?*'" He laughs.

"You've got a degree?" I can't even begin to hide my surprise. Dave works as a car mechanic. He's all roll-up cigarettes and oily jeans and tabloid newspapers. I can't imagine him at university.

"Yeah," he sighs. "Lot of good it did me."

"I was just saying to Rudy this morning how important it is to get a degree," Mum says pointedly.

"Oh, right, yeah," Dave says quickly.

"Why did you study English?" Annoyingly, my curiosity is outweighing my need to blank Dave and all that he stands for.

"I wanted to be a writer." He chuckles. "Thought I was gonna be the next Langston Hughes when I was a teen."

"So, what went wrong?"

"Oh, you know, life." He laughs again but this time it seems to be tinged with sadness.

I sit back in my seat and frown. I'm in the weird and unsettling position of actually being interested in Dave. *It's all a trap*, I remind myself. This whole dinner's just to butter me up before he moves in. But how long will it be before everything goes wrong? Before he walks out on us just like the others did? I cross my arms tightly in front of my chest. He might have wormed his way into our flat and Mum's affections but there's no way I'm letting him in. Why can't Mum see this too? Why does she keep setting herself up to get hurt?

"I don't know if there's something you dream of doing with your life, Rudy," Dave says, "but if and when you do, you go for it with everything you've got. Seize the day, as my old man always used to tell me."

You're not my old man so don't get any ideas, mate. "Yeah, OK."

Fighting the urge to ask Dave another question, I take out my phone to see if **@SpilledInk** has replied to my message, but there's nothing, only a text from Tyler: Yo amigo! How's it going?

Have you choked him with a chimichanga yet?

Not yet, I type back, but the night is young!

"Rudy," Mum says warningly.

"What?"

"It's rude to be on your phone when someone's talking to you."

"Sorry," I mutter, putting my phone away.

"It's OK." Dave smiles.

"Do you ever do any writing now, then?" I ask.

"Nah. Still get ideas though. Usually when I've got my head stuck under a bonnet trying to fix someone's engine. But I never bother writing them down. What's the point? That ship sailed long ago."

"Never mind, baby," Mum says, stroking his hand.

I fight the urge to say, *You should mind. You should do what matters to you.* "So you've given up on it, then?"

"I just don't have the time. Not with the shifts I work."

"Right." I make a vow to myself right here and now to never be a quitter like Dave.

CLEMENTINE

It turns out that it's very hard to flâneur when you're hoping to receive a reply to a message. In fact, I'm pretty certain flâneuring wouldn't have been invented if they'd had mobile phones back in the nineteenth century. As soon as the shock of **@FierceUrban** wanting to meet me wore off, I sent her a reply saying, **Yes – that would be great!** Ever since I sent it I've had to keep stopping and checking my phone to see if she's replied. So far, she hasn't. I wonder if maybe I was a little too vague.

I head down to the seafront and sit on a bench by the i360 viewing tower. The circular pod is at the top and, lit up red and gold, it looks like an alien spaceship against the night sky. I take out my phone and send another message to **@FierceUrban**: **I'm out in Brighton right now if you're free?** Then I reply to Becky's earlier message: **Sorry, out with a friend. x**

Even though I'm not actually out with **@FierceUrban** I could be. And that in itself makes me so happy.

RUDY

The rest of the meal is a buffet selection of boring and awkward. Thankfully, once Dave has run out of questions, he and Mum start droning on about plans to redecorate the flat. Just the mention of paint makes me long to be out on a darkened street with my spray cans. I make do with going to the toilet instead and draw a giant tortilla swallowing a man in Biro on the back of the cubicle door. Then my phone pings with a notification. **@SpilledInk** has sent me two new messages. She wants to meet. She wants to meet right now! In an instant my evening turns from dark to light.

Yes, I'm free, I reply instantly. I lean against the cubicle wall, my heart pounding. This could actually be happening.

Great! she sends back straight away, like she's been waiting to hear from me.

Where would you like to meet? I reply.

How about the entrance to the pier? she responds.

This is a good suggestion. There'll be loads of people around. Just in case **@SpilledInk** is some kind of poetic serial killer.

Cool. I can be there in 10.

Me too!

Great. See you soon.

I take a moment to come up with a cover story, then I head back into the restaurant.

"I've got a bit of an emergency," I say to Mum. "Well, Tyler has. Is it OK if I go and meet him for a hot chocolate?"

"Oh, I don't know." Mum frowns. "We're supposed to be having a meal."

"We've had the meal. And I won't be long."

"Go on, let her have some fun," Dave says to Mum. "She's hung out with us oldies long enough." For once I'm grateful for his campaign of butt-kissing.

"OK, but I want you home by ten-thirty," Mum says.

"Sure." I grab my coat and head for the door.

Outside, an icy wind is whipping in from the sea. I pull up the hood on my Puffa jacket and stick my hands deep into my pockets.

When I get to the seafront I huddle in a shop doorway across the road from the pier and text Tyler: I'm meeting @SpilledInk!

He replies straight away: When???

Now!!!

My phone starts ringing.

"Where are you meeting?"

"At the entrance to the pier. She messaged me just now to ask if I wanted to meet."

"That's great."

"I'll call you later and let you know how it goes."

"Good luck! I'd better get back to Assassin's Creed. I've just got onto the final level."

"Good luck to you too!"

I put my phone away and walk over to the crossing by the pier. The traffic is a lot quieter at this time in the evening so I've got a clear view. I don't have to meet with **@SpilledInk** if I don't want to, I remind myself. She has no clue what I look like so I can just walk by if I don't like the look of her. As I reach the entrance to the pier I glance at the row of kiosks. There are a handful of people dotted about but none of them are on their own. I keep walking, unsure what to do. I don't want to stand and wait because that would give **@SpilledInk** the advantage, removing my option to leave. I walk past the pier and keep walking for a couple of minutes, then I turn and head back. As I get close to the pier a girl walks over and taps me on the arm.

"Excuse me, have you got the time?"

I take my phone from my pocket and see that I have a new message from **@SpilledInk**. "Yeah, it's nine-twenty-seven," I say, not looking at the girl as I quickly type a reply to **@SpilledInk**: Here too.

There's a pinging sound as I send the message. I look up and frown. It's coming from the girl's coat.

"Thanks," she says, taking a phone from her pocket.

I stare at her. I can tell instantly that her clothes are all designer-label. They have that extra-luxurious look that even the best imitations can't replicate. I can just make out the edges of a pale blonde fringe poking from under her woolly hat.

The girl looks at her phone then looks at me. "Is it you?" she says, holding her phone out. "Are you Fierce Urban?"

Holy guacamole! as Tyler would say. I'm not sure what I was expecting but this girl is not it. She looks just like the kind of girls who bug me the most in school. The ones who look like dolls made of porcelain, with their perfect bodies and immaculate skin. The rich girls who never have to worry about things like money, or having enough clothes, or their mums moving people like Dave in to share the bills.

The porcelain white of the girl's face flushes pale pink. "Sorry, I think I've got the wrong person."

I'm so thrown by what she looks like I don't know what to say.

"Sorry to have bothered you." Her voice is perfect too, all light and melodic, like classical music.

I watch as she heads over to the doughnut kiosk and says something to the woman behind the counter. The woman starts filling a bag with doughnuts. That's one thing in her favour, I suppose. At least she isn't one of those doll-girls who obsesses over her weight. Then I think of **@SpilledInk**'s first poem. As unlikely as it seems, that girl wrote those words. She understood my pictures. Maybe I shouldn't be so quick to judge. The girl hands the woman some money and goes to sit on a bench. She takes out a notebook and pen. Old school. I approve. I move closer. She looks up and nods at me. Then she gets out her phone and taps something into it. This time my phone beeps. I look at the message.

Are you sure it isn't you???

I look at her and she grins. *Crap.* My cover's blown. I have no other option but to go over.

"Sorry. I – uh – just needed to be sure," I say.

"Sure of what?"

"Sure that you weren't some kind of crazed poet stalker."

She laughs. "So, what made you think that you could trust me?"

"The doughnuts." I nod at her bag.

"Oh, do you want one?"

"Yeah, go on." I sit down beside her and she offers me the bag. The doughnuts are still really warm. I take a bite out of one. "Oh wow," I mumble as the crispy, sugary coating gives way to the fluffy doughnut heaven beneath.

"They're amazing, aren't they?" **@SpilledInk**'s perfect, rosebud lips are now iced with sugar.

"Yeah." I take another bite. She's not the grungy, angsty poet I was expecting, but I get the feeling she's not exactly what she seems either.

"I – I really love your artwork."

Something inside me softens. "Thank you."

"It's so intriguing. I love that each piece has a really powerful message."

"Thanks." I hate to admit it but, despite **@SpilledInk** looking every inch like the kind of girl who'd normally be my arch-nemesis, this conversation is starting to feel enjoyable. I'm not quite sure what to do with this fact so I take another bite of my doughnut.

CLEMENTINE

I take a deep breath, trying to get my heart rate back to normal. So far, my meeting with Fierce Urban has not gone quite as I'd have liked. I can't help feeling she was disappointed when she realized who I was. I wonder if she was expecting me to look more edgy and cool; more like her, with her cat-shaped eyes and high cheekbones and silver nose ring, glinting like a star against her brown skin. As if to emphasize her coolness she stretches her long thin legs out in front of her. Her skinny jeans are paint-splattered and torn and she's wearing black DM boots with silver lightning bolts painted on the sides. I glance down at my own clothes and feel a wistful pang. I look so bland next to her. No wonder she pretended not to know me at first. All of my earlier courage starts draining from me.

"I liked your poems," she says, staring straight ahead.

"Really?" I wonder if she's just humouring me.

"Yeah. How do you know how to choose the exact words?" She turns to me. Her stare is intense, unflinching.

I look down into my lap. "Do you ever hear a voice in your head that doesn't sound like your own?" *Oh great, way to sound totally crazy!* "I mean, it's your voice, the same voice that tells you what to do all the time – like, the voice of your thoughts – but it comes up with an idea that doesn't feel like your own because it's – it feels like such a surprise." Despite the cold wind coming in off the sea my entire body is now aflame with embarrassment.

She grins. It's the first time she's smiled since we've met but I'm not entirely sure this is a good thing. For all I know she could be mocking me.

"I think I know what you mean," she says, "but I get an image rather than words."

I breathe a sigh of relief.

"Like, sometimes the idea for a picture will just pop into my head from out of nowhere."

"Yes, exactly! That's what writing poems is like for me. Well, when I have the right kind of inspiration, like your pictures. Sometimes it feels as if my poems already exist in some kind of magical creative realm and I just have to download them."

"Right." Thankfully **@FierceUrban** nods enthusiastically at my talk of magical creative realms.

"I'm Clementine, by the way. I mean, that's my real name."

"Oh, right." For a horrible moment I think she's not going to tell me hers.

"I'm Rudy."

"Cool." And it is cool, very cool. I'd much rather have a boy's name than a fruit's.

We sit in awkward silence for a moment, then her phone starts to ring.

"Hey," she says, answering it. "Yeah... Yeah... Nah, not really."

I wonder if whoever she's talking to knows about us meeting; if they're asking about me.

"Not sure, really. I'll let you know when I get home... Oh, ha ha, very funny... All right. Speak later." She puts the phone back in her pocket. "That was Tyler," she says, like this should mean something to me.

"Oh."

"He knows we were meeting. He wanted to know how it was going."

"Oh, right." I mentally rewind to her side of the phone conversation. She was hardly bubbling over with enthusiasm. But then, she doesn't strike me as the kind of person who would ever bubble over with enthusiasm. She seems way too cool to do over-eager. Unlike me.

Rudy shifts in her seat. "So, I was wondering ... would you be up for doing some kind of collaboration with me?"

"What, you mean like us working together?"

"We don't have to if you don't want to. I'm not bothered either way – it was Tyler's idea," she says.

"I think it's a great idea," I say quickly, still not exactly sure what the idea is.

"There's this French urban artist that I really like. She's called Miss.Tic and she always has words with her pictures, like a statement or a mini poem."

Finally I get what she's asking me and I shiver from a mixture of cold and excitement. "You'd like to use my words in one of your pictures?"

"Yeah. We could give it a go." She peers out from her hood. "What do you think?"

"I think that would be brilliant."

She coughs. "Yeah, we'll see."

I try and tone down my excitement to match Rudy's nonchalance. "So, how would we do it? Would we come up with an idea together, or do you want to create the image first and then I'll write the poem?"

She purses her lips. "Why don't you go first this time? Send me a poem and I'll see if I can come up with some artwork to go with it."

"Really?"

"Yeah. Why not?"

"OK. Is there anything in particular you'd like me to send you? Like, any particular theme?"

"I don't know, how about life?" she says with a shrug.

"OK." Thankfully at this point my phone starts ringing. It's the death march, the ringtone of doom I've assigned specially to Vincent.

"Cheery ringtone," Rudy says, raising her eyebrows.

"I only have it for my stepdad," I say. I'm tempted to terminate the call but Vincent hardly ever calls me, so I suppose I ought to make sure there hasn't been some kind of emergency. "Yes?" I say, answering the call.

"Yes, er, your mum asked me to ring you..." he says awkwardly.

"Why?"

"She was wondering what time you were going to be home from your friend's."

"I won't be long," I say.

"OK. See you then." Clearly he's as eager to end this exercise in awkwardness as I am.

"Yeah, see you." I end the call and stuff my phone in my bag. Rudy is looking at me and smiling, a genuinely warm smile.

"So, you'll send me a poem then?" she says, getting to her feet.

"Sure. I'll send you one tomorrow."

"Cool." She nods. "It was good to meet you, Clementine."

"It was good to meet you too, Rudy," I reply, in what has to be the understatement of the year, if not the century.

RUDY

"Uh-oh. You look like you might be in need of some caffeine." Tyler grins from behind the café counter as I drag my aching body over to him.

"I'm in need of *double* caffeine," I reply, slinging my school bag on the floor and pulling up a stool.

Tyler bangs the dregs of the coffee grounds from one of the scoops. "What's happened?"

"Double physics followed by PE happened." I rest my head on my hands on top of the counter. "Seriously, I just don't get why people say that exercise is good for you. I think I might have hypothermia and at least one cracked rib."

"Don't tell me, hockey?"

"Yep."

Tyler puts down the coffee scoop and winces in fake horror. "Stop it, please, you're making me have a rugby flashback."

"Oh, Ty, you're so lucky not to have to do PE ever again."

"Yeah" – Tyler lowers his voice and glances around at the handful of people in the café – "but now I have to deal with CFHs on a regular basis."

CFH is our code for Customers from Hell. "Oh dear. Bad day?"

"Put it this way, I won't be sorry if I never hear the words 'but is it gluten-free' ever again."

Tyler is so good at his job at Kale and Hearty and so cheery with all the customers it's hard to believe it's not what he really wants to do. "How's the fund for the mixing console going?"

"Slowly, but I'm working all the shifts I can get. Hopefully I'll have enough soon. So, has Tangerine sent you a poem yet?"

"Clementine!" I shake my head. "Not the last time I checked." I've been looking at my phone all day in the hope that Clementine would give me something positive to take my mind off school hell. I check again but there's still nothing. "It was a dumb idea anyway."

"No, it wasn't. It was my idea – and I don't have dumb ideas." He grins at me.

"Yeah, yeah." I flick a sugar cube across the counter at him.

As Tyler makes my coffee I take my pad from my bag and start sketching. I don't need Clementine and her poems, I remind myself. I don't need anyone to help me make my art.

"Hey, Rudy," Sid says coming out from the kitchen. His apron is stained with what looks worryingly like blood.

"Hey, Sid. What's going on back there, a vegetable massacre?"

"Yeah, man, I let those beetroots have it. What are you working on?" He looks at my pad. "Cool! Maybe I should get you to design my next tattoo."

"Do it," Tyler says, plonking a large coffee in front of me. "I'm getting her to design my first tattoo."

"You are?" I look at him, surprised.

"Of course."

My hockey-induced hypothermia starts thawing from the inside out at this latest development.

"Are you any good at drawing dragons?" Sid asks. "I'm thinking of getting one on my back."

"One what on your back?" Jenna says, coming through the front door laden down with bags from the cash and carry.

"A dragon tattoo," Sid replies. "I was just asking Rudy if she'd design one for me."

"That would be great," Jenna says, going behind the counter and kissing Sid on the cheek. Sid and Jenna are the only couple I know whose PDAs don't make me cringe.

"Seriously?" I look from Jenna to Sid.

"Of course." Jenna grins. "You're a great artist. Come on, Dragon Man, help me unpack these bags."

Sid and Jenna disappear into the kitchen and Tyler picks up a cloth and goes to clear a table. I take a sip of my coffee, and a chain reaction of ideas sparks to life inside me. Maybe that's how I could make money from my art – designing tattoos. There are loads of tattoo studios in Brighton. And I bet the people who work there don't have art degrees. I could be a tattoo artist by day and an urban artist by night. The thaw inside me spreads.

"So, what would you like for your first tattoo?" I call over to Tyler.

"I was just going to ask you for some ideas," he replies.

"Really?"

"Yeah. Something that will inspire me."

I turn back to my notepad. *Something that will inspire Tyler. . .* It would have to be sound-related.

A group of French students comes clattering into the café, laughing and joking. I pick up my pencil and start doodling a pattern of musical notes.

CLEMENTINE

By the time I get to the dance studio after school the fear that's been building inside me all day has made my throat so tight I can hardly speak. For so long now, I've been focusing on the promise of a role in the summer show as if it were some kind of golden ticket. But what if I haven't got it? What if I'm not going to be able to lose myself in months of rehearsals? What if my escape route has been blocked?

"Hey, Clementine," Bailey says with a smile – but is it a smile of congratulations or sympathy?

"Hey," I reply, my voice barely more than a squeak.

Jody and Abby are chatting away in the corner. How can they be so laidback and bubbly? Why aren't they struck dumb by fear too? I glance around; everyone looks so relaxed and happy, talking and laughing in their little groups, like islands, while I'm a lone swimmer, floundering in the sea. I look out of the window at the actual sea to try and calm myself down. The pale sun is starting to dip towards the water, the sky smudged with charcoal-grey clouds. I take a deep breath. And another.

"OK, guys," Bailey calls from the barre. "Can you all gather round?"

The chatter fades to silence. The islands of people form one large mass. I stand at the back of the group, breathing slowly to try and calm my hearbeat. *Please, please, please, let me have a part.*

"Now, the first thing I want to say is that you all did brilliantly at the audition and it was really hard to make our decision." Bailey beams her ultra-white, toothy grin around the group. I really hate this bit. I mean, is anyone actually consoled by being told they did brilliantly when they haven't been chosen?

"But obviously, there were only four roles that we were casting for, so some of you are going to be disappointed."

OK, OK.

"The dancers we decided to go for in the end are, Sophie ... Jada ..." Bailey pauses between each name as if she's announcing the winners on *Strictly. Just say them, please!* "Jody ..."

Clementine. Clementine. Clementine. I will her to say my name.

"And Abby."

Squeals of delight echo around the studio. The disappointment is a thud to my chest. And now it morphs into fear. I wasn't good enough. I'm not good enough. I don't have what it takes to be a professional dancer.

"Well done, girls," Bailey says. "I'll be sending you your rehearsal schedules by the end of the week. Now, let's get on with the class. I'm sure you all must be desperate to dance."

I can't think of anything I'm less desperate to do. I want to be as far away from here as possible, alone, so I can try and get my thoughts back under control. As the music starts and we get into our positions, my body follows numbly. But some kind of floodgates have opened inside. *I'm not good enough.* And not just at dancing. All day, I tried thinking of a poem to send to Rudy but everything I came up with felt dull and clunky. I can't be a true poet if I always need someone else's work to inspire me. I'm just a limpet, clinging to the side of someone else's talent. I'm not good enough to have any proper friends either. Today, I found out that Becky had been to the cinema at the weekend with Molly, without their boyfriends. They could have invited me – but they didn't. And then my thought spiral leads me to the biggest "I'm not good enough" of all. I'm not good enough for either of my parents to want me. Tears start burning in my eyes and blurring my vision, making me lose my step. Mum always puts Vincent before me, even though he treats her like crap and he's probably cheating on her. And my dad cared so little about me he moved to another country. Again, I miss my step. Even if I'd got a part in the show it was only ever going to be a distraction. It wouldn't have really changed anything. I miss another step and panic starts to rise up into my throat. I have to get out of here. I slip away from the group, grab my bag from the corner and without bothering to get changed, I pull my coat on over my dance gear and rush through the door.

Once I get far enough away from the studio I crunch my way across the pebbles on the beach towards the sea. The sun is low in the sky now, creating a pathway of pale gold light across the water. If only I could walk across it, to brighter, better things.

I breathe in the cold, salty air. *It's going to be OK*, I tell myself. It was only a show. It's not the end of the world. There will be other shows. But will I be good enough for them? And then a thought dawns on me that's so unexpected I'm not sure what to do with it. What if I've got it all the wrong way round? What if performing in shows isn't good enough for me? Do I really want a life of disappointment and rejection? A life of forcing my body into fitness regimes and rigidly choreographed routines? I'd been seeing the show as a distraction from Vincent and home but shouldn't life be about doing the things that you truly want to do? The things that make you feel free? I think of Rudy and her picture of the girl gagged and bound to the chair. Isn't that what a life of dance auditions would do to me? Make me feel equally trapped? I turn and start heading back up the beach towards the side street with her picture.

The street's busier at this time of day, with people heading to the restaurants or using it as a cut-through. I stand in a doorway opposite and gaze at the picture. I don't want to be that girl, tied and gagged by fear. Finally, words start coming to me, dropping like rain into my mind, washing the disappointment away.

Falling . . . Rising . . . Rising . . . Falling.
It's not about the falling. It's about the rising
Lessons . . . ladder . . . rungs

I pull my notepad from my bag and start writing.

RUDY

I don't hear from Clementine until almost ten o'clock. After a dinner of falafel and sweet potato fries with Tyler at Kale and Hearty I came back home and continued brainstorming ideas for his and Sid's tattoos, studiously ignoring the signs of Dave moving in – the boxes of records and books taking over every spare inch in the flat. By the time my phone vibrates with a message I've practically given up hope of hearing from Clementine again and assume it must be Tyler.

> Sorry – had a really crappy day and
> couldn't get any inspiration

My heart sinks as I read the message. She's bottling it. I knew it. My phone vibrates again.

> But then I went back and looked at your picture of the
> girl on the chair and it inspired me. It inspired this...

I stare at my phone expectantly until another message comes in.

It's not about the falling,
the hurting,
the crying. . .
It's about the rising,
Turn your lessons into ladders
and start climbing.

Straight away I love it. I love the fierceness of it. The way it commands the reader to get off their butt and do something. I'm about to reply that I love it when another message arrives.

Please don't worry if you don't like it. I'll totally understand.

I LOVE IT!!! I reply. **And after the day I've had, I needed it. Thank you!**

As I wait for Clementine's response excitement bubbles inside of me and a new picture starts coming to life in my mind. It's of my alter ego, Lightning Girl, climbing a ladder, high, high, up to the moon and stars, her eyes bright with hope. I could use the same silver paint for her eyes as I use for the stars. Everything about her will say Warrior. She'll wear her Afro like a halo. She'll— My phone vibrates.

Seriously???? OMG, you have no idea how
much that means to me. Thank YOU!

I think of Clementine and her perfect face and her perfect clothes and how at first she'd seemed to exude privilege but then I'd picked up on the sorrow hidden beneath. It's clear from her texts that life isn't all sweetness and light for her either. It's clear from the poems she writes that speak right to the heart of me. Much as I hate admitting that I'm wrong – about anything – maybe I was wrong to judge her. I quickly type her a message.

OK, so how about I sketch out an idea for our image then I'll show it to you to see what you think?

That would be great. Thank you!

No worries. Speak soon.

Cool. Thank you.

I fight the urge to reply, *Enough with all the thank yous*! and reach for my sketchpad instead. Lightning Girl will be wearing boots and skin-tight jeans. And she'll have the tattoo of a lightning bolt on her cheek. She'll exude power and strength and vitality. In my mind Lightning Girl smiles and high-fives me, as if to say, "Finally!"

CLEMENTINE

Normally, I hate Saturdays. They remind me of all I am missing – friends, a social life, my dream-boyfriend-who-probably-doesn't-exist, Luc. But not this Saturday. This Saturday, I don't have to sit in a café on my own and pretend that I'm mysterious rather than lonely. I actually have somewhere to go and something to do. This Saturday, I'm meeting Rudy. She's asked me to stop by the café where she works – a vegetarian place on Sydney Street. I'm so happy I don't even mind when Mum force-feeds me croissants *and* pancakes for breakfast. I don't say anything sarcastic when Vincent yells down the stairs that he won't be helping Mum with the weekly food shop, as he needs a lie-in, because he was out drinking till three in the morning. I don't say anything but I do think, *You selfish pig!* And I don't even get cross when Damon starts kicking my chair and flicking blueberries at me. Rudy wants to show me her idea for our image – that's what she called it in her message – *our* image. I still can't quite believe that she liked my poem enough to use it.

"Have you had second thoughts about the dance thing?"

Mum says, finally sitting down at the breakfast table. Her make-up barely conceals the dark shadows beneath her eyes.

"Not really." When I told Mum I hadn't got the part in the show I also told her that I wasn't sure if I wanted to dance professionally and that maybe I ought to leave the Academy.

"Once the disappointment fades you'll feel differently," she says breezily.

Why? I want to ask her. *Why are you so sure? Why do you think you know me so much better than I know myself?* But I bite my lip. Now is not the time to start an argument. Rudy has asked me to come down to the café early, before it gets busy. I choke down the last of my pancake.

"Right, I'm going to head into town. I need to buy a book for history," I say, to give my trip legitimacy.

"OK, love." Mum gazes into her coffee. She looks worn out and defeated.

"Are you OK?"

"Yes, yes, absolutely," she says quickly. "I was thinking maybe the four of us could go out somewhere together this afternoon — you know, as a family."

Once again I bite my lip and fight the urge to be sarcastic. "OK."

"Really?" Mum looks so relieved and surprised it makes me feel sad.

"Yeah, sure."

She places her hand over mine and gives it a squeeze. "Thank you."

* * *

It's raining, the kind of annoying rain that's more like a haze and totally umbrella-proof. I decide to try and be all Zen and embrace it. This only partially works as it's hard to embrace being wet and freezing. On a more positive note, Sydney Street is in North Laine, my favourite part of Brighton. Even on a dingy, drizzly day like today, it pops with colour – from the quirky shopfronts to the market stalls and the splashes of street art on every bin, lamppost and corner. I start feeling more excited with every step. Finally, in my boring Groundhog Day life, something interesting is happening.

Kale and Hearty is sandwiched between a shop selling crystals and a secondhand record store. A Van Morrison track is pumping out from the record shop. I recognize it because it's my dad's favourite song to drive to. I push away this thought and the pain it causes and look at the café. Every letter in the sign is painted a different colour and the "a" in "Kale" is an apple. I get a weird familiar feeling, kind of like déjà vu. But it's not because I've been here before, because I definitely haven't. Maybe it's because this is where I'm supposed to be. I really hope so. I push the door open and go in.

The interior of the café is even more colourful than the outside. The wooden tables and chairs are painted vibrant shades of yellow, red, blue and lime green. The warm air smells of a delicious mixture of coffee and cinnamon, and "Nevermind" by Nirvana is playing through speakers in the ceiling. A skinny guy with floppy brown hair and matching dark brown eyes stands behind the counter, tapping a knife and fork on the surface in time like he's playing the drums. I can't help doing a double take when I see him. He looks almost exactly how I imagine my dream boyfriend, Luc, to be. I blink hard, but he's still there. I haven't got so desperate that I'm now hallucinating imaginary boyfriends. The Luc lookalike is so engrossed in what he's doing I don't want to interrupt him. I scan the café for any sign of Rudy. About half of the tables are taken, mostly with people on their own, either tapping away on laptops or immersed in newspapers. I wonder if you need to order at the counter or if it's table service. I go up to the counter to be on the safe side. As I get there the guy reaches a crescendo with his knife and fork, rattling them against a coffee tin in a final flourish.

"Doesn't that sound awesome?" he says.

"Uh, yeah." I laugh. "Is – uh – is Rudy here?"

The boy's eyes widen. "Are you the poet?"

Annoyingly but oh so predictably, I feel the tips of my cheeks start to burn. I'd made a vow to myself that I'd be way cooler and more worldly this time when I met Rudy. This is not the best of starts. "Er, yes. I guess."

"You guess?" He tilts his head and looks at me questioningly.

"I am."

"Cool! Great to meet you." He extends his hand. His thin wrist is full of leather bracelets. I make a note to add a wrist full of bracelets to my mental picture of Luc. As we're shaking hands Rudy appears through a door behind the counter. She's got a scarf in a skull-and-crossbones print wrapped around her head like a turban and she's wearing an apron over her T-shirt and jeans.

"Oh, hey," she says. It's impossible to read from her noncommittal expression if she's pleased to see me.

"Have you prepped the fruit?" the boy asks her.

"Yeah, it's all done and in the fridge."

"Cool." He turns back to me. "Can I get you something to drink?"

"Sure." I quickly scan the blackboard on the wall behind him. "Could I have a hot chocolate, please?"

"What kind of milk?" he asks.

I look at him blankly.

"Soy? Almond? Oat? Skimmed? Semi-skimmed? Gluten-free?"

"Gluten-free milk? Is that a thing?" I stare at him.

"No, it's not." Rudy laughs. "Let's just say Tyler is highly intolerant of people's food intolerances."

Aha, so this is Tyler, the guy she was talking to on the phone the night we met. The guy who suggested we meet.

"No, I'm intolerant of people's *fake* food intolerances," Tyler corrects.

"I don't have any intolerances," I say. "Real or fake. So normal milk will be fine, thank you."

"No, thank *you*," Tyler replies with a grin.

"I'll just go and get my art folder," Rudy says.

"Wait till you see what she's done," Tyler says over his shoulder as he fills a metal jug with milk. "It's epic."

"Yeah well, I had Clementine's poem to inspire me," Rudy mutters before disappearing through the door.

Again, my cheeks burn. I take off my hat and coat. I scoured my wardrobe for something cool to wear today, something more edgy like Rudy, but practically my entire wardrobe is sportswear. I settled on a black hoodie and jeans, with bright turquoise high-tops. I rummage through my bag as if I'm looking for something, surreptitiously watching Tyler as he works. I wonder if he's Rudy's boyfriend.

"So, do you live in Brighton?" Tyler asks.

"Yes, well, Hove, actually, so not that far away."

"Cool." He takes the jug of milk over to the coffee machine and whips it into a froth. "I'm so glad you guys met."

"Me too." If only he knew how glad. Right now Rudy and the prospect of doing some kind of collaboration with her is the only bright spot in my life.

Rudy reappears holding a large black folder. "Shall we grab a table?"

"Sure." I follow her over to a small round table in the window and we sit down.

"This is what I've got so far," she says, unzipping the folder and pulling out some sheets of paper. "This is the ladder I'm going to use." She passes me a black and white photo. "And I'm going to have her climbing it." She passes me the drawing of a girl. Physically, it's similar to the girls in her previous pictures – she has an Afro and brown skin but in every other way she's different. For a start she's climbing, and there's a look of real determination etched into her eyes and mouth. Her outfit is brilliant. Skin tight jeans with silver DM boots and the tattoo of a lightning bolt on her cheek.

"I love it."

"Here's a mock-up of the backdrop," Rudy says, taking a large sheet of paper from her bag. "On the night we put it up I'll do this part in spray paint." The backdrop is painted black, with a dusting of stars at the top and the sliver of a silver moon. Rudy points to the stars. "She'll be climbing up to reach them." I watch as she places the photo of the ladder onto the backdrop, then places the cut-out of the girl on top.

"Wow!" I exclaim as the picture comes together.

"I thought I'd stencil your poem here." She points to a blank corner of the sky. I've done it in an old-style type-writer font but just say if you want me to change it." She takes another piece of paper from her bag. My poem's printed on it. She places it on the corner of the picture. "I was thinking of stencilling it in a bright colour, to make it really stand out," Rudy says. "Maybe red like the catsuit, or turquoise, like your trainers. I really like that shade." She looks at me. "So, what do you think?"

"It — it's amazing," I stammer. I've got the same weird feeling I had standing outside the café. The sense that this is exactly where I'm supposed to be and what I'm supposed to be doing.

"Are you sure?" Rudy's cat-like eyes scour my face, as if she's looking for evidence that I might be lying.

"Absolutely. I can't believe you got all that from my poem."

"Yeah, well, it was a bit like what you said about when you channel a poem. The picture came to me as soon as I read your words."

"It's great, isn't it?" Tyler says, arriving at our table with my hot chocolate and a coffee for Rudy.

"It's amazing!"

"Cool." Rudy sits back in her chair, the slightest of smiles on her face. "Now we just have to decide where to put it."

"What about on the wall by the seafront?" Tyler suggests. "Down by the kiosks."

"Could do," Rudy looks thoughtful.

"More people would see it down there," I say, finding it hard to believe that I'm actually having this conversation.

"What are you doing today?" Rudy asks.

"Me? Oh, nothing much." I instantly berate myself for sounding so boring. "Why?"

"Could you go on a recce down to the front? Find a patch of wall we could use?"

"Of course."

"Cool." Rudy puts the papers back in her folder. "I have to get back in the kitchen or Sid'll be threatening to put me in the juicing machine. Maybe you could message me later."

"Sure." I force myself to smile to hide the disappointment that our meeting is over so quickly.

"OK, great." Rudy picks up her coffee and gets to her feet.

As she goes back to the kitchen I sip my hot chocolate and try to process everything. Rudy is definitely hard to read, like a poem that's laden with mysterious subtext and hidden meaning.

"I reckon down by the old pier would be best," Tyler says, coming back over to clear the table next to mine.

"That's what I was thinking," I reply. "I'll check it out on my way home."

"I loved your poem by the way." Tyler stops wiping the table and looks at me.

It feels as if my body has turned to dandelion seeds, so light I could be blown away at any minute. "Really?"

"Yeah. It was like I needed to read it. I needed reminding."

"That's great. Thank you." I wonder what it was he needed reminding of doing.

"No, thank *you*," Tyler says, with a grin.

RUDY

"You didn't chat to her for very long," Tyler says, coming into the kitchen and heading for the fridge.

"Yeah, well, I'm at work," I reply, preparing to slice some lemons. "Don't want to get into trouble for skiving."

"You could have taken your morning break early if you wanted to chat to a friend," Jenna calls over from the sink where she's rinsing flour from her hands.

"She's not a friend, she's just someone … I've done some art for. I just had to check that she liked what I'd done and she did, so job done."

"She seems really nice." Tyler takes a container of strawberries from the fridge.

"Well, we'll see." I hack into the lemon. As far as I'm concerned Tyler is way too trusting of other people.

He comes over. "Are you sure you're OK, sis?" he asks quietly.

"Yeah, of course. Why wouldn't I be?" I feel a twinge of regret at lying to him but smother it down inside me. The truth is, I'm not OK. I'm not OK because Dave is moving in today. It was meant to be next week but this morning Mum had left me a note on the fridge: *GREAT NEWS! Dave moving in today! See you later, honey... xxxx.* So, when I get home from work this evening, he'll be there, invading my space, coming between Mum and me. I know he was moving in anyway but I thought I still had one more week of normality, of just Mum and me. For some annoying reason my eyes start swimming with tears. The knife slips and I slice into my finger. "Ow!" It's only a nick but the lemon juice really makes it sting.

"Uh-oh." Jenna comes rushing over. She's super health-and-safety-conscious. We have about ten first-aid kits at Kale and Hearty and the slightest injury has to be recorded in an "accident book" Jenna keeps on top of the fridge. She gets it now, along with the nearest first-aid kit. "Let's rinse it first," she says, leading me over to the sink.

I stick my finger under the cold tap and slowly it numbs the sting. Jenna pats my finger dry with some kitchen roll, then puts a sticking plaster over the cut. There's something so tender about the way she does this that it makes me want to cry again. What the hell is wrong with me? Why am I so emotional all of a sudden? It's not even like I'm due my period.

"There you go." Jenna looks up and notices my eyes filling with tears. "Oh, Rudy, what's wrong? Is it really hurting?"

"No, it's fine. I'm fine. I think it must be the lemon juice," I say feebly. Like, since when has lemon juice ever made anyone cry? If only I'd been chopping an onion.

Jenna looks at me for a moment, then gives my hand a gentle squeeze. "Why don't you have your morning break now?"

Why does she have to be so nice? It would be so much easier if she was a bitch of a boss, yelling at me for being careless. Then I could get angry, instead of feeling so pathetic.

"OK," I answer, feebly.

I go back into the café. Tyler and Sid are busy serving a crowd of customers by the till. I'm about to take a seat at the counter when I see that Clementine is still sitting at the table in the window, writing in her notebook. I wonder if I should leave her to it. But if she sees me sitting at the counter she'll think I'm ignoring her. And I wasn't exactly overly friendly before due to my whole breakdown about the Dave-moving-in thing. Maybe I should slip back out to the kitchen. But just as I'm about to leave she looks over and her face breaks into a grin. I force myself to smile back and go over to her.

"War injury," I say, holding up my plastered finger. "I've been told to go on my break before the lemons kill me. Don't let me interrupt you, though – if you're busy?" I nod at her notepad.

"Oh no, that's fine." She flicks the pad shut. "I was just having a writing rant."

"Really?" I sit down opposite her. Clementine doesn't look like she'd be capable of the slightest grump let alone a rant but I remind myself that this is the girl who has funeral music as her ringtone for her stepdad. Maybe perfect waters run deep.

"Yeah. It's been one of those weeks."

"Tell me about it."

We sit in silence for a moment.

"You can, if you want," I say. "Tell me about it."

"Oh, right." She looks out of the window, her cheeks flushing. "Do you ever feel like you've been cast as an extra in someone else's movie?"

"What do you mean?"

"I mean, when you look around at the people in your life and the life you're living it all feels wrong. Like, this isn't the way it was supposed to be."

A montage of random images flicks through my mind like a slide show: the apple in the art class, Dave, Mum lecturing me about going to university. There are so many things that don't feel right about my life but it never occurred to me that this might be down to some kind of divine casting mix-up. For as long as I can remember, I've accepted that life can be crap, that it's just the way of things.

"Sorry, does that sound a bit weird?" Clementine's face flushes redder

"No, not really." I look at her designer sweatshirt, her heart-shaped face and her pale blonde hair. Why, when she's been cast as the perfect princess, would she not want the life she's living?
"So, what kind of life do you think you should be living?"

"One where I'm free to make my own decisions," she replies instantly.

"Yeah, but isn't that every teenager's dream?" I feel a horrible pang of doubt. What if she's some spoiled brat who just wants to get her own way all the time? What if that's the reason she's unhappy?

"I suppose so. Do you know what I hate the most?" she says.

"What?" I hold my breath, praying she doesn't say something like, *I hate it when my parents don't give me a big enough allowance or buy me a second pony.*

"When adults ask you what you want to be when you grow up."

"Oh God, I hate that one too!" I pull my chair a little closer.

"Firstly, I hate the assumption that to be a 'grown-up' is some kind of aspirational thing. I mean the grown-ups I know are all so messed up."

"Yes!" I fight the urge to high-five her.

"And secondly, why are they so obsessed with what you want to do for a job? What if you don't know yet? And what if you don't want your job to be your entire identity?" Clementine's face is really flushed now and her eyes are sparking with anger. I feel the sudden urge to draw her, to capture the electrical charges pulsing beneath her perfect skin, bringing her to life, making her look way more interesting. "I have no clue what job I want to do when I 'grow up'," she continues. "All I do know is that I want to feel happy and I want to be free. And I don't want to be messed up like the grown-ups I know." She sits back and sighs.

"Yes, sister!" I raise my hand. For an awkward moment she doesn't understand what I'm doing but finally the penny drops and she laughs and high-fives me.

"Sorry. I thought I'd got all of my rant into my notebook but clearly I was still a little angry."

"Don't apologize. It's all good." And it is. I'm so glad I cut my finger and it brought me out here so we could chat. "That's why I loved your poem," I say. "It made me see a way out."

"How do you mean?"

"It made me realize that we shouldn't focus on the things getting us down, we should focus on how we can get back up again."

She nods. "It's funny. Even though I was the one who wrote it I still find it hard to actually do it!"

"I know, right? When I was working on the art for your poem I felt so empowered but then this morning…" I break off.

"What happened this morning?"

"I found out that my mum's boyfriend is moving in. I mean, I knew he was moving in, just not that it was going to be today."

"Oh God, you have my deepest sympathies."

"Yeah, I thought you might understand, after hearing the ringtone you have for your stepdad."

She laughs. "Absolutely. I think we need to take the advice of the poem and your picture. Let's not focus on the people and things that are getting us down. Let's focus on us and what we want to do and who we want to be."

"Preach!"

"Can I come with you?"

"Where?"

"When you do the artwork."

"Of course. I'd kind of assumed that you would."

Her face lights up. "That's great. When were you thinking of doing it?"

"How about Sunday night? It's a bit quieter then. Well, as quiet as Brighton gets. I go pretty late, though."

"How late?"

"About one in the morning."

I see a flicker of doubt cross her face before she quickly replaces it with a smile. "That'll be fine."

Tyler heads our way with a tray full of drinks and does a double take when he sees me. "Whoa!" he exclaims. "I thought you'd gone back to the kitchen."

"Yeah, well, I decided to take my break early."

He nods and grins knowingly. "Good idea."

I smile back at him. "Yeah, it was."

CLEMENTINE

I get home from Brighton just before midday, my head buzzing. Even though it's probably wrong to say this, I'm glad Rudy cut her finger and came back into the café. I feel so much better now that we've chatted properly and I was able to chip through her tough exterior, a little bit anyway. It was great when she started opening up about her mum's boyfriend moving in. It's good to know that we have evil stepdads in common. I'll have to recommend some evil stepdad ringtones. As I take my shoes off in the hallway I hear Mum's raised voice from the kitchen. I'm about to go and eavesdrop by the kitchen door when I see Damon sitting halfway up the stairs.

"Hey," I say, smiling up at him. Damon and I used to be really close. Until he was old enough to go to football and Vincent started paying an interest in him. Now that they're football buddies it feels as if there's a fracture through the middle of the family. Boys against girls. Men against women.

"Hey," he replies glumly. He's wearing his muddy football kit. Something is definitely up. Normally Mum insists he goes straight for a shower when he gets back – and his dirty clothes go straight in the washing machine. There's no way she'd let him sit like this on the pristine carpet.

"Are you OK?"

"Yeah." He shrugs but I can tell he's not, that there's a sadness in place of his usual swagger. I sit on the stairs and I hear the low rumble of Vincent's voice from the kitchen.

"I take it they're fighting again."

He nods.

"It's crap, isn't it?"

"Yeah."

I think back to how, when Damon was little, he'd come and snuggle up with me whenever Mum and Vincent had a fight. I move up to the stair he's sitting on.

"I don't like it when he drinks," Damon mutters, picking at a patch of dried mud on his knee.

"Me neither." Hope grows inside of me. This is the first time he's said anything negative about Vincent in ages. I put my arm around his thin shoulders. He relaxes into me. "What are they arguing about?"

"Dad not taking me to football this morning. Mum had to take me. He's only just got up. I'm glad he didn't take me anyway. He stinks of beer."

"How did it go?"

"We lost, two – three."

"Oh, sorry about that."

"Do you want to come and watch me play one week?" He looks at me hopefully.

"Of course. I'd love that."

Vincent's always made such a big deal of football being his and Damon's thing – a lads' thing – he's never once invited me.

"Really?" Damon looks so surprised it really upsets me.

"Of course! I'd love to see you play."

"Cool." Damon snuggles in closer. It feels so nice I don't dare move a muscle in case it makes him move away.

The kitchen door suddenly opens and Vincent comes marching into the hall. "OK, OK, have it your way!" he yells over his shoulder. When he sees us the shock on his face is almost comical. "Oh, all right? What are you pair doing there?"

"Having a chat," Damon says defensively.

"Oh, really?" Vincent looks from Damon to me. The whites of his eyes are stained red and his chin is flecked with grey stubble. "How do you fancy watching the Spurs game this afternoon, son? We can go round to Tommo's."

I internally groan. Tommo is a friend from Vincent's radio heyday. He used to read the sports reports on Vincent's breakfast show and he's one of his chief butt-kissers.

"I don't know," Damon says glumly. Vincent and I look at him in shock. It's unheard of for Damon to turn down an invitation to football.

"What do you mean?" Vincent splutters. "It's Spurs against Arsenal. How can you not want to see it?"

Mum appears behind Vincent in the hallway. She looks equally surprised to see Damon and me. "What's going on?" she says, looking at me.

"Have you said something to him?" Vincent glares at me.

"Like what?"

"I don't know. But there you are, looking as thick as thieves, and suddenly my son doesn't want to watch the football with me."

Adrenaline starts pumping through my body, causing a thumping sensation in my ears. "He's not only your son, you know."

"And what's that supposed to mean?" Vincent comes closer, bringing with him the sour smell of stale alcohol.

"He's Mum's son too and he's my brother."

"Half-brother," Vincent mutters.

"Yeah, thank God," I snap.

"Clementine!" Mum gasps.

"Well, that's nice, that is," Vincent says.

Damon shifts slightly away from me.

"I didn't mean I was glad that you're only my half-brother," I say to Damon. "I meant…" I break off.

"What? What did you mean?" Vincent stares at me.

"Never mind."

"Oh, but I do mind. I mind very much being spoken to like that in my own home."

"In your *and* Mum's home."

He lets out a snort of laughter. "Oh yeah, because she's contributed so much to the mortgage."

"OK, I think we all need to calm down," Mum says, taking hold of Vincent's arm. He shakes her hand away like it's an annoying insect.

"I think somebody needs to apologize," Vincent says, looking pointedly at me.

Anger burns inside me. "Yes, you're right, they do." I stare back at him.

"Clementine," Mum says.

"What?" I snap.

"Julia, I think you need to control your daughter."

"What, like you control Mum?"

An awful silence falls in the hall.

"OK, Dad, I'll watch the football," Damon says quietly. I instantly realize what he's doing is trying to keep the peace.

"You don't have to," I tell him.

"What the hell?" Vincent yells. He turns to Mum defiantly. "See, I knew she was up to something. I knew she was stirring."

"Trust me, if I wanted to stir, I'd have done it already."

Vincent leans in so close we're practically chin to chin. "Oh, really?"

My anger drains from me. There's a coldness in his eyes that sends a shiver right through me. All I want is to be away from him. "Never mind," I mutter. I get up and walk up the stairs, my heart pounding.

RUDY

Idiot Dave stands in the middle of the kitchen – *my* kitchen – waving a paintbrush at me. All the way home from work, I'd been preparing myself for this moment, hoping he'd be tucked away on the sofa or, even better, out somewhere with his friends. But no, he's standing in the middle of the kitchen, grinning like his moving in is the best thing that's ever happened.

"Hey, Rudy, your mum's asked me to paint the kitchen and I was wondering if you'd like to help."

I look at him like he's insane.

"I don't mean right now," he says, laughing. "I know you've been working all day. I was thinking maybe we could make a start on it tomorrow."

"On my one day off?" I go over and open a cupboard, more to have a reason to escape his grin than to actually get anything, but to my surprise, the cupboard's full of food.

"I did a food shop earlier," Dave says. "Feel free to help yourself."

Ah, right, he thinks he's going to worm his way in that way, does he? I shut the cupboard. "It's OK, I ate at work."

"I thought you might enjoy helping me decorate, as you're so into art."

Dave really, truly, is a complete idiot. "There's a difference between art and painting and decorating," I say.

"Well, that depends." Dave sets the paintbrush down and puts on the kettle. "Fancy a brew?"

I shake my head, even though I could really do with a tea. Dave always seems to bring out the *No, absolutely not* in me. "Depends on what?"

"On how we decorate it."

"Oh, yeah?"

"Yeah." He plops a teabag in a mug and pours in a dash of milk. Typical – he's the kind of tea-drinking monster who puts the milk in *before the water*! I can't wait to tell Tyler this latest development.

"I was thinking you might like to design something."

I frown at him. "What do you mean?"

"What if you did some kind of mural, here on this wall?" He points to the largest wall in the kitchen over, by the table.

"Are you serious?"

He nods.

"But what about Mum?"

"What about me?" Mum says, appearing in the doorway in her work uniform of skin-tight skirt and sky-high heels.

"Does she know about this?" I ask Dave.

"Absolutely."

"Know about what?" Mum says.

"Me doing a mural on the kitchen wall."

"Ah, yes." Mum smiles. "Dave thought it might brighten the place up a bit."

"But what about the housing association?"

To my surprise, Mum shrugs. "What about them? As long as we paint everything back to magnolia if and when we move out we're allowed to redecorate. And if it stops you from painting the wall behind your wardrobe…"

My stomach flips. "You know about that?"

"Of course I do. Do you think I can't smell the paint?" Thankfully, Mum starts cracking up laughing.

"But – why didn't you say anything?"

"You've got Dave to thank for that. I was about ready to kill you." She nudges him affectionately.

"I told her you needed a place to express yourself. So, what do you reckon?" Dave nods to the wall.

"And I get to design whatever I like?"

"Within reason," Mum says quickly.

"Why don't you sketch some ideas first," Dave says.

I know he's trying to suck up to me, but I can't help feeling excited. One thing's for sure, I definitely did not see this one coming.

"And of course we'd pay you," Dave says.

"You what now?" My eyes practically pop out of my head.

"You'll be an artist working on a commission. It's only fair that we pay you."

I look at Mum for proof that he's kidding, but she's nodding.

"Wow, uh, OK."

"Awesome!" Dave says, with yet another dimply grin. Already my mind is clicking into gear as the blank wall fills with possibilities.

CLEMENTINE

I walk along the beachside path aware of a weird kind of numbness. Ever since my argument with Vincent earlier I've felt unsettled. It was like a boundary was crossed between us today, one that there'll be no coming back from. In fact, things can only get worse. It's early evening. When I left the house Damon and Vincent were still at Tommo's and Mum was in the loft, no doubt manically sorting and cleaning. I stop opposite the old pier and gaze into the darkness at the inky black sea. I listen to the soothing rush of waves on the beach. *It's not about the hurting, it's about the rising,* I remind myself. But what if you've got nowhere to rise to? What if you're trapped in a situation where there's no magical ladder reaching to the stars to save you? I turn and look at the wall by the steps leading up to the road. It would be the perfect spot for Rudy's piece – *our* piece. As I correct myself I feel a bud of hope begin to unfurl. I take a photo of the wall and send it to Rudy:

> I think I've found the perfect spot. It's right by the old pier – by the stairs leading up to the road.

My finger hovers over the "x" – but I don't think Rudy and I are quite at the stage for kisses yet. A few seconds later my phone pings with a reply.

Are you there right now?

Yes.

I hold my breath and look at my phone.

Can I come and join you?

Yes, please do! That would be brilliant! I type, then instantly delete it and write "sure" instead. I don't want to seem over-keen.

I'll be about 5 mins.

OK.

I go up the steps and wait for Rudy by the cycle lane that runs along the seafront. The relief I feel at the prospect of seeing her again is so intense I almost feel like crying. I blink hard and stare at the sea. *It's going to be OK*, I tell myself. Groups of people walk past, laughing and chatting, off for a Saturday night out in town. One day I'll be old enough to do whatever I want to do too. One day I'll be free of Vincent. I try and focus on my dream life but fear keeps prickling. I've never felt afraid of Vincent before and I really don't want to now but there was something about the way he looked at me today; the contempt in his bloodshot eyes really unsettled me. I take out my notepad and lean against the railings.

YOU DON'T SCARE ME! I write in bold letters across the top of the page before falling down a rabbit hole of words and feelings. A few minutes later I'm snapped out of my writing trance by the rattling sound of wheels on the pavement. I turn to see Rudy flying towards me on a skateboard. She comes to a standstill and flips the board into her hand. She's wearing black jeans and Converse and a scuffed black leather biker jacket. The only splash of colour is a bright blue woolly hat, pulled down to her eyebrows.

"All right?" she says gruffly.

"Hey."

"Having another rant?" she nods at my notebook.

"Yes and no. I'm writing a ranty poem about misogyny," I explain.

She laughs. "That's good. Turn your anger into art."

"Exactly."

"Can I see it?"

"Oh – uh – well, it's still really rough."

"That's OK. I won't judge."

I hand the pad to her, thankful that it's dark and she can't see the embarrassment playing out on my cheeks.

Rudy whistles through her teeth. "Wow, who or what inspired this?"

"My stepdad," I say glumly.

"Sounds like a real Prince Charming."

"More like the evil old troll who lives under the bridge."

We laugh and Rudy pulls her jacket collar up against the cold. "So, where's this wall then?"

"Just down there." I lead her down the steps and point to the wall midway. "Think how many people would see it here."

Rudy nods. "And the good thing is, it's pretty secluded, so I should be able to do it without being seen. Especially if you and Tyler keep watch."

"Yes, of course." My skin prickles with excitement at the thought of helping Rudy, not to mention seeing Tyler again. Although how I'm going to get out of the house for one in the morning is a whole other question.

"Do you want to get some doughnuts?"

"Yes!" I answer so emphatically she raises her eyebrows at me.

"Sorry, it's just been one of those days. A definite doughnut day."

"I hear ya."

We start walking along the front towards Palace Pier.

"So, my mum's boyfriend moved in," Rudy says, staring straight ahead.

"Oh dear. What's he like?"

"He's an idiot."

We walk on in silence. I'm unsure what to say. I want to know more but I don't want to seem like I'm prying.

"He's trying really hard to make me like him."

"Really?" To me this doesn't seem like a bad thing. The thought of Vincent trying really hard to make me like him is laughable. Right from the start he was indifferent and now his indifference seems to have soured into out-and-out hatred.

"But I know it won't last," Rudy continues.

I want to ask what makes her so certain but I don't want it to seem like I'm challenging her.

"How old are you?" Rudy turns to look at me.

"Fifteen. How about you?"

"Same."

"Really?" I'm surprised. I thought Rudy was older. She seems so worldly.

"Yeah. What school do you go to?"

"Hove School for Girls."

"Right." There's a curtness about the way she says this that immediately makes me feel awkward. I get the sense Rudy doesn't have the best opinion of private schools.

"How about you?"

"Kemptown High."

"I know a couple of people who go there, from my dance school."

"Oh yeah, who?"

"Jody Blake and Abby Harwood." As soon as I've said their names I regret it. What if Rudy's friends with them and she asks them about me? They're hardly going to give me a glowing report.

Rudy stops walking. "Are you friends with them?"

"Not exactly, no."

"Good," Rudy says quietly, which instantly triggers a sigh of relief in me. We carry on walking.

"Those girls sum up everything that's wrong with society," Rudy continues.

"How do you mean?"

"I mean, they think the world revolves around social media likes and dumb celebrities."

I'm so relieved I start to laugh. "To be honest, I think they hate me."

Rudy grins. "Good, that's another thing we have in common."

"Another?"

"Yeah, as well as the whole idiot stepdad thing." Although Idiot Dave is not my idiot stepdad – at least not yet.

We reach the pier and buy a bag of doughnuts, then head down the steps to the beach, crunching our way across the pebbles to a sheltered spot beside one of the stone jetties. As the tide rolls in it brings a plastic carrier bag.

"This drives me nuts," I say, scrambling forward to fish the bag from the frothy water.

"What?"

"All of the plastic in the ocean. I just don't get why people don't care about the harm it's causing."

"Hmm." Rudy gazes out to sea. "Maybe we could get them to care."

"How do you mean?"

She turns to face me. "Maybe that's what we could do our next collab on, saving the the sea life."

"Yes! That would be awesome."

We continue eating our doughnuts in silence. Rudy is

staring out at the water, clearly deep in thought. The moment is so peaceful I'm filled with a sudden contentment and the sense that, however unlikely it might seem, she and I were supposed to meet.

RUDY

And straight in at Number One in the Cringe Top 40: grown-arse adults slow-dancing to Luther Vandross in the kitchen, *on a Sunday morning*.

"Morning, baby girl," Mum calls over Dave's shoulder as she spots me. "Are you joining us for breakfast?"

"Not if it involves joining your *Strictly* routine," I mutter.

Dave cracks up laughing. I head straight for the kettle.

"So, have you had any ideas for the kitchen mural yet?" Dave asks, thankfully disentangling himself from Mum.

"Not really," I reply, although the truth is, ever since he asked me, my mind's been popping with images.

"Well, let me know as soon as you do and I'll give you a lift down to Homebase to get some paints."

"The paints I use aren't sold in Homebase."

"Who fancies a bacon sandwich?" Mum says, taking a packet of bacon from the fridge.

"I'm vegetarian!" I exclaim.

"Yeah, but it's Sunday," Mum says.

"And?" I stare at her in disbelief. In her campaign to make

me eat meat again this is a new level of crazy.

"It's a day of rest."

"And?"

"And enjoying ourselves and giving thanks to Jesus."

"Try telling that to the pigs," I say, looking pointedly at the packet of bacon.

"It's organic and free-range," she says lamely.

"Great. So they were allowed to roam free before they were slaughtered. That's even worse. At least when they're all cooped up they're probably glad to be put out of their misery."

A look of defeat flits across Mum's face and I feel a twinge of guilt. I don't want to make her unhappy but I'm not going to sacrifice my principles.

"Where do you get your paints from then?" Dave asks.

"The art shop in Brighton."

He nods. "Fancy a trip there today, while your mum's at church? Maybe getting some new paints would inspire you."

I appear to be standing right inside the dictionary definition of "DILEMMA". The thought of a trip to the art shop fills me with joy but the thought of having to go with Dave feels all kinds of awkward. "I don't really have any money."

"No, it's on me. I told you," Dave replies, popping some bread into the toaster. "We're commissioning you to do this so we're paying."

Holy guacamole! My dilemma grows. "OK then," I mutter.

"Say thank you!" Mum says.

"Thank you," I echo.

CLEMENTINE

After the tension of yesterday, today has been surprisingly peaceful. This is mainly due to the fact that Vincent is having a "work meeting", aka all-day drinking session with his producer, and Damon has gone to his friend's birthday party. Mum is on the sofa with an industrial-sized bar of chocolate, mainlining one of those cheesy *Real Housewives* series. I'm lying on my bed about to start uploading my latest poem to Instagram when my phone pings. My first thought is that it might be Rudy, and just the fact that I might have got a message from someone who might potentially be a new friend fills me with gratitude. But when I check my phone I see that it's a message from Dad.

> Hey, sweetheart, how are you? All is good
> here, although it's freezing! Ada sends her love.
> Thankfully her morning sickness has finally come
> to an end. Love you and miss you. xxxx

As usual, when I get a message from Dad, it triggers a bittersweet mixture of emotions. My happiness at hearing from him is instantly soured by the fact that he's so far away and I can't be with him. And, ever since Ada got pregnant, a creeping sense of dread that he might not want to be with me once they have their new family.

I wish you were here... I type, then instantly delete it. There's no point telling Dad how sad I am and how tough things are here. He can't do anything about it.

All good here thanks. I miss you too. Really glad Ada's feeling better. Love you. xxxxx

I look at the time. It's almost six o'clock. Six hours until I meet Rudy and Tyler down on the front. Mum and Vincent usually go to bed early on a Sunday night so I'm hoping they'll be fast asleep by the time I slip out.

"Clementine!" Mum calls up the stairs.

"Yes?" I call back.

"Do you want to help me make the dinner?"

Cooking used to be the thing that Mum and I did together. But that was back when she and Vincent still got on OK. Over the past couple of years, as things have got more tense between them, Mum never seems to want help with anything.

"OK," I call and head downstairs.

The first thing I see when I come into the kitchen is an open bottle of wine on the counter. Mum is standing by the fridge, a half-drunk glass in her hand. Her cheeks are flushed and her normally immaculate eye make-up is slightly smudged.

"Hey!" she says, a little too cheerily.

"Are you OK?"

"Of course." She raises her glass. "I thought I'd have a little tipple, seeing as the boys are away. While the boys are away the cat will play," she says, her words slurring slightly.

I'm not sure what to make of this. Like everything else in her life, Mum's alcohol consumption is usually strictly measured and controlled. She never normally has more than one drink at a time. She's always the designated driver when she and Vincent go out – and even when he goes out without her, he'll usually call to ask her to come and pick him up.

"Dad messaged me," I say, deciding that it's probably safer to change the subject.

"Oh?" Instantly, Mum's smile fades.

"Yeah. Ada's feeling better now – you know, after her morning sickness."

"Great." Mum tops her glass up. "I'm so happy for her." She doesn't sound remotely happy, though.

"Are you sure you're OK?"

"Not really." Mum's shoulders crumple. "Oh, Clem. I don't know what to do." She says it so quietly I'm not sure I've heard her correctly.

"What?"

"I don't know what to do." She says it much louder this time.

"About what?" I ask, hardly daring to hope that she might finally be getting sick of Vincent.

"About my non-existent career, about my husband no longer finding me attractive, about my starting the menopause ten years too early – take your pick!" She downs a large swig of wine.

Yikes. As much as I want Mum to open up to me, this feels

like a bit too much information. "I'm sorry. Is there anything I can do to help?"

Mum gives a sarcastic laugh. "How can *you* help me? It's all right for you, you've got your whole life ahead of you. Your life is a blank slate. God, what I'd give to be your age again!"

"Seriously?" It blows my mind that anyone would want to be a teen. "But your life doesn't have to be like that. You can change it." I hold my breath, hoping I haven't said the wrong thing.

Mum gives a dramatic sigh. "And how do you suggest I do that?"

"You could get a job, build your confidence again." I feel as if I've strayed into a conversational minefield, where the slightest false move could result in a Mum explosion.

"What kind of job? I've been out of work for years. I'm on the scrapheap."

"No, you're not! You've got so much going for you. What about all of the years you worked as a radio producer? And you're still working for Vincent behind the scenes. Surely that must count for something."

Mum slams her glass down on the side and wine sloshes onto the counter. "I've been working as his effing skivvy!"

Wow. Mum never – *not ever* – swears. Things must be really bad for her to say "effing". She's also completely ignoring the wine spillage, which is now dripping from the counter onto the floor.

"Why don't you leave him?" It bursts out before I have time to rein it in.

"If only it were that easy. Where would we go? What would I do for money? I'm completely dependent on him."

"You could get a job. Seriously, Mum. You've got so much experience. We could start again."

"And who would pay your school fees?"

"I don't care about that stupid school. I could go to the comprehensive."

"But you're doing your GCSEs."

"Honestly, Mum, I don't care. I just want you to be happy."

Her eyes start shining with tears.

"I could help out. I could get a part-time job in a café or something."

Mum shakes her head. "I can't leave him. I've got nothing."

We both jump as the front door slams shut.

"Julia?" Vincent calls from the hallway.

Mum quickly wipes her eyes and smiles weakly at me. "Let's talk about this another time," she whispers.

I nod and give her arm a squeeze.

Vincent comes through the door holding a massive bouquet of red roses.

"I'm sorry, babe," he says, handing the flowers to Mum and completely ignoring me.

"They're beautiful," Mum murmurs. "Thank you."

My hope swirls away like water down a drain. "I'm going to go and do my homework," I mutter and quietly slip from the room.

RUDY

I meet Tyler in the stairwell just before midnight. He's crouched in the corner looking at his So Dark Fairy.

"Maybe this is what I should get as my first tattoo," he whispers.

"Seriously?"

"Yeah. I love it. I think it would look awesome on my arm."

As we head downstairs I can't help grinning. The thought of my artwork permanently etched upon another person's skin gives me even more of a buzz than thinking of it out on the street.

Outside, the rain has stopped and the sky is clear and starry-bright.

"You managed to escape from Dave then?" Tyler says as we start heading into Brighton.

"Yeah. He went to bed at nine, so that's something at least. Oh, Ty, it's been a nightmare today having to hang out with him."

Tyler grins. "I think it's quite sweet."

I glare at him. "Oh yeah? How exactly?"

"He wants to be friends with you."

"Yeah, well, I've got all the friends I need."

"What, me?"

"Yeah."

"What about the poet?"

"I suppose."

Tyler pulls a fake shocked pose. "Holy guacamole! You've doubled your number of friends in one week."

"Ha ha, very funny." I punch him lightly on the arm. "I wouldn't exactly call Clementine a friend. I mean, I don't really know her properly yet."

"Is she still coming tonight?"

"I think so. She hasn't texted to say no."

"Cool." There's something about the way Tyler is grinning at this news that sets off an alarm bell in me. I might be paranoid but he seems remarkably happy at the prospect of seeing Clementine and I'm not quite sure how I feel about this.

We turn onto the road running along the seafront and head past Palace Pier. This is the time I like the new pier best, when it's steeped in silence, with no gaudy lights and pumping music. The waves swish back and forth in the darkness below us and an icy wind races in off the sea. I pull my hood up over my hat. It's good that the weather's freezing though, as it's hardly going to encourage anyone to go for a late-night stroll along the beach. Tyler starts beatboxing. I swear that boy can make pretty much any sound using just his body. Once he gets his proper studio equipment there'll be no stopping him.

"How's the fund for the mixing console going?"

He sighs. "Don't ask. The telly broke so I had to buy a new one."

"Oh no! Couldn't your mum and dad have bought it?"

"They don't have any spare cash. Mum's just had her benefits cut and the Jobseekers people are on Dad's case."

"You're such a good son."

"Yeah, yeah."

"You are. One day it'll come together for you. Keep the faith, bruv." We link arms and he pulls me close and rests his head on mine for a second.

"Thanks, sis." We walk on in silence. It's as if the wind has whipped the city clean of people. Apart from the sea, the only sound is the rattle of discarded beer cans being swept along on the breeze.

"There she is," Tyler says, pointing ahead of us.

I see a small figure huddled by the railings opposite the old pier. When she sees us she waves in greeting.

"Hey," Clementine says as we draw close. She's wearing a black Puffa jacket, jeans and a woolly hat pulled down so low I can't even see her fringe.

"Hey." I unlink my arm from Tyler's. "You got out OK then?"

"Yeah. My mum and stepdad went to bed early." There's a bitterness to her voice as she says this that instantly makes me feel sympathy. I look from Clementine to Tyler.

"OK, are we ready, team?"

"Yes," Tyler and Clementine chorus.

"I was thinking that maybe one of you could keep lookout up here and the other one down on the beach."

"Sure," Tyler says. "How about I stay up here and you two go down there?"

"Sounds good to me. Is that OK with you?" I ask Clementine. She nods. "All right, let's do this."

As Clementine and I go down the steps I point to the pathway running parallel to the beach. "Can you go down there and see if anyone's coming?"

"Sure." She heads over to the path and gives me a thumbs-up. "It's OK, no one's coming."

"How about up there, Ty?" I call to him.

"All clear," he replies.

I take the can of black paint from my bag and give it a shake. Then I pull my scarf over my face to stop me inhaling the fumes and spray the wall until I have my night sky backdrop. Then I take the can of silver paint and add some stars and a crescent moon. Once I'm happy with the backdrop I take the pot of paste and rolled-up picture of Lightning Girl from my backpack. As I try to prise the lid off the pot my fingers tremble from a mixture of cold and excitement. I'm making my third piece of street art! Fourth, if you count adding the shorts to LADZ's Butt Cheeks of Shame. Finally, the lid comes free and I quickly slop the wall with paste. Then I wait a moment for the wind to drop, unroll the picture and smooth it to the wall. Just as I'm covering it in paste Clementine hisses, "Someone's coming."

Crap! I put the lid on and shove the paste back in my bag.

Clementine hurries over.

"How many people?"

"Just one."

"OK, let's pretend we're having a chat," I whisper. I'm so nervous the palms of my hands are actually sweating. We sit on the steps. Clementine huddles so close I get a waft of floral laundry detergent from her clothes.

"Do you want some gum?" I say, pulling a pack from my jacket pocket.

"No, thanks." She looks really scared. For some weird reason this makes me want to put a protective arm around her. I pop a piece of gum in my mouth instead. As soon as I start chewing my nerves calm. OK, so it's a bit weird that two girls are sitting here on the steps in the middle of the night in the cold but this is Brighton, the city where anything goes. I hear the footsteps approaching. Clementine huddles closer. A figure appears. It's a young guy carrying a sports bag. We sit frozen to the spot. He glances at us for a second, then carries on walking along the beach.

"Holy guacamole!" I whisper as he disappears from view.

Clementine giggles. "Oh my God, my heart was beating so loud I thought he was going to hear it!" She stares at the picture on the wall. "Wow, it looks amazing!"

"Thanks. I've just got to do the stencil of your poem and the tag." I open my backpack and take out some more cans. "Can you check the coast's clear?"

"Sure." Clementine goes back to her spot on the path and gives me a thumbs-up again.

"All OK up there, Ty?" I call softly.

"Yeah, all good," he replies.

I take out the stencil of the poem and attach it to the wall. Then I take the lid off the turquoise paint, pull my scarf back up over my face and quickly spray over the words. Once the poem's done I get the can of gold paint and spray my usual FIERCE tag beneath the picture. Below that I add a stencil of the word "ink" in typewriter font. I peel the stencils from the wall and step back to look at the finished piece. I've sprayed over the edge of the poem stencil in one corner but apart from that it's exactly how I imagined it. I shove the cans and stencils back in my bag. "OK, I'm done," I say quietly.

"It looks amazing," Clementine says, walking over. "I can't believe a poem of mine is actually in a piece of street art." Her mouth drops open in surprise. "You've changed your tag to Fierce Ink."

"*Our* tag," I reply. "I was trying to think of a way to combine our two names. Is that OK?"

"It's fantastic!"

"How's it going?" Tyler calls down.

"All done," I reply. "Come and see."

Tyler bounds down the steps. "Wow! That looks fricking awesome."

"Thank you," I say, pride glowing inside of me. "We'd better get going before someone else comes along."

Tyler takes some photos, then we head back up to the street.

"Great work, Fierce Ink," Tyler says with a grin.

"Thank you," Clementine says quietly. Then she suddenly grabs me and gives me a hug. I'm so taken aback I stand there stiffly, not moving, and she quickly lets go. Her eyes are shining in the orange glow from a nearby streetlight. "Seriously, thank you so much. This has been brilliant."

"Team Fierce Ink," I say, high-fiving her and Tyler.

"Team Fierce Ink," they both reply.

Down below a wave crashes on the beach as if the sea is cheering us.

CLEMENTINE

As I make my way back home I feel so happy it's as if I'm floating above the streets of Hove. The disappointment at not getting the part in the dance show, which had coiled itself round me like a rope, has finally fallen away. For the first time in ages, if not forever, I feel something close to free. And the best thing is that this feeling is coming from real life and not just a dream. An image of Tyler pops into my mind but I immediately push it away again. I have to ignore the fact that he looks as if he's just stepped out of my daydream. From the way he and Rudy turned up arm in arm tonight, I'd say they're definitely together. But it doesn't matter. At least I know now that boys like Luc really do exist.

It's only when I get to my road that nerves start chipping away at my newfound excitement. What if Mum woke up while I was gone? What if they hear me coming in? Thankfully, no lights are on. I sneak around to the back of the house. As I creep to the door I hear a rustling behind me and my heart practically stops. A fox darts across the lawn. I stand rooted to the spot until it's gone, my heart now racing. I put my key in the back door and turn it slowly. It only makes the softest of clicks but in the silence of the night it sounds loud enough to wake the entire neighbourhood. I step into the utility room and breathe in the warm, sweet-scented air. I shut and lock the door behind me and take off my coat and shoes, deciding to leave them down here. At least if I get caught coming upstairs I can just say I'd come down for a glass of milk or something. To add credibility to my cover story, I tiptoe into the kitchen and pour myself a glass of milk. Then I creep up to my room and hurriedly get changed into my pyjamas. I sit down on my bed, relief flooding through me. I did it. We did it! Team Fierce Ink.

The next morning I get up extra early. I'm going to go for another pretend jog to take some photos of our picture in daylight to use on Instagram. I'd been hoping I'd be up before anyone else but when I go downstairs I see Vincent coming out of the kitchen, wearing his tracksuit and trainers.

"What are you doing up so early?" he says. No "Good morning". No greeting.

"Going for a run," I mutter. "How about you?"

"Yeah, I'm going running too." He shifts awkwardly and I realize that he's probably having the same thought as me, that, in a normal situation with a normal stepdad we'd laugh at this coincidence and go running together. But instead, here we are in some kind of awkward stand-off.

"So, I'll be off then," he says, hurrying past me. I see the outline of his phone in his tracksuit pocket. I wonder if he'll be ringing the person he called "darling" the other day when he was meant to be running and I feel a surge of anger on Mum's behalf.

I have a glass of water, put a note on the kitchen table for Mum, telling her where I've gone, and head out of the door. As I run along the street I replay the events of last night and adrenaline starts pumping through my veins. Vincent might be the biggest a-hole to walk the planet but at least now I have Team Fierce Ink. I turn onto the seafront and get my first glimpse of the morning sun, burning gold on the horizon. *It's going to be a good day,* I tell myself. *I'm going to get a photo of some street art that actually features one of my poems.* The starlings that roost on the remains of the West Pier in the winter are waking up, swirling and looping through the pale blue sky. As the steps come into view it's hard to believe that I was here last night with Tyler and Rudy. It's all starting to feel like a dream, I wait for a gap in the traffic and run across the road. A couple of cyclists whizz by along the cycle lane. Normally, it annoys me that they zoom up on you out of nowhere but not today. Today, I don't think anything could annoy me. I run down the steps, taking my phone from my pocket. And then I stop, rooted to the spot.

"Oh no!" I'm so horrified at what I see I blurt my thoughts out loud.

Rudy's picture is still there but someone has sprayed red paint all over it. The girl's face is now completely obscured. You can no longer see her look of fierce defiance. You can no longer see the lightning bolt tattoo. They've sprayed all over my poem too. The only word that's still visible is "RISING" but streaks of red paint are trickling down it like blood. They've even covered our tag with what I assume is one of their own.

I look away, out at the sea. Why would anyone do this? Then I think of Rudy. How's she going to feel when she sees it? How am I going to tell her what's happened? I decide to send her a message.

Hi, I've got some bad news :(

Almost instantly my phone starts ringing. It's Rudy.

"Hey," I say.

"What's happened?"

"Someone's painted over the picture. They've sprayed all over it in red."

Rudy is silent. I hear the clatter of crockery in the background and remember that she works in the café on a Monday morning before school.

"They sprayed all over it?" She sounds weirdly brisk and efficient, like having her art ruined is a daily occurrence.

"Yes. And they wrote something over your – our – tag."

"What did they write?"

I look at the huge red letters obscuring FIERCE INK.

"I think it's another tag. It says 'LADZ'. L – A - D - Z."

There's silence from the other end of the phone, broken only by the chink of cutlery.

"Yes, I know how to spell it," Rudy says, quietly.

I stand in front of my picture, fighting the urge to scream. Although I got Clementine to send me a photo of it, it didn't prepare me for how I'd feel seeing it for real. I don't think anything could. I'd been prepared for the fact that none of my pieces of street art would last forever; that eventually they'd be worn away by the weather or replaced – but I'd not been prepared for this. A seagull screeches high above me, wrenching me from my daze. I look at how the paint has been concentrated in certain places – completely obscuring Lightning Girl's face and the words of the poem. And of course, the tag. I look at the huge letters now covering FIERCE INK.

LADZ

I don't get how he found it so quickly. Unless… I suddenly remember the young guy who walked past us last night. Could he have been LADZ? I trawl my memory for clues. He was carrying a bag – a large sports bag. Could he have been out last night doing a new painting? My stomach churns with a sickening mix of anger and dread. Whether it was him or not, the fact is, LADZ has found and ruined my picture. He must have recognized my FIERCE tag from the pocket of the shorts I sprayed on his stupid butt cheeks. But at least I added to his picture. At least I didn't destroy it. And I only did it because I found it offensive. There was nothing offensive about my picture of Lightning Girl. It was empowering. And now it's ruined. Disappointment crushes me. I'd felt so happy making that picture, visualizing myself climbing up my own ladder to the stars. But what was the point? Someone's always going to be waiting to knock me back down again. I turn and trudge away, up the steps.

I get to school late again. Not that I care. The worst that can happen has already happened. This time, when I come into art class, Ms O'Toole doesn't smile at me.

"This isn't on, Rudy," she says, coming over as I take my seat at the table. "You can't keep being late for lessons."

"I'm sorry," I mutter. Although, truthfully, the only thing I'm sorry about is that I have to be here at all.

"Well, maybe a detention will help you to get better at your time-keeping."

"What?" I stare at her. A stunned silence falls upon the classroom. Ms O'Toole never gives detentions. The closest she ever gets to disciplining anyone is when she raises her voice slightly.

"Detention here, with me, today after school," she says firmly. "Now, carry on working on your still-life piece."

"But it's not fair." As soon as I say it I regret it, as I sound like a brat. But it isn't fair. None of it is.

"I'm not going to argue about it, Rudy," Ms O'Toole says briskly. "I'll see you back here at three-fifteen."

By the time three-fifteen comes around I'm seriously tempted to skip the detention, and if it had been any other teacher, I probably would. Battling against the tide of students streaming out from every available door, I make my way to the art department. When I get to Ms O'Toole's classroom I'm relieved to see that it's empty. She must have forgotten about me. But just as I'm about to turn and leave, she appears from the storeroom, holding a handful of paintbrushes.

"Aha, Rudy," she says, cheerily, like she's invited me round to tea.

I wonder what she's going to make me do on this detention. I scan the room for any sign of fruit.

"Take a seat," she says, gesturing to one of the tables.

I slump down in a chair. Ms O'Toole puts the paintbrushes in one of the glass jars lining the shelf and comes over to sit beside me.

"Is something going on?" she asks softly.

"What do you mean?"

"I mean, is something causing you to be late? Is something going on at home – or personally?"

Normally, a teacher trying to be all best buds to get you to spill the beans makes me cringe but Ms O'Toole looks so genuinely concerned it makes me soften a bit.

"Or is it these classes?" she continues. "Have you gone off art?"

"What? No!"

Relief flickers across her face and this makes me soften even more.

"Well, that's something at least." She smiles. "You're a very talented artist, Rudy."

"Really?"

"Yes. And I think you have the potential to be an exceptional artist. I don't want to see you blow it."

"How do you mean?"

"I don't want your attitude to get in the way of your talent."

"It's not. I love art. It's pretty much all I think about, all I do."

Ms O'Toole looks at me thoughtfully. "I'd love to see some of the work you do – outside of this class, I mean."

"For real?"

"Of course."

I'm not sure what to make of this. For so long my art has fallen into two completely separate categories – school and personal – with zero crossover. I shift in my seat. "I could show you now if you like. I have some pictures on my phone."

"Absolutely." Ms O'Toole smiles broadly.

I relax some more. This detention isn't going at all how I'd imagined. I flick through the gallery on my phone until I reach the picture of the girl looking into the mirror. "I did this one recently."

I hold my breath while Ms O'Toole looks at the picture.

It doesn't matter if she doesn't like it, I tell myself, *I'm not doing it to impress teachers.*

"This is incredible."

OK, maybe I am doing it to impress teachers because Ms O'Toole's words seem to have set off some kind of happiness party inside of me.

I take the phone back and scroll through to the picture of the girl tied to the chair. "I did this one too."

Again, Ms O'Toole looks blown away and again, I feel stupidly happy. "Wow. These are very powerful pieces, Rudy."

"Thank you."

"Do you have any more?"

I nod and swipe through to the picture of Lightning Girl on the ladder, feeling an instant twinge of sorrow as I think of what's become of her. At least I have the photo to remember her as she was supposed to be. "This is my most recent piece."

"I love this!" Ms O'Toole exclaims. "What's written beside it?"

I zoom in on the poem. "My friend wrote a poem. Her words inspired my picture."

"I would love to see this piece. Would it be possible to bring it into class?"

I shake my head. "No. I – uh – it's actually on a wall. It's a piece of street art." I'm not sure whether telling a teacher you're a street artist and therefore effectively a law-breaker is such a great idea but then Ms O'Toole isn't any ordinary teacher. As if to reassure me she starts grinning.

"Is it here in Brighton?"

"Yeah. Well, it was but – but there's been an accident. It got ruined."

"Oh, what a shame." Ms O'Toole looks genuinely disappointed. "Thank goodness you've got this photo at least. Can you get a print of it?"

I stare at her, confused.

"I'd love to have a copy of this on my wall," Ms O'Toole explains.

All of the anger and pain and disappointment that's been curdling inside me dissolves away and I feel dangerously close to tears. I blink hard and look away.

"Rudy?"

I nod, not trusting myself to speak.

Ms O'Toole gently places her hand on my arm. "How about we make a deal?"

"What kind of deal?"

"You turn up to my classes on time and you make an effort with the exercises I set you – even if you find them deadly boring—"

"I don't…" She raises her eyebrows and I grin. "OK."

"And in exchange I come up with some extra-curricular material, tailor-made for you."

"What do you mean?"

"Now I've seen the kind of work you do I can point you in the direction of artists or techniques you might find useful and interesting."

I try not to let my mouth hang open in shock. "You'd do that for me?"

"Of course. I want you to succeed, Rudy."

"I – I don't know what to say," I stammer.

"Just say that we've got a deal." She smiles. "Then get out of here and get back to your art."

This has got to be the best detention ever! "Deal." I hold my hand out to her.

She takes it and shakes it firmly. "I have very high hopes for you, Rudy."

Her words echo in my head, carrying me like a sea breeze, up and out of school and all the way home.

CLEMENTINE

I trudge along the beach, kicking at the pebbles. Next to me, the tide crashes against the shore, as if it's mirroring my anger. For the first time ever, I feel the same sense of despondency about going to dance class as I do about going to school. All day I've been thinking about Rudy, wondering how she's feeling. And all day a creeping fear has taken over me – what if having her picture ruined makes her want to give up on street art? What if she no longer wants to collaborate with me? What will I do? I don't think I can bear my life returning to the boring nothingness it was before. When I get close to the studio I stop and look out at the sea.

"Please…" I whisper, not sure exactly what I'm asking for, other than a miracle.

Just then my phone beeps. A jolt of relief courses through my body as I see that it's a message from Rudy:

Team Fierce Ink meeting at Kale and Hearty
NOW! Hope you can make it…

I look back at the sea and laugh. My plea has been answered, in literally one second! *Unless, of course, she's calling the meeting to officially end Team Fierce Ink*, my stupid voice of fear chimes up. But I don't care. At least I'll have a chance to try and talk her out of it. I turn away from the studio and start walking back into Brighton.

By the time I get to Sydney Street a fine rain is falling and the café windows are steamed up. I hurry inside. Most of the tables are taken and the air is filled with chatter and the low hum of music. A thin woman with turquoise hair is standing behind the counter, slicing a cake. Beside her, a man with jet-black hair and multiple piercings is making a coffee, moving his body in time to the music. I'm about to go over and ask for Rudy when I hear a high-pitched whistle.

"Clementine!" Rudy and Tyler are sitting at a table in the far corner. I hurry over to join them.

"Hey," I say, sitting down.

"I'm really sorry about what happened," Tyler says to me.

"Yeah, it was crap," I reply. "I can't believe someone would do that. Or why."

"I do," Rudy says, looking slightly sheepish.

"What? Why?" I ask.

"Yeah, why?" Tyler stares at her.

"LADZ is another street artist and I…" She shifts uncomfortably in her seat.

"What have you done?" Tyler says in a mock scolding voice, like he's totally used to Rudy getting into trouble.

"He did this picture recently that I found offensive. It was of a woman's giant butt in a tiny G-string, so I – I *customized* it."

"You customized it how?" Tyler says, raising his eyebrows to me.

"I painted a pair of shorts on it."

"Oh man!" Tyler starts cracking up.

"I also might have added a caption," Rudy says sheepishly.

"Saying what?" I ask.

"Don't objectify women," Rudy mutters. "But he was objectifying them." She looks at us earnestly. "We are way more than butt cheeks."

"Amen, sister!" Tyler cries, before laughing again. I bite on my lip, trying not to giggle.

"It's not funny. I was taking a stand against misogyny." Rudy grins. Then she looks at me. "I'm so sorry. I also painted my FIERCE tag on the label of the shorts. He must have recognized it and that's what made him ruin our painting."

"Wow," is all I'm able to say, as I try to take in this latest development. In the last twenty-four hours I have not only become part of a street art collaboration but I also seem to have been plunged into a street art war. It's official — my life is no longer boring — and I'm overcome with relief.

"I'll totally understand if you don't want to work with me again," Rudy says, "but if you do, you'd better not bail," she adds, her dark eyes sparkling, "because Team Fierce Ink have work to do."

"We do? I mean — yes, of course! What kind of work?"

Rudy leans back in her seat. "We can't let him beat us. We have to keep going. And when you think about it, us not being beaten is exactly what our piece was about, isn't it? *'It's not about the hurting – it's about the rising'.*"

"*'Turn your lessons into ladders and start climbing',*" I add.

Rudy laughs and high-fives me. "All right then – shall we get working on our next piece?" She takes a sketchpad from her bag and opens it to a blank page. "What do you reckon we should do next?"

I truly cannot believe my luck at this turn of events. I had no idea Rudy would take it so well. It makes me feel ashamed for feeling so sorry for myself all day.

"What about what we talked about the other night on the beach? About people polluting the ocean with plastic."

"Great idea," Tyler says. "I was reading this piece on BuzzFeed on my lunchbreak that said that one hundred million sea creatures are killed every year because of plastic."

"What the hell?" Rudy exclaims.

"It's true," I say. "They're either eating it or getting tangled up in it."

The guy with the black hair and piercings comes over, holding an orders pad and pencil. "Can I get you guys any drinks?"

"Hey, Sid, I started working on some sketches for your tattoo the other night." Rudy flicks through her pad and shows him some pictures.

"These are awesome." He crouches down next to her and points to the page. "I love this one. Is there any way you could make the tail slightly longer?"

"Sure." Rudy starts sketching.

"Nice one." Sid stands up and grins at me. "Hello, I don't think we've met."

"This is Clementine," Tyler says. "She's a poet."

"Oh, I wouldn't say—" I begin.

"She's a great poet," Rudy cuts in, not looking up from her pad. "We're collaborating on some pieces."

"Really?" Sid looks genuinely interested.

"Yeah, look." Tyler takes his phone from his pocket and shows him what I guess must be a photo of our work from last night before it got ruined.

"This is epic," Sid exclaims.

"*Was*," Rudy mutters, still drawing. "Before someone ruined it."

"Shit!" Sid looks genuinely distraught, which restores my faith in humanity.

"That reminds me," Rudy says, looking up from her pad. "Would it be OK to use the office printer to make a copy?"

"Of course." Sid turns to Tyler. "Send it to me and I'll print one out now. Right, who's for drinks?"

We order and Sid goes over to the counter.

"Right, I'd better get back to work." Tyler stands up and puts his phone back in his pocket. I try to ignore how disappointed this makes me feel.

RUDY

I look down at a fresh new page in my sketchpad. What could I draw to symbolize how the ocean is being polluted? This is definitely pushing me out of my comfort zone but I love the challenge. Maybe I could sketch a selection of endangered sea creatures but that feels a bit predictable. I need something more powerful, something that represents the sea itself. The image of a mermaid pops into my mind. But this mermaid isn't all cutesy and Disney. She has glistening black skin and a glimmering blue tail and a thick mane of cornrow braids crowning her head.

Across the table from me, Clementine is writing in her notebook. Every so often she stops and chews the end of her pen, gazing into space, just like I do when I'm waiting for inspiration. I've always preferred to come up with ideas for my artwork on my own but this feels even better. As I watch Clementine gazing out of the window I think of her theory that poems already exist fully formed in some magical realm, just waiting for a writer they can use as a channel. I smile as I imagine our next piece of street art swirling around somewhere in the ether, waiting for us both to find it.

I look back at my pad and start sketching. I draw a rough outline of my mermaid rising up from the ocean, her braids streaming out behind her. Then I draw the outline of a staff in her hand, to give her even more of a warrior feel. I try to imagine the ocean as a person and how it would feel about all of the damage being done to it. I start adding detail to the mermaid's face: sorrow in her eyes, a frown line on her forehead.

"Wow." Clementine's voice breaks my concentration. I look up to see her staring across the table at my drawing.

"It's just a rough outline," I say, feeling suddenly self-conscious.

"It's brilliant." She looks back at her notepad and continues writing and I go back to my sketching.

When Tyler brings our drinks over he doesn't say anything; he knows better than to interrupt me when I'm in the flow.

I'm not sure how long we sit like this, me drawing and Clementine writing, but the next time I look up practically all the other customers have gone and Tyler's cleaning the tables.

Clementine glances up and smiles.

"How did you get on?" I ask.

"OK … I think." She flicks through the pages of her pad. "At first I just did one of my rants, like a stream of consciousness thing, but then I condensed it down into a poem." She turns a page and passes the pad to me.

I wonder if the moon cries
When she looks down at the ocean to pull in the tides
And sees all the carnage that humans deny…

"I love it," I exclaim, mentally adding a crying moon shining silver in the sky above my mermaid.

"She looks incredible," Clementine says, pointing to my sketch.

"Thanks. When I do the real picture I'll add a crying moon in the sky above her, to go with the words in your poem."

"That's a brilliant idea." Clementine grins at me, her eyes bright.

"For real?"

"Absolutely."

And in that moment, I'm so truly happy that nothing else matters. It's crazy to think that this morning I felt so down. Now, thanks to Ms O'Toole, Tyler and Clementine, I'm back to feeling like anything's possible.

"I'm so glad I met you," Clementine says softly.

"Yeah, well…" I clear my throat. "I'm so glad I met you too."

CLEMENTINE

I get home feeling full to the brim with excitement about our new piece of street art. A feeling which lasts precisely two seconds, the time it takes for Mum to yell my name from the kitchen when she hears me come in the front door.

"Yes?" I call back. I don't care what boring chore she wants me to do, nothing is going to get me down now after my meeting with Rudy.

When I reach the kitchen I find Mum peeling potatoes at the sink and Vincent sitting at the table scrolling on his phone.

"Where have you been?" Mum asks, putting down the peeler and rinsing her hands.

"Dance class."

Vincent clears his throat but doesn't lift his gaze from the phone.

"Oh, really?" Mum folds her arms. "So why did Bailey call to say you hadn't turned up?"

"What?" My mouth goes dry. Why would Bailey do that?

"She called me just now to tell me. She was worried about you. She said you walked out of class early last week."

I try and wrack my brain for some kind of excuse but my brain seems to have stalled.

"Did you?" Mum asks.

I nod. "I wasn't feeling well."

"You didn't say anything when you got home."

"I felt better by then."

Vincent clears his throat again. Why does he have to be here? I bet he's really enjoying this.

"So, where have you been this evening?"

"In a café." My brain slowly whirs back into life. It's not a lie. I just won't tell her about Rudy. "I was doing my homework."

Mum frowns like she just can't understand me. "Why didn't you go dancing?"

"I don't want to go any more."

"But you love dancing."

"Yeah, but I don't love dance school."

Mum sighs. "Is this all because you didn't get the role in the show?"

"Oh, for God's sake." Vincent puts his phone down on the table.

"What?" I stare at him.

"You didn't get the part so now you're throwing your toys out of the pram. You need to grow up, Clementine."

"*I* need to grow up?"

"Clementine," Mum says warningly.

"Yes, you do," Vincent says. "You can't just quit something the minute you don't get your own way. Especially not something that's costing me so much money."

"Yeah, well, if I quit think how much money you'll save," I mutter.

"Are you going to let her talk to me like that?" Vincent glares at Mum.

"Clementine, Vinnie spends a lot of money on your dancing."

"And her school fees," he adds.

I look at Mum, waiting for her to stand up for me. But she remains silent.

"I just don't understand why you don't want to dance any more," Mum says.

"Because I don't like the way it makes me feel," I say. "It used to be fun but now it's all about looking perfect and competing against each other in auditions."

"Oh, boo hoo," Vincent sneers. "See this is what's wrong with this generation. First sign of pressure and they want to give up. They're a bunch of snowflakes, the lot of them."

"Oh and you're so tough."

"Clementine," Mum warns.

"What?" I turn on her. "It's true. He's just a bully."

"That's charming that is!" Vincent exclaims.

"OK, Clementine, go to your room," Mum says.

"Gladly," I snap back. But as I turn and march from the room my eyes fill with tears. I should have known it was too good to be true the other day, when Mum talked about how unhappy she was with Vincent. I should have known that she'd let me down yet again.

RUDY

By the time I get back from Kale and Hearty Mum has gone to work but Dave is in the kitchen, making what smells like a curry.

"Hello, love," he says as I come in the door. "You hungry?"

Firstly, I'm not your love, I want to say. *And secondly, I'm not hungry.* But the truth is, I'm starving. I got so lost in drawing at the café I didn't think about having anything to eat and now my belly feels as hollow as a drum. It doesn't help that the curry smells delicious; the aromas of tomato, coriander and cumin are making me drool.

"A bit," I say, standing in the doorway, unsure what to do. The old soul tune playing on the radio wails to a crescendo.

Dave flips a tea towel over his shoulder and takes a pan from the stove. "Take a seat then. Dinner's almost ready." He obviously started cooking as soon as he came in from work, as he's still wearing his oil-splattered jeans and a sweatshirt advertising his car mechanic service.

I sit down at the table and take off my coat.

"How was school?" Dave asks as he spoons steaming heaps of rice onto a couple of plates.

"Crap, as usual."

"Did you have art?"

"Yep." For a horrible minute I think he's going to replay the whole school conversation from the other day.

"So, have you had any ideas for the mural?" Dave nods to-wards the kitchen wall.

"Yeah, I have actually." I spent my lunch break working on ideas for the mural and my next piece with Clementine.

"That's great!" Dave now ladles huge portions of curry over the rice. The sauce is the colour of sunsets, dotted with red and green peppers, baby sweetcorn and onions. Much as I hate to admit it, it looks and smells so good. "So, what are you thinking of doing?"

"I can show you if you like." I take my pad from my bag and open it to a sketched outline of Mum and me. We're standing on top of the silhouette of the Old Pier in Brighton holding hands. A murmuration of starlings swirls in the sky above us, spelling out the word "QUEENS".

"Wow," Dave says. "That's great." If he gets the subliminal message of the picture – that me and Mum don't need him; we don't need anyone – he doesn't show it. "You're very talented."

I want to kick myself for smiling. I wish he'd stop being so nice; it makes it really hard to keep my guard up. *But I must*, I remind myself. *For me and for Mum.*

Despite the soundtrack of sappy old soul and despite Dave continuing his campaign of niceness, dinner is surprisingly OK. And it's really cool not to have to make it myself for once, or rescue one of Mum's burned attempts at a meal. After doing the washing-up, I go to my room to work some more on my picture of the mermaid. After I've done a proper sketch, complete with a crying moon shining down on her, I take a photo of it and send it to Clementine.

Great, she texts back. I frown at the message. It's unlike Clementine to send a one-word message.

You OK? I reply. It takes a couple of minutes before her response comes through.

Not really. Few issues at home. I love your picture, though.

Stepdad issues?

Yes.

I think of how nice it was working with Clementine earlier, both of us lost in our own worlds of creativity and I have an idea.

I don't suppose you fancy coming over to mine one night this week, to help me with the picture?

As I wait for her reply my mind begins buzzing with reasons why I shouldn't have done this. *She probably isn't allowed out of her castle or wherever she lives in Hove. She probably wouldn't want to come here anyway. She probably—* My phone beeps.

I would LOVE that! Thank you. I've been grounded for the rest of the week but should be free again at the weekend. **#stepdadhell**

I instantly flinch at the thought of her stepdad putting her through hell. I quickly type a reply.

This weekend would be cool. Sat evening best for me after I finish work. You can stay over if you like…

That would be brilliant. Thank you! X

No problem.

I go over to my school bag and take out the folder Sid gave me. He ended up printing a few copies of the "RISING" artwork and poem. He and Jenna wanted to frame one for their flat and he gave the rest to me. I'm not sure if they were just saying they wanted one to try and make me feel better but it was cool of them to do that. And it's great that I've got a copy of the unspoiled artwork to keep. I stick one of the prints on my wardrobe door. Today has been such a weird day. A proper roller coaster. It started so badly, but it's ended OK. I look at the picture, preserved forever as it was supposed to be and I reread Clementine's poem.

> *It's not about the falling,*
> *the hurting,*
> *the crying…*
> *It's about the rising,*
> *Turn your lessons into ladders*
> *and start climbing.*

Once again, her words reach deep inside me. LADZ wrecking my picture might have knocked me down but he'll never stop me from rising back up again.

CLEMENTINE

All week I live my life as if it's a carefully choreographed routine, playing the obedient, remorseful daughter as if my life depended on it … or my Saturday night at least. I was so desperate to be allowed to stay at Rudy's at the weekend I decided it was worth the torture of sucking up to Mum and Vincent and doing whatever they told me to. I went back to dance class, apologized to Bailey for running out, numbly followed the routines. I worked hard at school, got all my homework done promptly. To console myself for this life of fakery, I spent hours lying on my bed and gazing out of windows, daydreaming about how my life one day will be. My daydreams are taking on a sharper focus now, as they involve people I actually know. Me and Rudy and Tyler all sharing a flat in Brighton, a buzzing hive of creativity. Every so often a rogue daydream will pop up – of Tyler and me cuddling up together on the sofa, or taking a walk, hand in hand, along the beach. I try hard not to think of what a terrible person I am, dreaming about my new friend's boyfriend. In the end I decide to see my inappropriate daydreams about Tyler like some kind of annoying medical affliction, something I have no control over.

I put off asking Mum if I can stay at Rudy's on Saturday night until Saturday morning. Thankfully Vincent has taken Damon to football, so I don't have to go through the excruciating experience of asking his permission. I find Mum arranging the books in the living room by colour.

I hover in the doorway and clear my throat. "Hey, Mum, would it be OK if I stayed at a friend's tonight?"

"Which friend?" Mum says as she completes a shelf of orange Penguin classics.

"A friend from dance class." I hold my breath, hoping that the dance class reference will make her more likely to say yes.

Thankfully, Mum's face lights up and she nods. "I don't see why not. Where does this friend live?"

"Kemptown. Her name's Rudy." I figure it's probably best to partially stick to the truth.

"OK." Mum comes over and gives me a hug. "I'm so glad you dropped that silly idea of quitting dancing." I stand there, stiff in her arms. It feels horrible not being able to tell her the whole truth. But then how long has it been since she's been able to tell her whole truth to me? She steps back and smiles. "Thank you, darling, for making such an effort this week. And I'm sorry about last week, the things I said about Vincent. I'd had too much wine. I was just being stupid."

I want to shake her, shout, *No, you weren't. You were being sane.* But I force myself to smile instead. "No problem," I say.

* * *

I set off for Rudy's at just gone six. We've arranged to meet at Palace Pier and walk up to her estate from there. I'm so curious to see where she lives it's practically killing me. All week, she's been sending me texts warning me about her mum's boyfriend. Although her mum will be at work tonight, Dave is likely to be at home, which is causing Rudy a great deal of frustration. Or, as she put it in one of her texts: Idiot Dave is seriously vexing me!

Rudy is already at the pier when I get there, her hood pulled down over her face, her cat-like eyes just visible, flicking back and forth, like she's keeping watch for some unseen enemy.

"Hey," she says when she sees me. Her hands stay stuffed in her pockets. I wonder if we'll ever get to the hugging stage in our friendship. I hope so.

"Hey," I reply. We start walking along the front together. "How's your week been?"

"OK."

I wait for her to say something else but she remains silent, walking and staring straight ahead. I remind myself that every time I see Rudy it's like this. It always takes a while for the conversation to stop stalling and start flowing. It's as if she needs to thaw out before opening up to me.

"I'm really looking forward to tonight." *Don't sound too intense, try and play it at least slightly cool,* I remind myself.

"Yeah, me too."

I breathe in the fresh sea air and fall into the rhythm of Rudy's long-legged stride. *So what if it's slightly awkward,* I console myself. *At least I've got a night away from home and Mum and Vincent. And anything's better than that.*

Rudy lives in a block of flats high up on the hill overlooking Kemptown. As we reach the entrance to the estate I turn and look back down. The lights of Brighton glimmer like jewels in the darkness, the pier twinkling like a wand reaching out into the dark of the sea.

"Wouldn't it be cool if mermaids like the one in your picture really did exist?" I say. "Like, if she was out there somewhere in the ocean."

Rudy stops and follows my gaze. "It would be amazing."

"Maybe she can exist, through us," I say.

"What do you mean?" Rudy turns her intense stare on me and I instantly feel self-conscious for sounding like a crazy person.

"Well, maybe we're channelling her by making this picture and poem." I hold my breath, praying Rudy doesn't burst out laughing.

"I like that idea," Rudy says thoughtfully. "Come on…"

She leads me across a small car park and into one of the blocks of flats. The entrance smells of cigarettes and bleach.

"We'll go up the stairs," she says, pointing to a door in the corner, "'cos the lift always stinks."

I follow her into the stairwell. This is the first time I've ever been on a council estate and it's different from what I was expecting. Cleaner. From things I've seen on the news and in documentaries I was expecting gangs loitering on every corner and graffiti all over the walls. But the walls inside the stairwell are pure white. Apart from… As we reach the fourth floor I spot a tiny figure in the corner.

"What's that?" I say, pointing to it.

Rudy grins. "It's one of my So Dark Fairies. I've been drawing them since I was a kid, started putting them up around the estate about a year ago. This one's based on Tyler. He lives upstairs."

I crouch down and look at the fairy. It's like looking at Tyler with wings and way cooler than any fairy I've ever seen. I feel a wistful pang. It must be so nice to have a boyfriend like Tyler to draw pictures of. And to have a boyfriend who lives just upstairs. Rudy is so lucky.

"I love it," I say, standing up again. "It looks just like him."

"He'd been nagging me for ages to make one of him," Rudy says with a laugh as she leads me out of the stairwell and down a narrow, harshly lit hallway.

A softly lit image of Tyler nagging Rudy to turn him into a fairy flickers into my mind like a scene from a romantic movie. *"Oh, please, please, make me a fairy,"* he whispers as he showers her with kisses. Oh my God, what is wrong with me?!

"Here we are then," Rudy says, opening a door at the far end of the corridor.

The first thing I notice about Rudy's flat is how nice it smells. A warming mixture of fried onions and incense, which is weirdly homely.

"So, this is the kitchen." Rudy leads me into the first room on the left.

It takes everything I've got not to show my shock. Although the room contains all of the standard kitchen things – oven, fridge-freezer, table and sink – that's where any resemblance to other kitchens end. The counters are covered in a random assortment of clothes and magazines and make-up and CDs and on the table there's what appears to be part of an engine, possibly from a car. All of the walls are painted bright emerald green, apart from the largest one, behind the table, which is painted blue and has the huge outline of the old pier drawn on it.

"I only just started working on that," Rudy says, following my gaze. As if drawing a giant mural in your kitchen is a totally run-of-the-mill thing.

"What's it going to be?"

"Me and my mum. I'm going to draw us on top of the pier."

"That sounds really cool." I look around the kitchen, try and drink it all in. It couldn't be more different to the pristine black and white kitchen at home. I love it.

"Hello, ladies." Behind us a man comes into the room. He's got dark brown skin and silver cropped hair and he's wearing a checked shirt and jeans. "You must be Clementine." He holds his hand out to me. There's a silver ring on his little finger that looks like a really small wedding band. "I'm Dave."

As I shake his hand he gives me a warm, twinkly-eyed grin. This is definitely not what I was expecting.

"Are you going out then?" Rudy says to Dave, although it sounds more like a command than a question.

"Yeah, thought I'd nip down the pub for a couple." He grabs a scuffed leather jacket from the back of one of the chairs. "I'll see you later."

"Bye," I say.

Rudy doesn't reply and opens the fridge.

"He's so annoying." she says as soon as we hear the front door close and Dave's footsteps echoing away along the corridor.

"Really?"

"Yeah."

My heart sinks. Dave had actually seemed genuinely nice. It makes me sick to think that he might be just like Vincent when other people aren't around; that he's horrible to Rudy.

Rudy takes a bottle of Coke from the fridge and a huge bag of tortilla chips from one of the cupboards. "Shall we get to work then?"

And just like that, the tension in me eases. "Absolutely."

RUDY

"'Scuse the mess," I say, as I open my bedroom door.

"Wow!" Clementine gasps as she follows me into the room. She had the same goldfish expression when she went into the kitchen. I'm guessing this place is very different from where she lives. "This is amazing."

I watch as Clementine walks into the middle of the room, to the one bit of carpet that's not covered in clothes or paints or sketches or books, and does a full 360, taking it all in. My radar is on high alert, programmed for any sign she might be judging, but she looks genuinely awestruck.

"This is just like my..." She breaks off, looking embarrassed.

"Just like what?"

"My dream bedroom," she mutters, her cheeks blushing.

I can't help laughing. "Seriously?"

"Yeah. My mum has this obsession with keeping everything clean and colour-coordinated and in its right place and I hate it. I fantasize about having a room like this. Not that I mean your room is messy..."

"It is messy."

"Yes, but it's a creative mess." Her face is so red now it's off the colour chart.

I stare at her, shaking my head.

We look at each other for a moment, then crack up laughing. As much as I can't quite believe I could ever be friends with someone who looks so much like the perfect princess, Clementine keeps on surprising me.

"OK, so I've pretty much got the artwork done." I point to the bed, where I've laid out the picture. "I just need to cut out the stencil for your poem."

When Clementine sees the picture she goes into a melt-down, clapping her hand to her mouth, her eyes wide. "This is amazing. Oh my God!" She looks so impressed it kind of floors me. "I love the colours and how scared the mermaid looks – and the crying moon. It's so sad – and so powerful."

"Thank you. I'm going to spray-paint the ocean backdrop and I thought it might be cool to stick actual pieces of plastic swirling around her, trapping her." I show Clementine the assortment of plastic packaging I've been saving all week.

"That's going to look brilliant." Clementine takes off her coat. She's wearing skinny jeans, Converse and a designer-label hoodie. Although her hair and skin are pristine as always, there are dark smudges of tiredness beneath her eyes.

"Do you want to help me with the stencil of your poem?" I ask.

"Sure. I'd love to."

I go over to my desk, and a sheet of card with Clementine's

poem printed on it in large typewriter font.

"All you have to do is cut around the edges of each letter."
I take the scalpel from my pen jar and start cutting out the first
letter. "See?"

"OK." Clementine sits down at the desk and I hand her the
knife. As she begins cutting the card, she pokes the tip of her
tongue out of her mouth in concentration. She looks really
sweet, like a little kid focusing on her colouring-in.

"Right, I just need to make a couple of finishing touches to
the picture." I put some music on, choosing a track with a chill-
out beat.

I glance over at Clementine, she's still bent over the stencil
deep in concentration, her feet tapping in time to the music.

"So, you like to dance then?" I say, remembering what she
said the other day about going to dance school.

"I love to dance but I'm not really loving my dance classes."
She looks over at me. "That's why I was grounded this week –
for not going."

"Really?" Another Clementine surprise. She so doesn't look
like the type to skive off lessons.

Clementine nods. "But my mum and stepdad won't let me
give it up because, of course, they know all about what's best
for me."

It takes me a moment to realize she's being sarcastic. "Yeah,
adults always *think* they know best."

"When did your parents split up?" Clementine asks, going
back to her cutting.

I add a sheen of green to the mermaid's braids to help them blend into the ocean. "When I was four."

"Do you see much of your dad?"

"I don't see any of my dad. Haven't seen or heard from him since he walked out."

"Oh no. I'm sorry." Clementine puts down the scalpel and for a horrible moment I think she's going to do something cringe like come over and hug me, but she stays at the desk.

"Do you not have any idea where he is?"

I shake my head. "Don't want to, though, so it's all good. How about your dad?" I ask, keen to change the subject.

"He lives in Germany. In Berlin. I see him most holidays but..."

"But what?"

"I wish I saw him more. He's so much nicer than my stepdad."

"Yeah, so what's the deal with him?"

"My stepdad?"

I nod.

"He's the biggest a-hole going."

I try not to double-take at Clementine's almost-swear word.

"He's so arrogant and he treats my mum like crap, or at least he has for the past couple of years. I mean, I get that she had a crush on him when she was a teenager and when she went to work for him it must have been amazing, working for one of her heroes, but still..." Clementine pauses to take a breath. "Sorry, I'm ranting."

"Don't worry, it's cool. How come your mum had a crush on him when she was a teenager?"

"He used to be a big-shot radio presenter back in the nineties. But now he hosts the mid-afternoon show on Radio Sussex. He's a cheesy old has-been."

There's something almost comical about seeing Clementine so mad. It's a bit like watching a super-cute toddler have a tantrum – all the rage seems so out of character.

"He sounds like a nightmare."

She nods. "So, what's up with Dave then? Is he like Vincent? Does he treat your mum badly?"

I think of the way Dave always looks at mum so adoringly and how he always laughs so loudly at her jokes and makes her endless cups of tea and calls her his Princess. It wouldn't be true to say that he treats her badly but he's still trying to get his feet under the table here.

"Not exactly. Not yet."

"What do you mean?"

"Well, I think he's using her – to get to live here." I feel an uncomfortable squirming in the pit of my stomach. Again, I don't know this to be absolutely true, but if Mum's previous partners are anything to go by… Both guys she was with after Dad used her and then did a runner. The last one even took our flat-screen TV when he left. Why should Dave be any different?

"Oh no, that's horrible."

"Yeah, well, that's life." I look back at the picture. "How are you getting on with the stencil?"

"Good, almost there."

Then I have an idea. "Maybe we could do it tonight, as it's

ready and you're here. Then you won't have to worry about your mum and stepdad catching you sneaking out."

"Oh … OK." Clementine doesn't sound completely convinced.

"It's all right, my mum doesn't get back from work till about four on a Saturday night, so we've only got Dave to worry about. Hopefully he'll crash out when he gets back from the pub."

"Where does your mum work?"

"At a casino by the marina."

Clementine nods. "Will Tyler come with us?"

"Nah, he's had to take his parents up to a family birthday party in London. He won't be back till tomorrow."

Clementine smiles. "OK." She still looks slightly nervous, though.

I push my own nerves from my mind. It will be good to do this on our own. To overcome our fear and live the message of our pictures.

CLEMENTINE

I know I don't have the worry of sneaking out of my own home
tonight, but I can't help feeling slightly jittery as Rudy and I creep
along the narrow hallway in her flat. Although Dave has been
really nice to us, bringing us chips when he got in from the pub
and asking me loads about my poetry, I somehow don't think he'd
be all that happy to catch us about to go out, especially if Rudy
is right and it's all some big act to suck up to her. As we get to
Rudy's mum's bedroom I hear the low rumble of Dave snoring
and it makes me want to giggle. I force myself to think of something sad – the fact that I won't be seeing Dad anytime soon and
I'm stuck living with Mum and Vincent. This usually does the
trick. I make my way along the rest of the hallway in glum silence.

Rudy carefully unlocks the door and we tiptoe out into the
corridor and down the stairs. My relief at having got out without waking Dave is short-lived. Walking through the estate at
this time of night is pretty scary. Somewhere in the distance
I hear a dog growling and barking. Rudy seems unfazed though.
"Have you got your phone?" she asks, pulling up her hood.

"Yeah."

"Cool. We need to get some photos tonight, just in case that idiot LADZ sees it and ruins it."

"Oh no, do you think he would?" I can't bear the thought of another of our pictures being ruined. "Maybe you shouldn't tag it, so he won't know it's us."

"No!" Rudy practically yells. "If we do that he'll have won."

"OK," I say, but I can't help thinking she's making a mistake, that this whole idea is a mistake. Rudy wants to paint the picture on a wall close to the station so more people will see it. The problem with this is that more people are likely to see us *doing it.* Even though the station is long closed by now, it's still right in the heart of the city. But Rudy is clearly on a mission. I have to half walk, half run to keep up with her as she strides along the street, her backpack slung over her shoulder. I think about how cool it will be to have one of my poems on a wall. I think about the message behind our piece and all the damage being done to the ocean. Rudy is right. We need to do this.

The streets are pretty deserted now but every so often we pass people weaving their way home from the clubs. Rudy keeps striding ahead, not one bit nervous. I wish I could be more like her. I wish I had her confidence. I wonder how Rudy would be if she lived with Vincent. I bet she'd stand up to him. I bet she wouldn't let him talk to her like she was a piece of dirt. We head down Sydney Street. It looks so strange late at night, drained of all the people and colour and noise. Every time we walk past a darkened alleyway I want to suggest we do the picture there but I don't want to seem chicken. Finally, we arrive on Trafalgar Street and start walking towards the station.

"How about down there?" Rudy says, gesturing to a side street just before the railway arches. It's dark and deserted and although it's visible from the main road, at least there are some shadowy doorways to hide in.

"OK."

"Let's do it here," Rudy says, almost as soon as we turn into the street, pointing to a blank piece of wall.

"Isn't it a bit too visible?" I whisper.

Rudy looks at me like I'm insane. "That's the whole point. We want people to see it." Then she nudges me and grins. "It's what our mermaid would want."

I give a nervous laugh. "That's very true."

"OK, we're going to have to do this one super quick." Rudy puts down her backpack and starts taking out cans of paint. "You keep watch, I'll get started."

I walk back to the end of the street and look up and down for any sign of movement. The hiss of Rudy's spray cans breaks the silence. Why is it so loud? Up at the top of the hill a car's headlights sweep across the road, thankfully turning off in the direction of the seafront. The waft of paint fumes reaches me. *Hurry! Hurry! Hurry!* Finally, the hissing stops.

"Is the coast still clear?" Rudy calls quietly.

"Yes," I whisper back. But for how long? Someone's bound to come along at some point. And then, as if my thinking it has made it happen, two women stagger into view at the bottom of the hill.

"Someone's coming," I hiss.

"Crap!" Rudy has got the picture of the mermaid out and is about to paste it to the wall. "How far away? Have I got time to put her up?"

"Yes, but be quick." I peer round the corner and watch the women weaving their way towards us. Then one of the women grabs the other's arm and they head off down a side street.

"It's OK, they've gone. Have you finished?" I whisper.

"Yeah, just got to stencil the poem." Rudy replies, her voice muffled by her scarf, which is up over her face like a mask.

There's a loud rattle, followed by more spraying.

I keep looking up and down the street. *Please, please, please, don't let anyone else appear.*

"OK, done," Rudy calls.

I hurry back to her. As soon as I see the artwork all of my fear fades. The mixture of Rudy's paste-up of the mermaid drowning in plastic wrappers against the painted ocean backdrop and the crying moon is incredible.

"Quick, get some photos," Rudy says, stuffing the paint cans and paste back in her backpack.

I reach for my phone and start taking pictures. "This is your best yet," I say. "It looks amazing."

"Oh, shit!" Rudy exclaims.

"What?" I stop what I'm doing and turn to see a sight that makes my blood run cold. A police car is turning into the side street and coming our way, the indicator light blinking bright orange as it pulls in beside us.

RUDY

I've always imagined – or liked to imagine – that if I ever got arrested for my street art I'd wear it as a badge of honour, a sign that I'd finally arrived as an urban artist, but as I sit in the back of the police car with Clementine, all I feel is dread. When the police first pulled up beside us I'd tried to play all innocent. *We were just on our way home. My friend loves taking pictures of street art, you should see her Instagram. Clementine, show them your Instagram...* But the stink of paint in the air was a bit of a giveaway and then, when they'd wanted to search my bag and I'd asked them if they had a warrant, well, things went rapidly downhill.

I stare out of the window at the lights of Brighton streaming by. It all feels so surreal. In the front of the car a message comes over the radio and the policewoman, who is definitely the Bad Cop of the duo, picks up the receiver and says something about perpetrators and being on their way. I sneak a glance at Clementine. She's staring straight ahead, ashen-faced, but as if she can sense my gaze, she turns and gives me a sad smile. I think of how this is going to make things a million times worse for her with her stepdad and it makes me feel horrible. I close my eyes, willing myself to stay strong and I notice something cold against my hand on the car seat. I open my eyes and look down. Clementine has linked her little finger in mine. It's such a small gesture but it feels so powerful, like we're joined by an unbreakable iron chain. I squeeze her finger tightly. We sit there like that, pinkie-linked for the rest of the journey.

When we get to the police station, Good Cop – a young, ginger-haired guy – takes us over to a desk, where a bored-looking police officer takes our names and dates of birth and our parents' details. I end up giving them Dave's phone number, as I can't bear the thought of Mum getting a call at work from the police. It'll be bad enough having to tell her what's happened when she gets home. Once we've given them our details, Bad Cop escorts us to a small room off the main corridor. It might not be a cell but with its harsh lighting and basic furniture it's not far from it.

"You're to wait here until we've contacted your parents," Bad Cop says, like we're a couple of annoying little kids who've been caught misbehaving in the park.

Next to me, Clementine shudders. I'm guessing she's thinking about her stepdad.

"It's going to be OK," I say as soon as Bad Cop has left the room.

"They're going to ground me forever," Clementine says glumly. "And Vincent…" she tails off.

"I'm so sorry," I mumble.

"What for?"

"For getting you into this. Don't worry. I'll let them know it was me who did the picture. You'll definitely get let off. I'm the one who committed the crime."

"We both did it," she says firmly. "Team Fierce Ink, remember."

I feel a lump building at the back of my throat. "Team Fierce Ink," I whisper.

Surprisingly, Dave is the first of the parentals to arrive. He comes into the room with Bad Cop, his shirt crumpled and half untucked in his jeans, looking like someone who just woke up from a really disturbing dream.

"Rudy, what the hell happened?" he says as soon as he sees me.

"As I said on the phone, they were caught defacing public property just off Trafalgar Street," Bad Cop says.

"We weren't defacing it," I mutter.

Dave looks at me and shakes his head almost imperceptibly, like he's trying to give me some kind of coded message. To shut up, I'm guessing. He looks back at Bad Cop. "I'm really sorry about this, officer. Would it be possible for me to have a word with you, in private?"

Bad Cop sighs but she leads him back outside.

"What do you think he's going to say to her?" Clementine whispers.

"I have no idea." I feel sick with dread. After the way I've treated Dave he has absolutely no reason to do me any favours and I very much doubt that his campaign of butt-kissing includes bailing out his girlfriend's criminal daughter.

The door opens again and this time Good Cop comes in with a man and a woman. The woman looks as if she's just stepped from the page of a magazine, airbrushed to perfection in her fake-fur jacket, heeled suede boots and skinny jeans. The man's one of those cringey old people who still thinks he's one of the kids, dressed in a designer tracksuit top and way-too-tight jeans.

"What the hell, Clementine?" he spits.

Clementine's mum puts a hand on his arm. "Clementine, what have you done?" she cries. Then they both look at me. My skin prickles from the obvious disdain in their gaze.

"She didn't do anything," I say. "I did it."

"There, did you hear that?" Clementine's mum says to the police officer. "I knew it had to be a misunderstanding. I knew Clementine wouldn't be involved in anything like this."

"You don't know anything," Clementine snaps, causing us all to look at her in surprise.

"Oh, I think we're getting a pretty good picture," her stepdad sneers. Wow, Clementine really wasn't exaggerating when she said he was a creep. My blood starts boiling and I glare at him.

"I don't understand," Clementine's mum says. Her whiny voice sets my teeth on edge.

"No, you really don't," Clementine mutters.

I want to high-five and hug her all at the same time. Instead,

I sit on my hands. The warmth I'm feeling towards Clementine rapidly fades as I realize that, after tonight, she'll probably never be allowed to see me again.

"What's that supposed to mean?" Clementine's mum says.

"She's being a spoiled brat again, that's what it means," Vincent says, making me want to punch him straight in his stupid veneered teeth.

Just at that moment Dave and Bad Cop come back into the room.

"OK, given the girls' age and the fact that it's their first offence, we're willing to let them off with a caution," Bad Cop says, sitting down opposite us. "But I can't stress enough that what you did tonight was a criminal act. You're going to have to find legal ways of expressing your art."

"Expressing their art!" Vincent snorts.

Dave looks at Vincent likes he's something gross he just scraped off his shoe.

"Thank you very much," Clementine's mum says to the policewoman.

"Yes, thank you," Dave echoes.

"Right, let's get out of here. I would like to get *some* sleep tonight," Vincent says.

Dave and Clementine's mum sign some paperwork and then we all trudge back out into the car park.

Vincent presses his key fob and the lights on a gleaming four-by-four flash on and off. "Say goodbye to your friend," he says to Clementine, spitting out the word "friend" like it's a maggot. Then he turns to me. "You stay away from her from now on, do you hear me?"

"What did you say?" Dave says, stepping in between us.

"I said, I don't want your troublemaker kid anywhere near her."

"Rudy's no troublemaker."

Vincent gives a sarcastic laugh. "Oh, really? So how come the first time Clementine spends the night with her she ends up getting arrested?"

"They didn't get arrested," Dave replies. "They were let off with a caution."

"Oh yeah, and you'd know all about police procedures, wouldn't you?"

It's all to obvious what he means by this and there's a terrible silence, like the moment after a bolt of lightning when you're waiting for the crash of thunder.

Dave takes a step closer to Vincent. For a moment I think he might actually deck him. Then he smiles and shakes his head. "I just figured it out."

"Figured what out?" Vincent asks, taking a step back.

"Who you are."

Vincent gives an arrogant smirk.

"Well, who you *used* to be," Dave continues with a laugh. "How the mighty have fallen, eh?" As I watch Vincent splutter and squirm I find myself in the bizarre position of actually wanting to hug Dave, or high-five him at least. He turns to Clementine. "You're welcome to hang out with Rudy any time."

"Thank you," she replies, with a weak smile.

Dave takes hold of my elbow. "Come on, Rudy, let's get out of here."

I don't say a word to Dave on the drive home. I'm too full of sadness and anger and guilt. It's only when he passes the turning for home and heads into the heart of Brighton that I look at him.

"Where are we going?"

"I want to see what all the fuss was about," Dave replies. "Off Trafalgar Street, was it?"

I nod numbly.

As we retrace the route Clementine and I took earlier my eyes burn with tears. I was so excited when we walked here before, so fired up at the thought of creating some more street art, but now that's all over.

"It's up there on the right, just before the bridge," I mutter.

Dave pulls over by the picture but I can't even bring myself to look at it. I hear him whistle through his teeth. "The one with the mermaid?"

"Yeah, she's meant to represent the ocean."

He winds down his window to take a closer look and I can't help looking too. As I do, I feel the slightest shiver of excitement. There's no denying it's really powerful.

"You did that?" Dave says.

"Yeah. And Clementine wrote the poem. We wanted to make something that would stop people dumping their crap in the sea."

Dave laughs but it's not mocking like when he laughed at Vincent; it's more a laugh of surprise. He turns the engine off and shifts in his seat to look at me. "OK, here's the deal," he says. "We won't mention this to your mum…"

"We won't?"

He shakes his head. "As long as you promise you won't do this again."

My heart sinks but I force myself to nod.

"At least not anywhere it's illegal."

"What do you mean?"

"There are places in Brighton where street art's allowed, you know."

"Yeah, but you have to be really good to be allowed to paint there."

"You *are* really good. Better than really good."

"Seriously?"

Dave nods. "Seriously. But you have to be smart too, smarter and better than the rest of them, know what I'm saying?"

I think of what happened in the car park; the way Vincent talked to Dave and the way Dave kept his cool and laughed in his face. Vincent probably wanted Dave to punch him so he'd end up getting arrested. But Dave outsmarted him. He didn't get triggered by his racism; he rose above it and laughed in his face.

"I know what you're saying." Then I remember Dave asking the policewoman if he could have a chat with her. "What did you say to the policewoman – when you went out of the room?"

His face clouds over. "I recognized her. She was a sister of a friend of my wife. Let's just say I called in a favour for old times' sake."

At the mention of Dave's ex-wife I can't help flinching. I wonder if he left her the way my dad left Mum and me. "Where's your ex-wife now then?"

"She's dead. Died of breast cancer, four years ago. Put up a hell of a fight, though."

"Oh no. I'm really sorry." I'm so shocked I have no idea what to say.

Dave smiles at me but his smile is tinged with sorrow and, instead of seeing a butt-kissing, wannabe stepdad, all I see is someone who really gets my pain. Finally, the tears that have been threatening since the police showed up start spilling down my face.

CLEMENTINE

Vincent speeds along the roads back home as if he's tearing around a racetrack. At one point he almost goes straight through a red light.

Mum places her hand on his leg. "Take it easy, darling."

"Take it easy?" he snaps. "Take it easy? After the night I've had, easy is the last thing I'll be taking."

That doesn't even make any sense, you imbecile, I think. As per usual what's happened tonight is going to be all about Vincent.

"Not only do we have to come out in the middle of the night to bail out your daughter but I then get threatened by her new friend's reprobate dad."

"He didn't threaten you," I say indignantly.

"Oh no you don't!" Vincent screeches the car to a halt and turns to glare at me. "You don't say a word, do you hear me?"

I look at Mum. She stares straight ahead out of the window.

The one good thing about hitting rock bottom is that you have nothing left to lose. "Or what?" I say to Vincent.

"Clementine," Mum warns.

"You can't stop me from speaking," I say. We all sit in

silence for a moment, in an awkward stalemate.

"Give me your phone," Vincent says, turning right round to face me.

"What? No."

"Give me your phone." he repeats.

"Mum."

"She needs to be punished."

To my horror, Mum nods in agreement. "Give him your phone."

"No! I need my phone. I need it to message Dad."

"You can borrow my phone if you need to contact Dad. Vincent's right: you need to face the consequences of your behaviour."

Vincent gives me a defiant smirk and holds out his hand. I feel like spitting in it.

I turn my phone off, thankful that I thought to set a password. I ignore Vincent's outstretched hand and give the phone to Mum.

Vincent turns the key in the ignition and we roar off up the street.

RUDY

"What the actual Jeff?" Tyler stares at me, his mouth gaping, as I finish the sorry tale of Saturday night.

"Jeff?" I say, momentarily thrown from my tale of doom.

"Instead of 'eff'," Tyler explains. "According to my parents I swear too much, especially when I'm driving. But they weren't the ones having to drive in London – only two months after passing my test. But that's not important. I can't believe you guys got caught by the po po!"

"Oh my God, Ty, gangsta so doesn't suit you!"

Tyler gives me a sheepish grin. "Sorry. Seriously, sis, that's so crap."

I'd texted Tyler yesterday to let him know that something bad had happened but I'd put off telling him the gory details until we were face to face at work this morning.

"Yeah, it wasn't exactly the greatest of weekends." I start slicing a cucumber for the salad.

"I can't believe you got arrested," Tyler says, continuing with his breakfast prep.

"Who got arrested?" Sid says, coming into the kitchen with a tray of plates.

I shoot a warning glance at Tyler but he doesn't see. "Rudy. On Saturday," he says.

Great, now my boss is going to think I've got a criminal record.

"I didn't get arrested. I got let off with a caution," I say quickly, unsure if this is really any better news for my employer to hear.

"For doing what?" Sid asks, looking shocked.

"My street art."

"No way!" Sid shakes his head but in a way that would suggest he was more impressed than horrified.

"It was worth it, though. Look." Tyler shows him his phone. After I'd texted him yesterday he went to see the picture and sent me some photos. I'd messaged Clementine a couple of times yesterday with the photos but got no reply. I've been trying really hard not to think about what this could mean.

"Wowsers!" Sid exclaims. "Rudy, this is excellent."

"Thank you." But his praise only makes me feel sadder, because it's a reminder of what could have been, if only Clementine and I hadn't been caught.

"Can I print a copy of this one too?" Sid asks. "Jenna and I framed the other one over the weekend and hung it in our hall. This would look great next to it. We'll have a matching pair."

"Sure," I say numbly. I know I should be flattered but ironically it would be a lot easier if he wasn't raving about my pictures – a lot easier to give up on my dream.

* * *

When I get into school the feeling of sorrow grows. Much as I hate to admit it, Dave was right: I can't afford to get caught by the police again. Next time there won't be a warning. I'll have to wait until I'm older to do more street art. But what will I do until then? For the first time in my life I feel as if the fight's gone out of me. Art class is all about Van Gogh. I try to look interested but inside my head sadness and confusion build. It doesn't help that Van Gogh's first name was Vincent. Every time Ms O'Toole says his name it makes me think of Clementine's evil stepdad and my stomach clenches. I'm hoping to slip out at the end of class but Ms O'Toole comes over to me.

"Did you remember to make me a print of your picture?" she asks.

I nod and take it from my folder.

Ms O'Toole smiles and I have to look away. The last thing I need is for her to start raving about it like Sid. "Thank you. It looks great. And I have something for you too." She goes over to her desk and comes back with a book. There's a photo of a young guy on the cover wearing a jacket that's a patchwork of colour. He's staring so intently into the camera it's like he's looking right out of the book at me.

"Have you heard of Jean-Michel Basquiat?" Ms O'Toole asks.

I shake my head.

Her face lights up as if she's about to share the world's greatest secret with me. "He was an artist in New York in the seventies and eighties. He started as a graffiti artist and then he went on to work in mixed media. As soon as I saw your piece last week

I thought of him. I think you're going to love him. He was one of my main inspirations when I first began making art."

I look at the book, at the spine that's fraying and the well-thumbed pages. It seems really dumb to say this but I've never thought of Ms O'Toole before she became a teacher; Ms O'Toole as an artist. It would never have occurred to me that she'd be a fan of an artist like the guy on the cover. I had her down as liking artists like Constable and Vincent Van Gogh. "Would it be OK to borrow the book?"

"You can have it," Ms O'Toole says.

"What – but, don't you want it?"

"I've read it to death and, besides, I think Basquiat would have wanted you to have it."

"Would have? Is he dead?"

Ms O'Toole nods and she looks so sad for a moment it's like she'd lost a close friend.

"Thank you."

"You're very welcome! I hope he inspires you the way he inspired me."

I look back at the young guy on the cover of the book, the cigarette burning between his fingers, the cluster of dreads erupting from the crown of his head, and I feel a weird spark of recognition ignite deep inside me.

CLEMENTINE

Much as I was relieved to leave the house this morning, by the time the school day's over I'm practically itching with frustration. Losing my phone is like losing a limb. No exaggeration. Not only because I haven't been able to message Rudy but I'm now without my lifeline of Instagram. Mum told me that "if my behaviour improves" she'll return my phone at the end of the week. I feel as if I'm living in some weird alternative reality, where standing up to bullies is deemed bad and being an arrogant creep is rewarded. I'm not going to let them beat me, though. I can't.

So, as soon as the school bell rings, I hurry into Brighton. As I race past the station my heart rate quickens. *Please, please, please . . . yes!* Our picture is still there and untouched. After what happened to the one by the beach I've been terrified that LADZ might have found this one and trashed it too. I don't think I'd have been able to take the disappointment. I jog down the hill to Sydney Street. I know that Rudy works at the café on Monday mornings, but I'm hoping she'll have called in on her way home from school too. I burst through the door into the steamy heat.

Tyler's behind the counter, playing imaginary drums with a pair of straws. He looks seriously cute. *No, he doesn't!* I reprimand myself. Rudy's the only one who should have thoughts like these about Tyler.

"Clementine!" he exclaims when he sees me. "How are you doing?"

"OK, I guess." I go over to the counter. "Is Rudy here?"

He shakes his head. "Not yet, but she should be any minute. She's been really worried about you."

"She has?" Relief floods through me. I'd been so worried that Vincent and the way he behaved at the police station might have put her off.

"Yeah. She was trying to get hold of you all yesterday."

"My mum and stepdad confiscated my phone."

Tyler squirms. "Ow!"

"Tell me about it."

"Hot chocolate?"

I shake my head. "I can't stay. I've been grounded as well. I just wanted to let Rudy know that I'm not ignoring her."

"Well, I guess you can tell her yourself." Tyler grins over my shoulder and I turn and see Rudy.

"Clementine!" she calls, running over. She stops for a second before grabbing me in a hug. Her thin arms are surprisingly strong.

"I'm so glad I caught you," I say. "I can't stay. I've been grounded. And my mum's confiscated my phone."

"I was wondering why you didn't reply to my messages."

Rudy looks so relieved I have to fight the urge to cry with gratitude.

"Yes. I'm so sorry. Do you have an email address? At least then I'll be able to contact you."

"Sure. Can I have a piece of paper, Ty?"

Tyler tears a couple of pages from his orders pad and Rudy and I exchange email addresses.

"Aha, it's the dynamic duo!" Sid exclaims, coming out from the kitchen. "Here you go, I got some prints for you too," he says to Rudy, handing her a brown paper bag.

Rudy takes out some A4 sheets. They're prints of our mermaid picture.

"Wow, they look awesome!" says Tyler.

"I know, right," Sid agrees. "I seriously think you girls could sell these."

"Really?" Rudy looks at him and then at me.

"Sure. If I saw them in a shop I'd buy one."

"Me too," Tyler agrees.

"Might be a safer option too," Sid chuckles. "Not quite so illegal."

We all laugh and the tension from the past couple of days drains from me. If only I could stay here, surrounded by people I care about, people I can be myself with.

RUDY

After Clementine goes I get Tyler to make me a mocha – I'm in need of some comfort sugar and froth – and I sit at a table in the window. It was so nice to see Clementine, and so cool to think that she would run all this way just to see me. I can't believe her stepdad took her phone, though. That's got to fall under the trade description for child abuse. I think of Dave and how he stood up to Vincent outside the police station, and how cool he's been ever since, not breathing a word of what happened to Mum. For the first time since he came into our lives I actually feel something close to lucky. I'm trying really hard not to get freaked out at this development.

I take out the book Ms O'Toole gave me and read the blurb on the back. The words send a shiver up my spine.

> "When Basquiat was sixteen, he and his friend Al Diaz formed the infamous graffiti duo SAMO. They displayed their work in New York's Lower East Side in the late 1970s, when it was a melting pot of hip-hop, punk and street art. Their artwork was known for its enigmatic messages."

Like a reflex reaction, I fish my phone from my bag to message Clementine.

Google Jean-Michel Basquiat, I type, before remembering that she doesn't have her phone so I send her a quick email instead, then I continue reading. *"Basquiat went from being homeless to earning tens of thousands of dollars from his paintings in just a few years. By the 1980s his artwork was being displayed in galleries and museums around the world."* I open the book and dive in. By the time Tyler comes over to collect my empty cup I know two things. One: I am not going to give up on my street art. Two: I wish I'd been living in New York in the 1970s. Oh, and two point five: I wish I could have known Jean-Michel Basquiat.

"You OK?" Tyler asks.

"Yeah." I look at him and smile and it's only partially a lie. Things might not be OK right at this moment. But, thanks to Team Fierce Ink and Ms O'Toole and Jean-Michel Basquiat, I know that one day they will be.

CLEMENTINE

Thankfully, when I get home everyone's out. Vincent's at work and Mum has left a note for me on the kitchen table. *"Gone food shopping."* I have a thought that instantly makes my pulse race. I could look for my phone. The most obvious place it would be is Mum and Vincent's bedroom. Even though no one's home I can't help creeping across the landing like a cartoon character in a haunted house. The bedroom smells of a stuffy mix of Vincent's aftershave and Mum's perfume. Mum's side of the room is immaculate, the rose-gold alarm clock, white china angel and box of tissues on her bedside table arranged with the symmetry of an art exhibit. In contrast, Vincent's bedside table is a mess of coins and a phone charger and a folder of documents.

I look in Mum's chest of drawers. The good thing about her being such a neat freak is that I can tell immediately that my phone isn't among the rows of tightly folded tops and underwear. I go over to Vincent's drawers and open the top one, my heart pounding. And there it is, on top of his colour-coordinated T-shirts. I turn it on and notifications start flashing up on the screen. There are loads of messages from Rudy and loads from Dad too. It turns out Dad had been trying to ring me. Is everything OK? his last message reads. Can't get hold of you and your mum's not answering her phone or returning my messages. xxx

Reading this makes me so angry. It's one thing to stop me talking to my friends but Mum and Vincent can't stop me from talking to my dad. I call his number, willing him to be available. He answers almost immediately.

"Clem! Are you OK?"

"Yes, I'm so sorry I didn't get back to you… Vincent confiscated my phone."

"He did what? Why?"

"It's a long story."

"Go on, tell me."

It's so nice to hear the concern in his voice. I sit down on the edge of the bed. "I've made friends with this girl called Rudy. She's an artist – a street artist." I tell him all about our collaborations and the night the police picked us up.

There's a silence, which fills me with dread. What if Dad reacts the same way as Mum and Vincent? What if he's angry with me? I hear Ada's voice in the background and Dad starts saying something to her in German. Then they both laugh. My dread turns to anger. Are they having some kind of private joke? "Dad?"

"Sorry, love. I was just telling Ada what happened."

I don't know whether to be relieved or confused that they seem to have found it funny.

"Were you charged by the police?"

"No, they let us off with a warning."

"OK, well, that's good." I love the way Dad's always so calm about everything but it only makes me miss him more. Annoyingly, I start to cry.

"Clem, are you OK?" Now he sounds really worried, which only makes me cry harder.

"No, not really," I splutter. "I'm so sick of living with Vincent, Dad. He's such a bully."

Dad starts to say something but I can't hear properly and his words ring around my ears like feedback. I can barely breathe. Vincent is standing in the bedroom doorway, his face creased with fury.

RUDY

I get home hyped on inspiration. Losing myself in the colourful world of Basquiat has got my fingers itching and twitching to paint. I go straight to the kitchen and look at the outline of my mural on the wall. Mum is at work and there's no sign of Dave. *There's no sign of Dave.* An old fear sparks like a match inside me. *What if he's gone?* Then I see a note on top of the pile of his records on the table: *Rudy, I had to go and fix my mate's carburettor. Veggie spag bol in pot on stove. See you later, Dave.* The fear flickers out. I look at the pot on the stove but I'm too hyped up to eat, plus I need to take advantage of having the flat to myself for a bit. I go to my bedroom, get changed and fetch my paints.

I'm so lost in my painting I don't hear Dave come back till he's standing in the kitchen.

"Bloody hell!" he exclaims, looking at my picture.

"What?" My hackles rise. Looking at Basquiat's work inspired me to get more adventurous and so I've made Mum and me into a patchwork of colour. Does Dave think it looks stupid?

"This is brilliant," he says.

"Really?" I scour his face for any sign that he might be faking.

But he nods, deadly serious. "It's so bold. It's got a really abstract feel to it. I love it."

I bite my lip but I can't stop myself from grinning.

"I reckon you might have just added a few grand to the value of this property." Dave laughs. "Just as long as you remember me when you're rich and famous. Speaking of which…" – he fishes a flyer from his jeans pocket – "I picked this up in town today, thought you and your mate might be interested."

I take the flyer. It's from the cosmetics company Bare-Faced Chic and designed like an old-style WANTED poster. My eyes skim the text…

WANTED

**Street artist to create a mural for
the wall of our Brighton store to
commemorate our tenth anniversary**

The blurb on the back explains how to enter the competition.

"So? What do you reckon?" Dave looks at me questioningly.

"Do you really think we'd be in with a chance?"

"Of course. And you know what? Even if you didn't win, it's something to aim for and at least you'd never be left wondering, what if?"

There's something about the way he says this that makes me think he's speaking from personal experience. I'm guessing he sometimes wonders what might have happened if he'd carried on writing.

"True." I nod in agreement. "Thank you. I'll ask Clementine when I see her."

"Great." Dave goes over to the stove and lifts the lid on the pot of bolognese. "Did you have any dinner?"

"Nah, I forgot all about eating once I started painting."

Dave laughs. "I used to get like that when I was writing."

"Really?"

"Yeah. I'd lose myself for hours. You want me to heat you some of this?"

"Please." My stomach growls on cue, as if it just remembered it was hungry.

Dave lights the hob and brings a couple of bowls over to the table. He looks shy suddenly. "I just want to say thank you."

"What for?"

"I know it can't be easy, having me move in when it's been you and your mum for so long." He glances at the mural and I realize that he did get the underlying message. But rather than this making me feel triumphant it makes me feel shoddy and mean.

"It's not that bad," I say. "You're kind of growing on me."

"What, like a fungus?" Dave grins.

"Exactly," I say, and we both start proper laughing.

CLEMENTINE

Every time I think it's impossible for me to hate Vincent more, he stretches my hatred to new limits. When I first saw him standing in the doorway I assumed he was going to go crazy. But of course, he's too clever for that. No, clever's the wrong word. Clever's too positive. Vincent is far too *sly* to let Dad see his true colours. So instead of yelling, he asked me very calmly if he could speak to Dad. I handed over the phone and sat there on the bed feeling every possible kind of awkward as Vincent explained, oh so calmly, that he'd had no option other than to confiscate my phone, because I'd fallen in with the "wrong crowd" and it was "in my best interests" that I wasn't able to contact them. "As her stepdad you must appreciate that there will be times when I need to discipline her," he said. "But I really don't like her going through my private possessions to find her phone… yes, 'fraid so." At that point he actually looked at me and grinned. I wanted to yell at Dad, *don't fall for his lies, he twists everything.* But before I knew it, Vincent was ending the call. "Cheers, mate. I really appreciate your understanding."

When he said that, I felt like a prisoner who'd just been

handed a death sentence. Vincent had cut me off from the one person who might have been able to save me. After he ended the call he put my phone in his pocket.

"I don't know why you bothered calling him," he sneered. "He couldn't give a shit about you. He didn't even stay in the same country as you, that's how little he cares."

"He moved to Germany because he married Ada," I said.

"Exactly. He put some bird before his own child. There's no way I'd ever do that to Damon. Like I told your mum, there's no way she'd ever take that boy away from me."

I wonder why Vincent would have had a reason to say this to Mum. Did Mum threaten to leave? And is this another reason why she keeps staying? Because she's scared Vincent would try and take Damon from her?

Then doubt about Dad started sneaking into my mind. Why had he moved to another country if it meant he couldn't see me regularly? Why hadn't he persuaded Ada to move to the UK? As if sensing my defeat, Vincent went in for the kill. "So, if I were you I'd stop pushing your luck, OK?"

I nodded, too numb to say anything, and went straight to my room, where I've been ever since.

Mum was notified of my latest misdemeanour as soon as she and Damon got home from shopping.

"I'm so disappointed in you," she said, from my bedroom doorway.

Not nearly as disappointed as I am in you, I thought, but defeat had got my tongue.

It's still got it. I can't even bring myself to read some of my beloved Emily Dickinson's poetry. What's the point? The hope perching inside my soul has keeled over and died.

RUDY

"I've come up with a cunning plan," I tell Tyler at work on Saturday.

"Uh-oh. Is this cunning plan likely to get you arrested again?" Tyler starts slicing a loaf of sourdough.

"Firstly, I didn't get arrested and secondly, no. At least, I don't think so."

Tyler laughs and pops a couple of slices of bread in the toaster. "Go on then, what is it?"

"I'm going to try and find out where Clementine lives. I need to talk to her about the street art competition." I hang up my coat and put on my apron.

Tyler frowns. "Can't you just email her?"

I shake my head. "Nah, I can't risk her evil stepdad seeing it. She hasn't replied to the other emails I've sent."

"But what if her evil stepdad sees you?"

"I'm not scared of him." I put my hands on my hips to emphasize my point. "And I'm really worried about her."

It's been five days since I last saw Clementine at the café. She was so determined to stay in touch with me it's obvious something bad has happened. Something bad beginning with V.I.N.C.E.N.T.

Tyler fetches a couple of butter portions from the fridge and puts them on a plate. "Do you know her surname?"

"No, but I know his. He's a radio presenter on one of those cheesy stations that plays *easy-listening* music." I mime air quotes around the words "easy listening".

Tyler grimaces. "Those stations should be banned from the airwaves."

"I know, right? So I did a Google search and I found out that he lives in Albion Avenue in Hove."

"Great sleuthing, sis. Did you find out the house number?" Tyler checks his order and puts a mini jar of marmalade on the plate beside the butter.

I shake my head.

"So, what are you going to do? Call at every house?"

"I can't. Stepdad from Hell might answer."

Tyler frowns. "What's your cunning plan, then?"

"I'm going to stake-out the street."

Tyler's eyes widen. "What, like in a cop movie?"

"Exactly. And, if you're not doing anything tomorrow, I'd like you to come with me."

Tyler laughs. "Do you ever do anything standard? You know, like go for a walk or see a movie?"

"Why see a movie when you can live your life as if it's a movie?" As soon as I say this I think of what Clementine said to me about feeling as if she'd been cast as an extra in the wrong film. If my cunning plan works I can hopefully make her feel like she's the star in the right one.

"How are we going to stay undercover on this stake-out?" The toast pops up and Tyler puts it on the plate.

"I'm not sure. I was thinking we could hang around at the end of the street, or walk up and down it or something?"

"Yeah, that wouldn't look suspicious at all." Tyler raises his eyebrows at me.

"I've got to do something. I'm really worried about her."

Tyler scrunches his mouth up, the way he always does when he's thinking. "All right, leave it to me. I've got an idea."

"Really?" Relief flows through me.

"Yep. When were you thinking of going?"

"First thing in the morning? We need to get there before any of them are likely to go out."

"OK."

"Seriously?" I'd been kind of dreading asking Tyler, as I wasn't sure if going on a stake-out might be a test of our friendship too far.

"Sure. But I'm only going to help you on one condition."

"Of course, what is it?"

"I get to be the hard-drinking, wise-cracking, burned-out cop on the stake-out."

"Who am I then?"

"You're the sensible one, devoted to your family. The one who's about to retire, until you get paired up with a maverick like me."

I start cracking up laughing.

He grins and hands me the toast. "Now take this to Table Ten."

Tyler calls for me at eight-thirty on Sunday morning. I told Mum and Dave that we were going to London for the day to visit some art galleries and we wanted to get an early start to beat the crowds. We head across the car park to Tyler's parents' car, which he's managed to borrow for the day. It's one of those cars with doors at the back that slide open. Tyler's mum is in a wheelchair full-time now because of her MS, which was a major factor in Tyler learning to drive as soon as he could. Tyler opens the passenger door for me.

"It's so cool your parents have lent you their car for our stake-out," I say as I get in.

"Yep. I told them it was only fair, after all the driving I did for them last weekend. Of course, I didn't tell them I was going on a stake-out." Tyler turns the key in the ignition and an old-school Oasis track starts playing on the stereo.

"What did you tell them?"

"That we're going birdwatching in Worthing."

"Birdwatching!" I practically shriek. "Dude!"

"What? I had to think of something on the spot. Anyway, I've always thought birdwatching would be kind of cool. Here, can you take this?" He hands me a carrier bag and starts to pull out of the car park.

"What is it?" I ask.

242

"Binoculars, the birdwatching tool that can also come in very handy on a stake-out … if Clementine lives in a long street."

"Genius!" I exclaim.

"Yeah, well, you don't get to be a hardened maverick cop like me without a touch of genius." He grins. "My mum also made us a load of sandwiches, which I'm aware is not the kind of thing a hardened maverick cop would ever say on a stake-out, so can we just pretend that they're not there … until we get hungry?"

Albion Avenue is one of the roads off the high street in Hove that cuts down to the sea. When we get there the overcast sky is lightening from gun-metal to ash-grey. Tyler pulls into a space at the top of the street, giving us a view all the way to the sea. But today I'm too nervous to pay any real attention to the sea. Like most cunning plans, this one was great when it was in my head but now we're actually here all I can think about is what might go wrong. Mainly, Clementine's idiot stepdad seeing us out here and calling the police. I pull up my hood and sink down in my seat.

CLEMENTINE

I'll never forget the day I found out that there was no Father Christmas. This really annoying kid in my class called Daniella Boardman announced the terrible news one lunch break when we were in Year 2. At six years old, I was nowhere near ready to deal with a spoiler of this magnitude. I've been feeling a similar sense of devastation all week, only this time it's like I've lost my belief in everything. It hasn't helped that I'm having the worst period ever. Sometimes I think my cycle does this deliberately – as if my period waits for the worst possible moment to strike, like the day of an audition or PE, or this week.

I lie on my bed and gaze up at the ceiling. It's only just gone seven on Sunday morning. I'd been hoping that if I stayed up late binge-watching a Netflix series I'd sleep in late this morning and lose half the day. But my stupid period cramps woke me and now they won't go away. I briefly consider writing a poem about periods, titled something like, "Why Does My Womb Hate Me?" but I push the words from my mind. What's the point in writing poems if I'm not able to post them? If I'm not able to see the one person who believes in them, who believes in me? When I think of Rudy the pain in my lower stomach radiates through my body. I close my eyes to stop the tears that are threatening. I feel terrible for not contacting her but I can't risk getting her into more trouble. After re-confiscating my phone Vincent reminded me that I was banned from having anything to do with her. He told me he had friends in high places in the police and that if he caught me making contact with her, he'd get her charged with vandalism and defacing private property. I'm not entirely sure how true that is, but I can't risk finding out. Anyway, Rudy's probably already forgetting about me. It's not as if we'd known each other ages, and she has Tyler. She never really needed me, not the way I needed her. Tears slide down my face. I've cried so much this week I'm amazed I've got any tears left. How are tears made? Why does sadness make us cry? I start going down a rabbit hole of thoughts, then stop myself abruptly. Who even cares?

From the landing I hear Mum waking Damon up. Vincent is taking him into London for the day, to see the football. That's something at least.

"Dad! Dad! Are you awake?" I hear Damon cry excitedly.

I feel a bolt of hate go through me. It's so unfair that Vincent can play the doting dad to Damon when it suits him, while taking away that option from my own dad and me.

RUDY

"Are you thirsty?" Tyler says, stretching out in his seat. "I could murder a can of Coke."

"Me too." I sigh.

We've been on our stake-out for over two hours now and there's been no sign of Clementine. There's been no sign of anyone. I'm starting to regret coming here so early. I mean, who in their right mind gets up before nine on a Sunday anyway? I yawn.

"Shall I nip down to the high street?" he asks. "See if there's a café open?"

We've already eaten the sandwiches his mum made us. We ate them in the first half-hour.

"OK. Thanks, Ty."

Tyler gets out of the car and I watch in the wing mirror as he trudges up the road. As his reflection disappears from view I feel a wave of gratitude. He's probably really regretting giving up his one lie-in of the week to come on this wild goose chase with me but he'd never say it. I'm so lucky to have him as a friend. I see a sudden movement on the other side of the street and my heart skips a beat. But it's a false alarm; it's just a paperboy. I watch as he goes up the steps to a house and pushes a rolled-up paper through the ornate letterbox. The houses in Albion Avenue are four storeys high and painted white. A general rule of thumb in Hove is that you can tell how rich the street is by how white the houses are. In Albion Avenue the houses are as white as freshly fallen snow. The only splashes of colour are from the front doors, all regal shades, like burgundy and navy blue. I wasn't far off when I imagined Clementine living in a castle. What I didn't realize was that she was being kept there against her will. There's another sign of movement and I sit up straight in my seat. A few houses down on the left a door opens and a boy comes out. He looks about nine. I watch as he leaps down the steps onto the pavement, then goes up and does it again.

"Hurry up, Dad, we'll miss the train," he calls.

Clementine hasn't mentioned having a brother and I'm about to mentally cross the house off our list of possibles when Vincent appears at the top of the steps. I recognize him instantly from the unnatural brown of his dyed hair. He and the boy are wearing matching football scarves. As they start heading up the street my heart pounds. We're parked on the same side as them; they're going to walk right past me. I slide off my seat and into the space beneath the dashboard. As the voices get louder I hear the door on the driver's side open. "What are you doing?" Tyler says, staring at me.

"Shh!" I put my finger to my lips.

Tyler gets into the car and places the drinks on the dashboard.

Vincent's voice is now level with us. He's saying something about free kicks.

"Was that him?" Tyler asks as the voices fade off up the street.

"Yes. Have they gone?"

Tyler checks the rear-view mirror. "Yep."

I wriggle back up into my seat. "That was close!"

"I can't believe I missed it." Tyler shakes his head. "Did you see which house they came out of?"

"Of course I did." I look at him and grin. "It's a perk of being the sensible, family-loving cop – I never leave the scene of a stake-out, not even for a can of Coke."

CLEMENTINE

About a minute after I hear Vincent and Damon go off to the football Mum comes to my room, clad from head to toe in Lycra, ready for her Pilates class. I assume she's going to ask me if I'd like any breakfast, as per the usual routine, but instead she sits on the end of my bed.

"Clementine, can I ask you something?"

"OK."

"The artwork your friend did, the one the police caught you doing…"

"Yes…"

"Was it by the station in Brighton?"

"Yes."

"Down the side street by the bridge? The picture of the mermaid in the ocean?"

I nod cautiously, trying to work out where this might be leading.

"And you wrote the poem that went with it?"

"Yes." I prepare myself for yet another telling-off.

"Do you write a lot of poetry?"

"Yes. And when I had my phone I used to post them to Instagram too." As soon as I say it I regret it. I don't want her knowing about my Instagram page. She's bound to tell Vincent.

"Really?" She looks genuinely surprised. "I'd like to see them."

OK, this has got to be a trick. If I show her the page she'll make me take it down, or Vincent will, at least. "Why? So you can make me take them down? Don't bother. I've stopped writing. You've won, OK?"

Mum recoils when I say this. "It's not a case of winning."

I sit up and glare at her. "Of course it is! It's all about him winning."

"Him?"

"Vincent. He's not happy until everyone's doing exactly what he wants them to. Can you really not see it?"

Mum's about to say something when the doorbell rings. "Wait there," she says, like I'm going anywhere.

I lie back down and listen to the soft tread of her steps down the stairs and into the hallway.

"Clementine," Mum calls up the stairs a few seconds later.

I frown. There's no way it can be for me. Can it? I get out of bed. "Yes?"

"There's someone from your dance school at the door. They want to speak to you."

I go out onto the landing feeling completely confused. Why would someone from my dance school come here? How would they even know where I live? I've never brought anyone from the Academy back here.

"It'll only take a minute," a young guy's voice calls out from the door. I gasp in shock. It sounds like Tyler.

I race into my room and pull a hoodie on over my pyjamas.

"Come inside for a minute, keep the heat in," I hear Mum say.

I hurry downstairs and see Tyler standing in the hallway. His hair is down, tumbling in brown waves around his jaw-line, annoyingly making him look even more like Luc from my dreams.

"I've got to get ready for Pilates," Mum says, hurrying past me. "We'll finish our chat when I get back, OK?"

"OK," I murmur but all I can think is: what is Tyler doing here? And how did he find me? And why did he tell Mum he was from the Academy?!

"Hello, Clementine," Tyler says with a massive grin. "I hope you don't mind me calling round like this but I just had a couple of questions about the – uh – ballet routine."

The thought of Tyler doing any kind of ballet routine makes me bite my bottom lip to stop myself laughing. "Yes, of course."

"Hello," he whispers.

"What are you doing here?" I whisper back.

"Rudy sent me." He coughs and takes a phone from his pocket. "OK," he says loudly. "How many – uh – pirouettes do we have to do before I lift you in the pax de deux?"

"Do you mean *pas* de deux?" I say, now fighting the urge to scream with laughter.

"Yep, that's the one."

"Erm, four."

"Four? That's great." He moves closer. "Rudy's outside."

"Really?" I blurt out, way too loud.

Tyler frowns. "Yes, it's great that it's four because – uh – four is my favourite number."

Now it's impossible to stop grinning. Rudy is outside. Somehow they managed to find me. *They cared enough to find me.*

"Are you going to be home alone any time soon?" Tyler whispers.

"Yes," I whisper back. "Mum's about to go to Pilates."

"Great." Tyler hands me the phone. "Put this in your pocket."

I look at him blankly.

"So we can contact you," he explains.

"Ah, right." I shove the phone in my pocket as I hear Mum's footsteps on the stairs.

"Thanks so much, really looking forward to dancing with you," Tyler says loudly.

"Yes, me too." I open the door to let him out and quickly scan the street for any sign of Rudy, but the pavement is empty.

"See you soon," Tyler whispers before bounding down the steps.

I go back in and shut the door behind me, feeling full to the brim with excitement and relief.

RUDY

"Well?" I look at Tyler hopefully as he gets back into the car.

"Well, the ballet dancing cover story worked a charm – until I forgot what that stupid pas thingy was called."

"Did you see her?" I practically yell.

"Yes, I saw her."

"Cool!" I exclaim. "And did you give her my phone?"

"Yep."

The tension that seemed to have turned my entire body to stone eases slightly. The first stage of my cunning plan is complete. "How was she?"

"I didn't get the chance to ask, her mum was hovering about in the background. Clem looked pretty tired though."

"Did she seem pleased to see you?" All week I've been fighting the nagging doubt that Clementine might have done a disappearing act because she couldn't be bothered to hang out with me any more.

"Oh, for sure." Tyler nods enthusiastically. "And she seemed really pleased when I told her you were out here."

"She did?"

"Yeah. And her mum's about to go to her Pilates class, so she'll be on her own soon."

"Great! Right, time for Stage Two." I hold out my hand and he passes me his phone. I quickly send a text to my phone. Thankfully, Tyler reminded me to turn off the password setting before giving it to Clementine.

Hey! We're just outside waiting for your mum to go out. See you VERY soon!

"Come on," I say, staring at Clementine's front door, willing it to open. Tyler's phone vibrates with a message.

OH MY GOD! THANK YOU!!! XXX

The words send a jolt straight to my heart, like the time Clementine linked pinkies with me in the police car. She *is* happy to hear from me.

"Here we go," Tyler says, nodding towards the house.

I watch as Clementine's mum comes down the steps and gets into a bright red sports car. Like everything else in this street it's polished to perfection. Tyler puts on his cap and pulls it down over his face before Clementine's mum drives by. "Now I feel like I'm on a proper stake-out," he says with a grin.

"Right, let's do it!" I say.

"Don't you want to wait a few minutes?" he asks. "Check the mum isn't going to come back for something?"

"No, I do not." I hand him his phone. "Call me if any of them come back."

"Will do."

I get out of the car and start running towards Clementine's house. The door swings open the second I knock on it.

"Oh, Rudy!" Clementine exclaims. "It's so good to see you!"

"You too," I reply. "Oh wow, you look terrible!"

"Thanks!" she says, pulling me into the hall.

"Sorry – I didn't mean…" She really does look terrible, though. The whites of her eyes are streaked with pink and the roots of her hair are greasy.

Thankfully she starts laughing … or is she crying? Her eyes are suddenly shiny.

"What the hell's been happening?" I ask as Clementine closes the door behind me.

"I went through Vincent's things to find my phone and he caught me."

"No way!"

"Yep. But that's not the worst of it. I was on the phone with my dad and Vincent told him what happened with the police. He tried to make out that he was just being a good stepdad confiscating my phone; that he was trying to save me from a life of crime."

"Shit."

"Exactly. And now I can't even speak to my dad." Clementine looks at the front door nervously, like someone might come through it at any minute. "Shall we go into the kitchen, so we're by the back door, just in case…"

"Sure. But don't worry, Tyler's keeping watch outside. He's going to call straight away if anyone comes back."

"Cool."

I follow her along a grand hallway. The floor is tiled in black and white squares like a giant chessboard and a huge chandelier hangs above us, sparkling silver. The kitchen runs the entire width of the back of the house. It's practically the size of my whole flat. As I look around at the huge cooker, the island-style counter in the middle of the room and the industrial-sized fridge-freezer, all beautifully illuminated by golden spotlights in the ceiling, anger prickles at me. It's the feeling I get when I'm reminded of how unfair life can be. But Clementine isn't a part of this privilege, I remind myself. She's a prisoner of it.

"Would you like anything to drink?" Clementine asks.

"Nah, I'm good," I reply. "So, what are you going to do?"

"What do you mean?"

"About him?" I glare at a huge framed black and white photo of Vincent staring down at us from the far wall. "You can't let him get away with this. You can't let him stop you from speaking to your dad. It's bad enough that he's made you stop speaking to me."

Clementine gives me a weak smile. "I hate that he's made me stop speaking to you."

Hearing this makes my heart sing with relief.

"I wanted to message you but Vincent – he told me that if he caught me having anything to do with you he'd go to the police."

"What the Jeff?"

"What the *Jeff*?" Clementine grins and my cheeks burn.

"Sorry, it's one of Tyler's stupid sayings. I'm clearly spending way too much time with him!"

"Right." Clementine's smile fades.

"What did your stepdad mean when he said that he'd go to the police? Does he seriously think it's illegal to be friends with me?"

"He said he knew people in high places, that he could get them to charge you for defacing private property."

"Wow." I look back at the portrait on the wall and fight the overwhelming urge to deface Vincent.

"I didn't want to get you into trouble." Clementine leans against the counter in the middle of the kitchen. It's horrible to see her like this, so pale and drawn. It's like someone's taken a giant eraser and rubbed away all of her colour. I need to bring it back.

"Firstly, I really don't think he can do that. I mean, I know he was some kind of big shot, like back in the seventies..."

"Nineties," Clementine corrects me.

"Yeah, whatever. He was a big shot in the last century. No, scrap that, in the last millennium, but now he's nothing but a has-been. When I was trying to find out where you lived I saw all these stories online about him. Apparently no one's listening to his show any more. He's just a loser looking for someone to pick on." I step closer to Clementine and take hold of her arms. "And we're not going to let him win."

CLEMENTINE

"Dave gave me this – he thought maybe we'd be interested." Rudy takes a folded-up flyer from her jeans pocket and hands it to me.

"A street art competition?" I murmur as I scan the words.

"Yep. What do you reckon?"

"You should go for it."

"What do you mean, me? *We* should go for it."

"But how can I? I've been banned from seeing you."

Rudy sighs and I feel horrible. But there's no way I'd be able to enter any kind of competition with her. It would be way too risky. All of the excitement I felt at seeing her and Tyler has disappeared. They'd be better off carrying on without me.

"Do you want to use my phone to call your dad?" Rudy asks, breaking the awkward silence.

"I can't. He lives in Germany. It would cost a fortune."

"Text him my number then. Ask him to call you."

"I don't know." Vincent's words ring in my mind like one of the annoying jingles from his show. *He couldn't give a shit about you. He didn't even stay in the same country as you, that's how little*

258

he cares. "I don't think my dad cares that much, to be honest."

"What? Why?"

"He lives in Berlin."

"So? Do people who live there not care about their kids? Is it like a Berlin thing?"

I laugh. "No, it's not that. It's…"

"I thought you said you see him most holidays."

"I do."

"And he calls you every week."

I nod.

"That doesn't look like not caring to me. And trust me, I should know – I've got a degree in uncaring dads. No, actually, make that a PhD."

Rudy's smiling but I can tell it's masking years of pain.

"Do you never hear from your dad?"

She shakes her head. "No, never."

"And you have no idea where he is?"

"Nope." She looks down at the floor, scuffs the toe of her boot against the counter. "And do you want to know the really pathetic thing?"

"What?"

She pulls a wallet from her pocket, opens it and fishes out a photo. "I still carry this around with me, just in case." She passes the photo to me. It's of a man in a pork-pie hat and tight-trousered suit grinning at the camera, his eyes cat-like, just like Rudy's.

"Just in case?" I ask softly.

"Just in case I ever do see him. So I'll recognize him," she says quietly. She takes the photo back and shoves it in the wallet. "Anyway, I know all about having a dad who doesn't give a shit and your dad doesn't sound like that, not at all. You need to tell him what's going on. How can he help you if he doesn't know the truth?"

I nod. It's like Rudy is unravelling the knots of confusion Vincent tied me in, helping me find my way back to the truth. I look at her phone, lying on the counter in front of us. "Shall I send him a text then?"

"Yes!" Rudy exclaims.

I grab the phone and type quickly:

Dad, please can you call me on this number immediately. It's an emergency. Clem xxxx

I put the phone back down and stare at it. Every second that ticks by is a reminder of what Vincent said to me. *He . . . tick . . . doesn't . . . tick . . . care . . . tick . . . about*— The phone lights up with an incoming call.

I grab it and answer it. "Dad?"

"Clem? What's wrong?"

Rudy grins at me.

"Oh, Dad, everything!"

RUDY

As Clementine tells her dad the terrible truth about Vincent – about how he'd taken her phone and banned her from seeing me and how he generally makes her life a misery – I nervously pace up and down the kitchen. For all I know her real dad might not give a damn. But I had to do something, suggest something that might help. I just hope it wasn't all for nothing.

Clementine falls silent and I hear the tinny echo of a man's voice on the other end of the phone but I can't work out what he's saying. I study Clementine's face to try and work out if the conversation's going well. Her eyes start filling with tears. *Crap!*

"OK," she says. "No, it belongs to my friend Rudy… Yes, the artist…"

What is he saying? The suspense is practically killing me.

"Thank you… OK… No, no, don't say anything… OK. Thank you… Love you too." She ends the call and puts the phone on the counter.

"Well?" I practically yell.

"He was so upset."

"In a good or bad way?"

"A good way. He's going to call Mum later. He wants to talk to her about what's been happening with Vincent and he wants me to come to Berlin next week, during half-term. I hadn't planned to go, as I'd been auditioning for a dance show and I wasn't sure if I'd get a part. But I didn't, so I can." She smiles at me, her eyes gleaming.

Even though it's great to see Clementine look happier I feel a sudden pang of sorrow. It must be so nice to have a dad who actually wants to see you, who gets upset when you're hurting, who tells you he loves you. I notice something flashing on the counter. It's an incoming call on my phone, but this time from Tyler.

I grab the phone and answer it.

"Where the hell have you been? Enemy incoming!" he yells, like he's playing Call of Duty. At the other end of the house I hear the front door slamming.

"Oh no!" Clementine gasps. "Quick." She hurries me into a little room off the kitchen, housing a tumble dryer and washing machine. Thankfully, it also contains a back door, which Clementine unlocks. "You can get to the street down the passageway on the right," she says, then she grabs me in a hug. "Thank you," she whispers in my ear. "I've really missed you."

"I've really missed you too," I whisper back.

CLEMENTINE

I race back into the kitchen, my heart pounding. Please, please don't let it be Vincent. Mum comes in and puts her car keys on the counter. She looks really stressed. Oh no, did she see Rudy coming in?

"You're back early," I say, fake calmly.

"I kept thinking about what you said," Mum says. "About Vincent."

"Oh?" OK, this is good. She clearly didn't see Rudy.

Mum looks at me, her expression deadly serious. "I don't want you to feel like that."

"Like what?"

"Like he makes me feel – defeated." She goes over to the fridge and pours us both a glass of juice and takes them over to the table. "How did you and the artist girl get to know each other?"

I instantly feel a prickle of suspicion.

"This isn't a trap," she says, as if reading my mind.

"Online." I go and join her at the table.

"How?"

"I like to write poems inspired by pieces of street art I see in Brighton. I take a photo of the artwork and post it on Instagram with my poem. She was one of the artists I used for inspiration and she saw my post and messaged me."

"I see." Mum's expression is impossible to read.

"She's really nice, Mum. She's not a criminal. She's so talented."

"I can see that."

I look at her, puzzled.

"I really liked the artwork she did, at Brighton station... I loved your poem too."

"Seriously?"

"Yes." She takes a sip of her juice. "I feel like I've let you down," she says in a voice so small I can barely hear it.

"What do you mean?"

"I wish I could leave – take you and Damon away from this – from him – but I can't."

"Why not?"

"He's the one with the career, and the money. He told me that if I ever left him I'd never see Damon again, that he'd go to court for full custody."

So I was right. That *was* one of the things Vincent's been threatening Mum with. I'm about to say that there's no way any right-minded judge would give Vincent full custody but then I remember what he told me about going to the police about Rudy, and how I'd believed him. I have an idea. "Can I show you something? I'll need to borrow your phone though."

"Sure." Mum takes her phone from her handbag and passes it to me.

I do a quick search for my Instagram page and the picture Rudy and I did down by the seafront before it got damaged. "Read this," I say, zooming in on my poem and handing her the phone.

"Did you – did you do this?" Mum asks.

I nod. "Read the words."

I wait while Mum reads.

"You wrote this?"

I nod. "You mustn't believe what he tells you. If you want to leave him you should."

Mum shakes her head. "I can't. But there is something I can do." She stands up. "Wait here."

I sit in the kitchen, trying to process everything that's happened this morning. I think of Rudy and Tyler turning up out of the blue. The conversation with Dad. And now Mum finally opening up to me. This morning when I'd woken up, everything had felt so hopeless, like nothing would ever change, but I was wrong. Change can come at any minute – even when you're least expecting it. Mum reappears in the kitchen.

"Here." She hands me my phone.

"But what about Vincent?"

"I'll deal with him."

"Are you sure?"

Mum nods. "You're *my* daughter, not his." She looks back at her phone, at my Instagram feed. "Your generation are amazing."

"What do you mean?"

"You're so fearless."

"We're not, Mum."

"But look at what you and your friend did. That takes real courage."

It's been so long since I've had a conversation like this with Mum that hasn't been overshadowed by Vincent I don't really know how to react or what to do.

"Back when I was your age there was this thing called the ladette culture. It was meant to be all about empowering women but nothing really changed. The men still got to be the stars of the show – in Vincent's case, literally." Mum sighs. "I was the producer of his show. I was the one who came up with all the ideas that made it such a success. There were loads of talented women at the radio station but most of them were hidden behind the scenes."

"Couldn't you do that again? Go back into radio producing?"

"I don't think so. Vincent says things have really changed."

Hmm, I bet he does. "Maybe we shouldn't believe everything Vincent says. I mean, he's hardly been a huge success on the radio without you, has he?"

I see a flicker of recognition in Mum's eyes.

"Seriously, Mum. You need to start thinking about you."

RUDY

As we head out of Clementine's street Tyler glances across at me. "So, how was she?"

"Not good. And she can't do the competition with me."

"You're kidding."

"No. Her stupid stepdad has banned her from having anything to do with me. He says if she does he'll call the police on me."

"What the Jeff!"

"Can you stop saying that!" I snap.

"Hey, what's up?" Tyler reaches out and touches my arm.

"Nothing. Everything. I don't know." I slump back in my seat. "I'm sorry." Even though it was great to see Clementine, and she was so pleased to see me, the sadness that started in her kitchen is souring everything. I shouldn't have shown her the photo of my dad. I hadn't looked at it in ages. Seeing his face again ... it's like I've taken the lid off the pain I'd been storing away and now I can't get it back on again.

Tyler pulls over to the side of the road. "OK, what is it? What's wrong?"

I stare through the window at the dark murky sea blending into the pale murky sky – the perfect colour chart to match my mood.

"I just…" I don't know what to say. Tyler knows about my dad leaving but I've never told him about the pain it caused me. I've never told anyone. "I'm just fed up about Clementine's stupid stepdad."

"Are you sure that's all?" Tyler gives me one of his X-ray stares. Damn him and his Jedi mind powers. But I can't tell him the truth, it's too pitiful.

"I don't want to lose Clementine, you know, as a friend," I mutter.

"But why would you lose her?"

"She's not allowed to see me. And she's going to Berlin next week, to stay with her dad for half-term. She got him to call her on my phone so she could tell him what's been going on."

"But that's just for a week, right?"

"Yeah but…" A horrible thought occurs to me. What if Clementine has such a great time with her dad she doesn't want to come back? What if she asks him if she can move there?

"What if she ends up moving there?" I make the mistake of looking at Tyler and my stupid eyes fill with stupid tears.

"Moves there? Why would she move there?"

"Because she's so unhappy here. Because of her troll of a stepdad and her dumb-ass mum. Because her dad cares about her and wants her to be happy."

Tyler looks so upset at the prospect of Clementine moving

away, it stops me in my tracks. Why should he care so much?

"Why are you so bothered?" I stare at him.

His face flushes and he looks away. "It's been nice … hanging out with her."

"Do you like her?"

"No! Well, yes, I—"

"Oh my God!" I undo my seat belt.

"What? What's wrong?"

"Not everything's about romance, you know." I have no idea why I said this. It's as if my anger and fear have formed a crazy potion inside me and it's bubbling out all over the place. The thought of Tyler and Clementine as a couple is practically as bad as her going to Berlin. Where would I fit in? I open the car door.

"Where are you going?" Tyler says.

"For a walk. I need to clear my head." *Don't slam the door. Don't slam the door*, I tell myself as I get out of the car. But I can't help it. Hothead Rudy is now in full gear. I slam the door and march off down the street. Part of me wants Tyler to get out of the car and come running after me and hug me and tell me it's all going to be OK. But after a few seconds I hear the rev of an engine and he speeds away.

Don't cry, don't cry, don't cry, I repeat in my head in time with my feet. This is what I hate the most about life – the way things can fall apart at any second and without any warning. I turn sharply and head down to the beach. Thankfully there's hardly anyone down here as the weather's so crappy. I march over the banks of pebbles towards the sea. Then I take the photo from my wallet.

I think again about Clementine talking to her dad on the phone and how he was so worried about her and wanted to see her. *He wanted to see her.* He didn't just leave with no warning and no explanation. He stayed in touch. He still sees her regularly. I look at the photo of my dad, at his stupid grin and the way it seems to be mocking me. Why do I want to be able to recognize him? He's never coming back to me. *He's never coming back.* I hold the photo in front of me and tear it in two. Then I tear both halves in two and I keep on tearing until the pieces are the size of confetti. A wave comes crashing in, licking at the toes of my boots. I pull my arm back and fling my last reminder of Dad into the sea.

CLEMENTINE

Mum and I end up chatting for ages about my collaborations with Rudy and the work Mum once did as a radio producer. I'm hoping that getting her to remember who she used to be will help her remember who she really is. She's just finished telling me about an award she won for the first show she ever produced when she looks at the kitchen clock. My heart sinks. She's bored of chatting. She's thinking about something else she needs to do; something else she needs to clean most probably. I prepare myself for the inevitable disappointment.

"Come with me," she says, getting to her feet.

I follow her upstairs and into the spare room at the end of the landing. She fetches a pole from the wardrobe and uses it to open the loft hatch in the ceiling, then pulls the ladder down. I haven't been in the loft for years but Mum spends loads of time up there, clearing and sorting, when she runs out of things to tidy and clean in the rest of the house.

"Come on," she says.

I sigh as I follow her up the steps. I can't believe that after the heart-to-heart we've just had she wants me to help her sort out the loft. Surely there's nothing left to do.

Mum turns the light on.

"Oh, wow!" In this day of shock twists, the loft has to be the biggest of all. It's like the polar opposite to the rest of the house. For a start, it's the only room that isn't arranged symmetrically, and there's no sign of white either. The walls are lined with storage rails and boxes and the carpet is only visible in patches, in between piles of books and clothes and CDs and framed pictures. Even though it's a large space it's made cosy by the low sloping roof.

"This is my haven," Mum says, with a shy smile.

"Really?" It's hard to imagine neat-freak Mum feeling at peace among all this chaos. I follow her over to a pile of boxes in the far corner.

"You talking about your friend Rudy made me think of Gina," Mum says.

Gina was Mum's best friend forever. Pretty much literally. Their mums met on the maternity ward right after giving birth to them and instantly bonded. They went to the same schools and even the same university. Gina was like a member of the family – I even called her Aunty Gina when I was little – but she and Mum lost touch a few years ago.

"We had such great adventures together." Mum fetches a photo album from one of the boxes and hands it to me. "This was when we went on a road trip around Scotland – we were eighteen. We wanted to do Route 66 in America but we couldn't afford it." She laughs.

I flick through the photos. Mum is barely recognizable, not just physically, with her soft curves and long, curly hair, but emotionally too. She looks so happy. The final picture in the set is of Mum and Gina perched on the bonnet of an old-style Mini, their arms draped around each other's shoulders, their heads thrown back, laughing.

I look from the picture to Mum now and her toned, thin, Lycra-clad body. It's as if all of her soft edges have been chiselled away. "Why did you and Gina lose touch?"

"We kind of drifted apart after I had Damon. And then Vincent had an argument with Tony, her husband, so it all got a bit awkward."

"Right." I look back at the picture. I've never seen Mum looking this happy and carefree. I can't help wondering if Vincent's argument with Tony was intentional – separating Mum from Gina so he could wear her down.

"Aha, this is what I was looking for." Mum hands me an envelope of photos. They're of crowds of people holding banners at a demonstration. The words "WAR" and "PEACE" feature a lot.

"Here we are." Mum points to a couple of young women with brightly coloured peace symbols painted on their faces.

"Is that you and Gina?" I stare at the picture in disbelief.

Mum nods. "It was at the Stop the War demo in 2003 – against the threatened Iraq War. It was the largest protest march ever held in London – not that it made any difference. We still went to war, but it felt so good to be a part of it." Mum sighs. That was two years before I was born. She was still with Dad then. She was still happy. "Your dad was there that day too," she says, as if reading my mind. "He was the one who took the pictures."

I flick through the photos to a close-up shot of Mum leaning against a red phone box. It was clearly taken when she wasn't looking. She's smiling at something out of shot and she looks so beautiful, so natural. I wonder if Dad saw her beauty too; if that's what made him take the picture. "Do you have any photos of Dad on the march?"

Mum shakes her head. "Vincent…" She breaks off. "I got rid of them when I married Vincent."

I look around the loft, at the rails of Mum's old clothes, the piles of books and the CD collection. It's like being at some kind of weird museum exhibition: "The Former Life of Julia Grayling". "I don't understand…" I say, not wanting to upset her.

"What?"

"Why did you let Vincent change you so much?"

"It's complicated," Mum says quietly. "I was in love in the early days. He was so funny and exciting to be around. He made me feel really alive."

Much as it's making me cringe to hear her talking about Vincent like this, I take comfort from the fact that at least it's in the past tense.

"But then, after I had Damon and I gave up work, everything changed. *He* changed and I…" She trails off again.

I feel a weird mixture of anger and sorrow. Anger that

Vincent not only stole my dad away from me, he took my real mum too. And sorrow that I never really knew the fun, happy Mum from the photos – or at least I was too young to remember her. But maybe it's not too late. Maybe I can find her again.

"Why don't you get in touch with Gina?" I say. "I bet she'd love to hear from you."

"Oh no, I can't." Mum looks genuinely horrified at the prospect.

"Why?"

"We parted on pretty bad terms."

"But all of this has to count for something." I gesture at the photos.

"Maybe."

"You're still that person, Mum, that person in the photos."

She laughs drily and puts the photos back in the box. "Come on, we'd better get back downstairs."

I follow her down the ladder, vowing to myself that I'm going to help Mum find her real self again and no one, not even Vincent, is going to stop me.

RUDY

After my ceremonial burial of my dad at sea I stomp along the seafront back to Brighton. I can't believe Tyler and I have had a fight. We never fight. I keep checking my phone to see if he's messaged but there's nothing and I don't know what to say to him either. How do I explain that the thought of him liking Clementine filled me with fear? I can barely even understand it myself. It's not as if I *like* Tyler – just the thought of it feels gross, due to the whole honorary sibling thing. It was more the fear that I'd end up losing them both if they got it together. One of my favourite old-school hip-hop groups, De La Soul, once did a song about three being a magic number. But there's nothing magic about it if two of the three get loved up. Then it's just plain awkward.

I'm so lost in my thoughts that it's only when I see the old pier, like a black line drawing against the paper-white sky, that I realize I'm now dangerously close to my ruined picture. I know that looking at LADZ's handiwork is the worst thing I could do right now but hey, I'm in the middle of the world's greatest self-pity party, so I have a perverse desire to add to my misery. But as I approach the steps I see that my ruined picture has completely disappeared and there's a brand-new one in its place. The new picture is so good it stops me dead. It's of two young guys dressed in hoodies, low-slung jeans and snapback caps, leaning against a wall. One of them is saying to the other in a speech bubble: Are you all right, mate? And stencilled at the bottom are the words:

MATES, LOOK OUT FOR EACH OTHER
#SUICIDEPREVENTION

I feel a weird sense of relief. If my picture was going to be covered up with anything, I'm really glad it was this. But then I see something that causes my breath to catch in the back of my throat. In the very bottom corner of the picture is a tag – the LADZ tag. Wait… *What*??

CLEMENTINE

I lie on my bed and listen to the thunderous rumble of Vincent's voice downstairs. He and Damon have just got back from London and I'm guessing from his raised voice that Mum must be telling him she's given me back my phone. Fear nips at me. What if he comes up and takes it back? What if he makes Mum's life even more of a misery? I've got no time to lose.

I quickly go onto my Facebook app and do a search for Gina. Thankfully, her surname is Hermet rather than something super common like Smith, so I'm hoping there won't be too many to sift through. As I wait for the search results to load, I pray that Gina isn't one of those older people who doesn't do social media. Thankfully, only three results come up and I spot her profile immediately. Her bright auburn hair is now cut into a short bob but I can tell instantly from her smile that it's her. I click on the option to send her a message, then bite my bottom lip. What should I say?

In the end I decide to try the honesty-is-the-best-policy policy, and tell her that I'm worried about Mum. From what Mum said earlier, it sounds as if they fell out pretty badly, so

I need to say something that will hopefully convince Gina to give their friendship another chance. I write about Vincent and how he's worn Mum down. I write about how shocked I was to see the photos of her and Mum when they were younger and how much happier Mum seemed then. I write that I'm scared for Mum and I don't know what to do. By the time I've finished the message I feel weirdly lighter. For years, I've carried the reality of what's been happening at home, like a terrible secret. Finally telling people the truth feels like a huge weight being lifted. But is it right to tell Gina? Wouldn't it make Mum angry to know that I've told her such personal stuff?

I hear the rumble of Vincent's voice again and a door slamming and before I can talk myself out of it, I press SEND. Almost immediately my phone bleeps with a new message. My spirits lift as I see that it's from Dad.

Hey, just wondering if your artist friend would like to come with you to Berlin? I'd love to meet her. And don't worry about the money. I'll pay for her flight. xxxx

RUDY

I end up staring at the new picture by LADZ for so long I can no longer feel my fingers or toes from the cold. When I'd seen his picture of the giant butt cheeks I'd assumed he was just some sexist idiot who didn't really care about anything meaningful but clearly I was wrong. Just like I was wrong to lash out at Tyler before. Annoyingly, I hear Mum's voice in my head, sharing one of her favourite Jesus quotes: *"If someone slaps you on the one cheek, honey, turn to them the other also."* Jesus didn't say "honey", by the way, that's just how Mum likes to personalize her sermons to me. I usually hate it when she says this, especially as she's got just as much of a hot temper as I do, but maybe sometimes it's right to not lash out. If I hadn't painted the shorts on the butt cheeks LADZ wouldn't have ruined my picture, and if I hadn't accused Tyler of being some kind of romance addict we'd still be hanging out. A terrible thought occurs to me. What if he doesn't want to be my friend any more? I need to make amends – for everything.

The first thing I do is find the LADZ account on Instagram and request to send him a message. It takes me ages to come up with the right words.

Hey, I'm sorry I painted the shorts on your butt cheeks –
even though I still believe it's wrong to objectify women. Just
saw the piece you've painted by the beach. If my picture had
to be covered up with anything I'm glad it was this. Truce?

Two hours later, I'm knocking at Tyler's door, armed with what I hope will be the perfect peace offering. Tyler's dad, Kevin, answers. He looks pale and his eyes are ringed with dark shadows. He's looked this way ever since he lost his job. And I know that his worry affects Tyler too. I feel so crappy for having snapped at him when he's got so much to deal with and he's been nothing but the best of friends to me.

"Hello, Rudy," Kevin says, opening the door wide to let me in. "He's in his room."

I breathe a small sigh of relief. At least Tyler hasn't told his dad to ban me from entering.

I head past the living room, where I can hear one of Tyler's mum's favourite quiz shows blaring from the TV. Part of me wants to go in there and join her and pretend to be really excited about John from Milton Keynes knowing that there are fifty states in America, to avoid the awkwardness of what's to come. But I can't. I have to put things right. I take a deep breath and knock on Tyler's door. There's no reply and my heart sinks. He doesn't want to see me. Then I realize that he doesn't even know it's me and that he's probably listening to music on his headphones and hasn't even heard me knock. I don't want to barge in on him, so I take my phone from my pocket and call him.

I hear movement from inside the room and start counting the seconds, praying he'll pick up.

"Hello." His voice comes at me in a weird kind of surround sound, through the phone and the door.

"Hey," I say softly. "I'm really sorry."

"That's OK." He sounds quiet. Sad.

I turn and lean against the wall beside his door. "I was being an idiot. I was scared I was going to lose you."

"Why would you lose me?"

"Because I have a habit of losing the people I love the most." It's so hard for me to utter these words I'm practically whispering.

"You'll never lose me, Rudy. You're my Jedi sis."

"Thanks, bruv." I'm so choked up my voice comes out like a squeak.

"Wait a second. Where are you?" I hear more movement from the bedroom and Tyler flings open the door. "What are you doing out here?" he says, looking totally bewildered.

"Delivering some of your favourite fajitas," I say, holding out a takeaway box from Dos Sombreros. "And waiting for a hug," I add, looking down at the floor. Within a second his thin arms are wrapped around me.

CLEMENTINE

I'm so excited at Dad's message I have to call Rudy immediately. The phone rings a couple of times before it's answered but there's only silence.

"Rudy?" I say cautiously.

"Clementine? Holy guacamole! Have you stolen your phone back again?"

I laugh. "No. My mum got it back for me."

"Seriously? How come?"

"She was feeling really bad about everything and we had a really good chat. But that's not why I'm calling. I'm calling because I've got some exciting news. Well, an exciting question. At least I hope it will be."

"What is it?"

"My dad just messaged."

"Oh, right."

"He asked if you'd like to come to Berlin with me! He said he'll pay for your flight."

More silence. I'm hoping it's from excitement rather than disappointment.

"So, what do you think? Would you be able to get a few days off from the café? You'd love Berlin, seriously. The street art there is amazing. Maybe it could inspire us in our competition entry…"

"You want to do the competition?" Now Rudy definitely sounds excited.

"Absolutely. I've decided that I can't let Vincent win, but I'll tell you all about that when I see you. So, what do you think? Would you like to come to Berlin?"

"But don't you want some quality time with your dad? Wouldn't I get in the way?"

"Of course not! I'd love you to come … if you want to?"

There's another pause and then I hear her laugh. "Of course I want to! Wow, I can't believe this is happening."

I try and maintain my cool, even though I'm so excited I want to bounce up and down like Tigger. "Great. I'll be in touch again tomorrow, to sort out the flight details."

"Amazing." There's a beat of silence. "Thanks so much." I'm not sure if it's a crackle on the line or Rudy's voice cracking with emotion.

"That was Clementine," I say to Tyler as I end the call.

"Yeah, I figured." He immediately looks awkward.

"I'm so sorry about what I said earlier. I was really out of order."

"It's OK." He prods at his fajita with his fork. "I'm not obsessed with romance, you know."

"I know. I don't know why I said that. I was being really stupid." I look down at my lap to try and hide my embarrassment. "It's just that I panicked. I don't want to lose you – as a friend, I mean. It's not that I like like you or anything. I mean, the thought of you and me together is kinda gross…"

"Thanks!" Tyler laughs.

"I'm sorry!" I groan.

"You could never lose me as a friend," Tyler says, now deadly serious. "I mean it. You're my sister." He shifts along the bed and gently leans against me.

My entire body exhales with relief.

We sit like that in silence for a moment, both staring straight ahead. Then Tyler turns to me. "I think you're pretty gross too, to be honest," he says with a grin, and we both start chortling like kids.

I get home from Tyler's nice and early, to catch Mum before she goes to bed. Now that I've got things sorted with Tyler I'm so excited about a potential Berlin trip. I'm so happy, in fact, that when I find Mum and Dave cuddled up on the sofa watching a movie it doesn't make me cringe at all – well, only a little bit. But of course, I should have known it was all too good to be true. Instead of beaming with joy at my news, Mum immediately frowns.

"What do you mean, her dad will pay for you?" She purses her lips and gives me one of her death stares. "Does he think we're some kind of charity?"

"No. I think he was just trying to be nice."

"Oh, really?" Mum gets up from the sofa and starts pacing. "I've never even met this man before. Or his daughter."

"You were at work when she came round," I say.

"She's a lovely girl," Dave adds.

Mum shakes her head. "Yeah well, lovely she may be, but we're not accepting their charity."

"What if I paid for it myself then?" I offer. "I could ask for an advance on my wages from the café."

"You can't go swanning off to another country to stay in some strange man's house."

"He's not a strange man, Mum. He's my friend's dad."

"No, Rudy, I'm sorry. I'm not happy about this."

"Why don't we sleep on it?" Dave suggests, standing up and putting an arm round Mum's shoulders.

Mum shakes his arm off. "The only thing I'm sleeping on is my bed and if you want to be sleeping there too you'd better stop right now with trying to help her get her way. I mean it."

Dave looks at me and shrugs helplessly.

I think of Clementine going to Berlin on her own and her dad asking her to move in with him. Without me there she might agree. She might feel as if there's nothing here for her. And all because Mum's too proud to accept so-called charity. The injustice of it all eats into me. I treat Mum to a death stare of my own. "I might never see her again and you don't even care."

"Oh, sweet Jesus, enough with the melodrama." Mum sighs and shakes her head. "She'll only be away for half-term. You'll see her when she comes back."

I turn and walk from the room, too angry to say what I'm thinking: *But what if she doesn't come back?*

CLEMENTINE

The first thing I do when I wake up on Monday morning is check my phone, hoping I've got a message from Rudy. But there's nothing since the message she sent last night:

Won't be able to come to Berlin. Really sorry.

WHY????? I'd replied but I'd heard nothing more from her. And still there's nothing. There's been no reply from Gina either. I try to ignore the fear now bubbling away inside me and I get out of bed. I have to go and see Rudy.

Once I'm dressed I come out onto the landing and lean over the bannister to see if I can hear Vincent in the kitchen. A cough from behind me makes me jump. I turn and see him standing by his bedroom doorway in his tracksuit. It's the first time I've seen him since Mum gave me back my phone and ungrounded me. I'd stayed in my bedroom all of last night to avoid him.

"Morning," he says curtly.

"Morning," I mutter, swallowing down my fear. In a couple of days I'll be in Berlin, I remind myself. I'll be free from Vincent, for a few days at least. If only Rudy was able to come with me. *Maybe she doesn't want to come with you*, my inner voice taunts, like some kind of trainee Vincent. I push the thought from my mind. I'm going to go and see Rudy at the café and get to the bottom of it. Part of me wants to head straight out the door but I need to let Mum know I'm going. I don't want to give her or Vincent any reason to ground me again.

When I get to the kitchen I'm surprised to see Mum still in her dressing gown. She's usually up and dressed before anyone else. Must be because it's half-term. In another twist, Vincent is actually making his own breakfast, angrily shaking some cereal into a bowl.

"I'm just popping into town to get some travel toiletries for Berlin," I say to Mum.

"OK, honey. See you later."

Vincent slams his bowl down on the counter. Pathetic. I grab a banana from the fruit bowl and head out the door.

Outside, it's the first sunny day in what feels like ages. Everything looks so much better, brighter. The sea is sparkling and the people I pass look so much lighter too. It's as if the whole of Brighton is shaking off the heavy coat of winter. It's only when I get to North Laine that I start feeling nervous. I hope Rudy won't mind me turning up out of the blue but I didn't want to give her the chance to turn me down in a message. When I get to Kale and Hearty it's bustling with people having breakfast. I see Sid clearing one of the tables and go over to him.

"Hey, is Rudy in today?"

He looks at me blankly for a moment before his face lights up with recognition. "You're the poet!"

"Yes, I am." It's so cool to be greeted in this way my tension fades slightly.

"Hold on a sec." I wait as Sid goes behind the counter and calls into the kitchen, "Rudy!"

"What's up?" Rudy appears in the doorway wearing a white apron over her T-shirt and jeans.

"Visitor for you." Sid gestures at me.

"Oh."

I study Rudy's face, unsure if she looks shocked or unhappy to see me. Either way, she isn't smiling. My heart sinks.

"I'm sorry to bother you at work," I say as she comes over.

"Don't be silly. What is it?"

"I just … I was wondering… Is there any way you'd change your mind about coming to Berlin?"

"It's not that I don't want to come," she says quickly.

"Then what is it?"

"The money." She looks down at her feet.

"But my dad said—"

"I can't accept his money."

"Oh."

"I was going to ask if I could get an advance on my wages." Rudy lowers her voice. "But I'd be leaving them in the lurch as it is, going away at such short notice."

What she's saying makes perfect sense but there's something

about the way she's saying it that feels off somehow, like she's not being totally straight with me.

Tyler appears behind the counter and looks over at us. Then I realize the real reason Rudy doesn't want to go – she'd rather be here with him. I feel a hot flush of embarrassment at my stupidity.

"OK, well, I'll get out of your way then…"

"You're not in my way."

I'm so embarrassed now I can barely see. I turn to go. "I'll see you next week, when I get back – if you want?"

"Of course. Look I—"

"Have a good week." I hurry out of the café, overwhelmed with disappointment.

RUDY

"OK, what did that onion ever do to you?" Tyler calls across the kitchen as I bang my knife down over and over again until I've chopped the onion on my board to smithereens.

"It didn't, it's just an innocent victim, caught in the crossfire of my stupidity," I mutter.

"Want to talk about it?" Tyler wipes his hands on his apron and comes over.

"I feel like such an idiot."

"Hey, that's no way to talk about my Jedi sis." He nudges me playfully.

"Why not? I deserve it."

"Is this something to do with Clementine's surprise visit?"

I nod.

"I'm not allowed to go to Berlin with her."

"What? Why?"

"My mum had one of her hissy fits. She thinks letting Clementine's dad pay for my flight would be accepting charity. Anyway, it's too short notice. She's going tomorrow. I wouldn't be able to get the time off from this place."

"Who says?" Sid appears in the kitchen at just the right – or wrong – moment. "Seriously, do you want some time off?" he asks, coming over to me.

"She's been invited to go to Berlin," Tyler says, clearly appointing himself my official spokesperson.

"Oh wow, that's amazing." Sid's face lights up. "Berlin is incredible. You'd love it there."

"Yeah, well, don't worry about it," I reply. "I can't go."

"If you're worried about taking time off I'm sure we could cover for you," Sid says.

"Absolutely," Tyler agrees.

"Honestly, it's all good. Forget I ever said anything."

"All right then." Sid places his hand on my shoulder. "But if you change your mind just let me know. You haven't had any time off in ages. You're more than entitled to it." I feel myself deflating like a burst balloon as he goes back into the café. I know he's being nice but that only makes it worse.

"I'll lend you the money," Tyler says. "You can take it from my mixing console fund."

"No way!"

"Think about it at least."

"But my mum says no, so..."

"Since when have you let that stop you?" Tyler says with a grin.

CLEMENTINE

My flight to Berlin is due to take off just after midday. I take the train to the airport, turning down Mum's offer of a lift. Things between her and Vincent are so tense now I don't want to add to it. Besides, I need the chance to decompress. There's something about train journeys that really helps me sort out my thoughts, something so soothing about watching the world stream by outside, putting distance between me and my problems. I still haven't heard from Gina so I'm guessing I never will. Hopefully my trip will inspire me to come up with some other way to help Mum.

When I get to Gatwick I follow the route to the terminal on autopilot. I've been making this journey for three years now and as soon as I turned fourteen, I started doing it by myself. Mum used to freak out at the thought of me flying on my own, even though she'd drop me off at one end and Dad would pick me up at the other. I'm not sure what she thought was going to happen. I mean, airports have got to be one of the safest places in the world, what with all the security. Normally, when I travel to Berlin on my own, I like to pretend that I'm already living my dream life and I'm off on some kind of adventure as a world-renowned dancer or poet, but today I'm finding it impossible to slip inside a dream. Thoughts of Rudy and Mum keep blocking me.

I stop by a tall stand advertising the Tourist Information centre, right in front of the departures board. My eagerness to leave the house means I'm super early. I'm about to head to Check-in when my phone starts buzzing. When I see that it's a call from Rudy I almost drop the phone in surprise. I haven't heard from her at all after our awkward encounter in the café yesterday.

"Hello," I say nervously.

"Hey, where are you?"

I frown. It sounds like her voice is coming from behind me. I walk around the stand. Rudy is there, looking down at the floor, her phone clamped to her ear. "I'm right here," I say.

When she sees me her face lights up.

"What are you doing here?" Her backpack is on the floor, the big one she uses when she's doing her street art.

"Coming with you to Berlin … if the invitation's still open?" There's a nervousness beneath her usual tough exterior.

"What the…?"

"Jeff?" she says and we both start laughing.

"How? I mean… I thought you said your mum… My flight leaves in a couple of hours… Y-you don't have a ticket," I stammer.

"Who says?" Rudy taps something on her phone and passes it to me.

There's an airline ticket on the screen. I check the flight number and check my boarding card to double-check. It's for the same flight as mine. "But how…?"

"Dave. Turns out he's not such an idiot after all." Rudy grins. "I'm really sorry about yesterday. My mum told me I wasn't allowed to go but I was too embarrassed to tell you. It seems Dave had a word with her last night and somehow convinced her to change her mind. He brought me up here this morning and told the airline I'd be travelling with you and luckily they still had some seats free. They booked me on the same return flight as you too. Hope that's OK?"

I feel like someone who just won the lottery, without even realizing they had a ticket.

"You do still want me to come, right?" Rudy asks. It's weird seeing her look so nervous.

"Of course I do. Oh my God, this is amazing." I want to hug her so badly but I manage to stop myself.

Dave comes striding over, holding a cup of coffee. "Aha, you've found her," he says when he sees me. He holds up his phone. "I just need to get some info from you, Clementine. Got to keep Rudy's mum happy – or stay off her hit list, at least."

Rudy grins. "Thanks so much for doing this."

"No problem. It's not every day you get the chance to see Berlin. I spent a summer there, back in the nineties," he says to me. "Just after the Wall came down. It was one of the best times of my life."

I nod in agreement, although it's weird to think of Berlin

positively. For so long I've resented it as the city that took my dad away from me. "What do you need to know?"

"Your dad's name and number and address. She wants his email too, for some reason."

"Sorry about this," Rudy says, looking embarrassed. "It was the only way she'd let me go."

"It's fine," I laugh. I don't care what her mum needs to know, as long as it means Rudy can come with me. Once I've given Dave the information I message Dad and tell him the good news. Thankfully he doesn't seem fazed by this last-minute change of plans. Can't wait to meet her, he replies.

"Right then, you two had better get going through security," Dave says. "I'll hang around here for a bit, have another coffee. So, if there are any issues just call me."

"Will do," Rudy says. She looks at him for a moment, then grabs him in a hug. "Thank you," she mutters, before pulling away and looking at the floor.

"You're welcome." Dave grins. "Have fun. But no getting arrested 'cos I won't be there to bail you out."

"We didn't get arrested!" Rudy and I chorus and all three of us start laughing.

Rudy swings her backpack over her shoulder and we head to security, my skin tingling with excitement and disbelief.

RUDY

I decide not to tell Clementine that I've never flown before. It was embarrassing enough having to tell her about Mum almost banning me from going to Berlin. I don't want her to think I'm a total kid. One thing I definitely wasn't prepared for was the Security guard. Talk about an attitude problem. As I hand the guy my passport he stares at me like it's got "INTERNATIONAL DRUG-DEALING TERRORIST" stamped right across it. *Don't say anything; don't do anything,* I tell myself, fighting the urge to yell, *What exactly is your problem, mister?* Thankfully, he finally stops staring at me and I'm allowed through. I meet Clementine by the conveyor belt and pretend to be completely unfazed as we wait to collect our things. The truth is, I'm anything but unfazed. I can't believe this is happening.

Once we've got our bags we head into the departures lounge and over to a café. As I watch the barista get our hot chocolates I think of Tyler and Sid and Jenna. It was so good of Sid to give me the days off. We take our drinks over to a table and talk about Berlin, and Clementine lists all the places she wants to show me. I try to concentrate on what she's saying but all I can think of is that soon we will be up in the sky in what is essentially a giant tin can. The more I think about it, the more I don't understand how planes manage to fly. It's completely unnatural. Where is Tyler when you need him? I bet he knows all the science behind it. I bet he'd be able to reassure me.

"Penny for your thoughts," Clementine says.

"What?"

"I was just wondering what you were thinking about. You looked so deep in thought."

"Oh, I was just thinking about Tyler."

"Ah." Clementine looks up at the departures board. "OK, better go – our gate's been called."

I quickly finish my drink and follow her out onto a long concourse. By the time we get to our gate I feel as if we've walked halfway to Berlin. If only we could walk all the way. As I look out of the window at the huge plane outside my mouth goes so dry I can barely swallow. We sit in the waiting area for ages but as soon as a heavily made-up woman in an airline uniform tells us it's time to board it feels like our wait is over way too soon. The woman starts calling out seat numbers. Thankfully, when Dave booked my ticket they were able to put me next to Clementine. I'm not sure how I'd cope with the fear now threatening to suffocate me if I had to sit next to some random.

Finally, it's our turn to walk along the gangway to the plane. My pulse starts pumping a fierce beat. Seeing the plane does nothing to calm me. Up this close it's huge. I don't get how it can defy the laws of gravity. And I can't work out why the flight

attendants who greet us are so smiley. How can they put themselves through this terror every day? But at least they're getting
paid for it. Unlike the rest of us, who are actually paying for the
privilege of being scared to death. On and on my fear rants.
We find our seats and I copy Clementine and put my bag in the
overhead locker. As soon as I sit down I put on my seat belt. Not
that it's going to help, if it actually came down to it.

"Are you OK?" Clementine asks.

I nod, my mouth too dry to speak.

"Do you like flying?"

I shrug, like I'm all *whatevs*, when really I'm all *WHAT THE
HELL*???

Thankfully she changes the subject and starts talking about
this poet she loves called Emily Dickinson. I half listen, half
continue to have a meltdown.

Once everyone is seated the pilot, whose name is Jeremy
and who sounds like one of those mega posh dudes in the royal
family, tells the crew to prepare for take-off. At this point my
fear is so intense it's like there's a massive bass drum pounding
away inside me.

The plane heads over to a runway and the engine starts
to roar. I sit back in my seat and silently say Mum's favourite
prayer, even though I think religion's for losers: *Help me, Jesus...
And sorry for not believing in you*, I quickly add. The engine's
roar gets louder and the plane picks up speed. I look out of the
window at the airport whizzing by. The ground starts slipping
from view and the nose of the plane tilts upwards.

"I love this bit," Clementine exclaims.

The noise and the speed mingle with the adrenalin coursing through my veins. The plane climbs higher and higher. It's like being in a rocket. And now we're in a cloud. We're actually in a cloud! And then suddenly, there's a flash of sunshine. The plane levels out. The sky is brilliant blue and the snowy-white clouds below us look like a magical kingdom made from marshmallow. My fear turns into a high. And suddenly, I love flying. I turn to Clementine and grin.

"I love this bit too."

CLEMENTINE

Thankfully, by the time we land in Berlin, Rudy seems to have stopped thinking about Tyler. All the way here I fought the urge to ask her about their relationship. If anything, she's got happier and happier as we've got further from the UK and by the time we touch down in Germany, she's more animated than I've ever seen her.

As soon as we get through Customs I take her to buy a Welcome Card – a pass that gives you unlimited travel on Berlin buses and trains – then we follow the walkway outside to the station.

"This is so cool," Rudy murmurs as we walk past the airport pub, which has been made from wooden beams to look just like an alpine lodge.

"Bratwurst…" Rudy reads from a sign as we walk past a stand. "Is that like the German equivalent of a hotdog?"

"Yes and they're everywhere," I reply.

"Cool." Rudy's eyes are saucer-wide. If she's this impressed with the walk between the airport and the station, she's going to love the city.

"We've still got a couple of hours till we meet Dad so I thought

I'd take you to my favourite place. I have a feeling it might be your favourite place here too."

"Cool," Rudy says again.

When we get to the station a train to the city centre is waiting at the platform. We get on and sit down and Rudy stares all around, drinking every detail in. Seeing her expression reminds me of the first time I came here and how weird it felt, being surrounded by signs and announcements and people speaking a different language.

"Is this your first time in Germany?" I ask.

Rudy nods. "It's — it's my first time anywhere — abroad, I mean."

"Really?" I'm not able to disguise my shock. "Hang on a minute. Does that mean you've never flown before?"

Rudy shrugs but I can tell she's embarrassed and I wish I'd never said anything. "Yeah, well, I've always been too busy — with school and work and stuff."

"Sure. That makes this even better then. I'm honoured that your first trip abroad is with me." As soon as I say it I worry that it sounds too over the top but thankfully Rudy grins.

"Yeah, well, so you should."

We settle back into a comfortable silence and I gaze through the window as the green of the Berlin suburbs gradually fades into the grey of the cityscape. When the train gets to Alexanderplatz I nudge Rudy. "This is our stop."

I lead Rudy out of the station and around the corner and point across the road. "Here we are." I point to the first of the brightly coloured murals. "It's all that's left of the Berlin Wall, which used to separate the east of the city from the west. When they tore the Wall down in 1991 they kept this part and turned it into an art gallery. Artists came from all over the world to paint murals on it."

Now Rudy looks impressed. "Wow."

The traffic lights change and we cross over. Rudy gazes at the first mural, then off down the street. The wall stretches further than the eye can see. She looks back at me, for once her expression is soft and unguarded.

"I think this might be the best day of my life," she says quietly, before turning to look back at the picture.

RUDY

Walking along the Berlin Wall gives me the same feeling I got when the plane was taking off. With every mural we look at, my spirits soar to a higher altitude. There are so many different styles of artwork on display here, from bold abstracts that remind me of Jean-Michel Basquiat, to cartoon characters and more muted pictures in pastel shades of grey and blue.

"This is one of my favourites," Clementine says as we reach a painting of a wall bursting open and a sea of faces pouring through. The colours are beautiful. The soft yellow, pink and peach of the faces contrast sharply against the dark blue background and the stark white of the wall. It reminds me of what the Berlin Wall used to be for and it sends a shudder through me.

"Can you imagine if something like this happened in the UK?" I say. "Like, what if the government decided to build a wall between Brighton and Hove and we weren't allowed to see each other just because of where we lived?"

"I know. It's horrible, isn't it?" Clementine replies. "But that's why I love this gallery. It's proof that building walls between people doesn't work."

We walk on. In spite of the cold, grey weather there's still quite a lot of people about, stopping to take photos and selfies. Up ahead of us a small crowd has gathered around a dark-haired, heavy-set man sitting on a crate in front of a small card table. He's doing the classic magic trick where the crowd has to guess which of three beakers a ball is under. He's not very good, though. As he whisks the beakers round, the bright blue of the ball is clearly visible beneath the yellow one. Sure enough, one of the people watching guesses correctly and wins ten Euros.

"It's all a con," Clementine whispers as we walk past. "He gets his friends to pretend to play and win to make it look really easy. Then, when someone else plays, he moves so quickly you can't see where the ball is and he ends up taking their money."

There's something really grim about this; turning the Wall – and everything it should symbolize – into a place to con people out of money. We carry on walking and come to a painting of an old-style white car bursting through an eggshell-blue wall.

"That was the kind of car the East Germans used to drive," Clementine explains.

I look at the tag at the bottom of the picture. It says Birgit K. It sounds like a woman's name. I imagine what it must be like to be asked to create a piece of art for somewhere as iconic as this, not to worry about anyone destroying it, or arresting you. I take a photo of the painting to send to Tyler, and we carry on walking.

"This is probably the most famous of all the murals here," Clementine says as we get to a close-up painting of two men kissing. The most impactful thing about the painting is that the kiss seems so unlikely. The men look so old and strait-laced, and they're dressed in the kind of formal suits managers would wear to a business convention.

"Do you know who they are?" I ask.

"I think they were the Soviet and East German leaders," Clementine says. "Hang on, I'll check." She takes her phone from her pocket. "Yes, that's right. Apparently it was based on an actual photo of them kissing." Clementine points to the words painted along the bottom. "And apparently that says 'God help me to survive this deadly love affair'."

"Wow."

This is definitely the most popular of all the murals, with more people than ever clustering around taking pictures, some of them kissing in front of it.

"It's funny, isn't it?" Clementine says, breaking me from my trance. "Politicians think they have all the power, but really it's the artists. The artists speak the truth."

I pause for a moment, to really let her words sink in, as if I'm taking a mental photograph of this moment. Because I never want to forget it. I never want to forget this place and all it represents. I never want to forget this feeling of finally arriving where I was always supposed to be. And then, before I can stop myself, I grab Clementine in a hug.

CLEMENTINE

I arranged for us to meet Dad by the television tower. As soon as the huge structure looms into view, glowing white against the darkening sky, Rudy gasps.

"It's Berlin's equivalent of the Eiffel Tower, or Nelson's Column in London," I explain.

"Or the Clock Tower in Brighton," Rudy laughs. "It looks like a giant wand." She takes her phone from her pocket and takes a photo of it. "I've got to send a picture to Tyler."

The only downside of Rudy's enthusiasm about Berlin is that she keeps sending photos of things to Tyler and this keeps setting off little wistful pangs inside me. If only I had a Tyler to send things to. Or *the* Tyler to send things to. *No. No. No.* I push my wistful thoughts from my brain.

"It was built back in the days of the Wall," I tell her, remembering what Dad told me when I first came here. "Europe didn't allow East Germany to have enough airwaves to broadcast television programmes, so they built this themselves. I think it was their way of saying, we don't need you."

"Like a giant 'eff you'." Rudy laughs.

"Exactly."

Rudy turns slowly in a full circle, taking in the shops and the station and the concourse crowded with commuters making their way home. "This place is so interesting."

I wait for her to say, "I wish Tyler could see it" but she doesn't. Instead she just smiles. But it's not her usual cocky smile; it's a lot softer, shyer. "Thank you so much for inviting me."

"Thank you for coming. I was…" I break off, unsure if I ought to say it.

"What?"

"I was really disappointed when I thought you couldn't come."

"Me too."

"I mean, I know we haven't known each other all that long but…" Again I run out of words.

"But?" She looks at me.

I think of how she hugged me earlier and I decide to risk sounding over the top and uncool. "But I think you're great and I'm so pleased we're friends—"

"Clementine!" Dad's voice interrupts me. I turn and see him striding across the precinct towards us. As usual, his tie is askew and his coat is flapping open. Dad's one of those people who look scruffier the more they try to look smart. The tension of the last few weeks, which I'd been wearing like a protective skin, begins to slip away.

"Hey, Dad," I call, my voice suddenly wobbly.

As soon as Dad reaches us he hugs me. I inhale the trace

of his aftershave. I feel myself shrinking back to a smaller version of me; one who used to curl up for hours on his knee. Dad lets go and turns to smile at Rudy. "And you must be the infamous Rudy."

"Dad! She's not infamous!" I say, my cheeks beginning to burn.

"Yes, I am." Rudy grins.

"It's great to meet you," Dad says, holding his hand out in greeting.

Rudy takes his hand and shakes it vigorously. "Good to meet you too, sir."

Dad laughs. "No need for that. Valentino will be fine – I always wanted to be called Valentino."

"That's not your name?" Rudy looks confused.

"It is – it's his idea of a joke," I say, cringing.

"Oh, right." Thankfully Rudy laughs and actually sounds like she means it.

Dad claps his hands together. "So, are you guys hungry?"

"Yes!" Rudy and I say in unison.

"Great. I told Ada we'd meet in that Italian place by the station. Then maybe over dinner you can show me some of your artwork," Dad says to Rudy, "if you've got any pictures on your phone?"

"Sure."

"I still can't believe you got arrested."

"We didn't get arrested!" I exclaim.

"We got let off with a caution," Rudy says.

"Well, whatever. So, how long have you been doing street art, Rudy?"

As we make our way across the precinct and Dad and Rudy fall into conversation it feels so bittersweet. If only my life could always feel this happy, and this easy.

RUDY

It turns out that Clementine's dad is really nice and the evening flies by as he and his partner, Ada, tell me all kinds of cool facts about Berlin. By the time we get back to their apartment, which I'm relieved to see is way closer in size and appearance to my flat than Clementine's house in Hove, I'm feeling that weird kind of wired-tired from all the excitement and travelling.

"We've set up an airbed for you in Clem's room," her dad says, showing us into a room next door to the lounge. Although he's called it Clem's room, there's no real sign of it being hers. No pictures on the wall, or books on the shelves. There's even a cot in the corner.

"Oh," Clementine says, looking really surprised.

Her dad smiles as he follows her gaze. "Yes, we're getting ready for the new arrival. I hope you don't mind but we were thinking of painting this room yellow – to make it look more like a nursery."

Clementine's doing this strange impression of a smile but I can tell it isn't for real. I can see the hurt in her eyes. Over the years I've often wondered if my dad has got a new family somewhere and that's why he no longer cares about me. It's a horrible feeling.

"Are you OK?" I ask as soon as her dad says goodnight and leaves the room.

"Yeah." She sits down on the end of her bed. "I just wish…"

"What?" I sit down next to her.

"I wish I didn't feel so alone," she says.

"What? You're not alone," I exclaim. "You've got me for a start."

"I know but sometimes I wish I had – this is going to sound really pitiful…" She breaks off, her face flushing.

"Go on…"

"I wish I had someone special," she practically whispers, "like Dad has Ada and you have Tyler."

"You do know that Tyler and I – we aren't together. He's just my friend – well, more like a brother."

"Really?" Her face breaks into a grin. The kind of goofy grin someone gives when they've just been handed a surprise gift.

But although the thought that she might like Tyler gives me a sinking feeling, I realize something even stronger. True friendship is about putting someone else's happiness above your own fears. If Clementine and Tyler do like each other I've got to figure out a way to deal with it.

CLEMENTINE

Rudy and Tyler aren't together. It's weird because even though this news made me ecstatically happy at first, the feeling soon faded. Ever since Rudy hugged me earlier, by the Wall, I've felt like our friendship has moved onto a new, deeper, level and I don't want anything to ruin that. She and Tyler might not be going out but they're so close, it would still feel really awkward if anything were to happen between him and me. I'm just about to get ready for bed when my phone pings with a Facebook message. As I take it from my pocket I tell myself not to get excited – it could be from anyone. But it's not – it's from Gina.

"Oh, wow," I exclaim under my breath.

"What is it?" Rudy asks.

"I've got a message from my mum's old friend." My fingers are trembling as I click on it. What if Gina's angry that I contacted her? What if she's telling me she wants nothing to do with Mum? As the message opens I catch a glimpse of the word "lovely" and I relax slightly and start to read.

Dear Clementine,
It was such a lovely surprise to hear from you! And I'm
sorry it's taken me so long to reply – your message had

gone into my "other" folder on here, as we aren't Facebook friends. I was very upset to hear about your mum – not to mention angry! Reading your message was confirmation of my worst fears about Vincent. The minute your mum fell pregnant with Damon he started trying to control every aspect of her life – even down to the friends she had – or didn't have. Anyway, I would love to meet up with her again. I've missed her so much and feel terrible for giving up on our friendship. Just let me know what you want me to do. Sending you lots of love,
Auntie Gina xxx

I put my phone down and sigh.

"What is it? What's happened?" Rudy asks.

"My fightback against Vincent has officially begun."

RUDY

On our second day in Berlin, Clementine and I take the bus to the Jewish Museum. As soon as we sit down at the back of the bus I feel my phone vibrate. I assume it's yet another of Mum's messages checking that Clementine's dad isn't a mass murderer and he hasn't baked me up into a pie or something, but when I check I see that it's an Instagram message … from LADZ. My heart instantly starts to race. For a second I think of ignoring it – I don't want anything to ruin my time in Berlin – but if I don't read it I'm just going to be stressing about what it might say. I click the message open.

> No worries. I'm sorry for ruining yours too. Maybe
> I'll run into you one of these days. Peace.

"Is it your mum again?" Clementine asks.

I shake my head. "No, it's LADZ."

"What?" Clementine's eyes go saucer-wide. "As in the guy who ruined our picture?"

I nod and tell her about the message I sent him.

"What did he say?" she asks. I show her my phone. "Wow."

"I know." Even though I'll always think LADZ's butt cheek picture was stupid I can't help feeling a wave of relief.

"What do you think he means about running into you one of these days? Do you think he wants to meet?"

I shrug my shoulders like I don't care but there's something about his words that is making me have to fight the urge to grin. I picture LADZ and me sitting on a bench by the seafront, and me schooling him in the evils of misogyny.

"Well, at least we know he won't ruin any more of our art… If we're ever able to make any more," Clementine adds wistfully.

"Oh, we will," I say, looking out of the window, my mind buzzing with determination and excitement.

The Jewish Museum is in a residential neighbourhood lined with tall apartment blocks. It looks like one of those super posh stately homes you get in the countryside back in England, with an ornate cream façade and a red-tiled roof.

"There's a whole newer part to the museum at the back," Clementine says as we cross the road. "The architect who designed it wanted the building to make a statement."

"What do you mean?"

"It's hard to explain. You'll see when we get inside."

We walk through the entrance straight into airport-style security. As I follow Clementine through the body-scanner, the implications are instantly sobering.

We leave our coats and bags in the cloakroom and walk through to the newer part of the museum, where the architecture dramatically changes. It's like no building I've ever been in before, with jagged corridors and sloping floors. The exhibits are arranged along long corridors lined with glass cases, each displaying some kind of object or photo, every one telling a story. Each corridor is called an Axis of something. The Axis of Emigration tells the stories of the Jews who fled Berlin at the start of the war.

I stop in front of a glass case containing a handmade card, decorated with a dried, pressed violet. The description next to it tells the story of a couple called Ernst and Rosa Jakubowski who emigrated from Berlin to Italy. Ernst was arrested at the outbreak of the war and taken to some kind of prison camp. He'd sent the card to Rosa from the camp to celebrate the arrival of spring. The flower is faded now and the card is yellowing with age but there's something so beautiful about it. Even though Ernst was trapped inside a prison camp, even though he'd been torn away from his wife and family, he still had the urge to create. And he created something full of joy and hope. I feel a weird kind of energy rising inside me. Even in the face of the worst kind of evil, people can create beauty. People *must* create beauty.

I carry on reading and my heart practically cracks in two. Ernst was deported to Auschwitz and died on a death march from the camp. I swallow hard to try and stop myself from crying. I look back at the flower on the card. I think of what Clementine said yesterday at the Wall, about artists having the power because they speak the truth. I think of how many people must have seen this card and its terrible, beautiful truth. And I make a silent vow to never stop telling the truth through my painting. For the sake of Ernst and all the fierce artists who came before me.

Next to me, Clementine winces as she reads Ernst's story. We walk on in silence.

When we reach the end of the corridor we go into a narrow, triangular-shaped room. It's empty and the walls reach up the entire height of the building and the only light is coming through a slit in the ceiling. There's something suffocating about it, like being in a prison. I think back to what Clementine said about the person who designed it wanting the building to make a statement and I realize that this entire place is a work of art. But reading these personal stories is shattering. The families who were torn apart. The love stories with such tragic endings. It makes me feel ashamed for getting so stressed about Tyler liking Clementine and for being so selfish.

We reach another weird triangular-shaped room. In this one there's a huge stone trough filled with faces made from flat metal discs. A sign on the wall explains that it's a memorial to all the victims of war. As I look at the sea of faces it reminds me of the painting of all those faces bursting through the Berlin Wall. But these faces aren't joyful, their mouths are wide in expressions of fear. I shiver at the horror of it all but also at the power of art to make me feel like this.

As we leave the room I turn to Clementine. "How did the Nazis get away with it? How were they able to kill so many Jews?"

"I don't know." Clementine shakes her head. "They tried to wipe out anyone who didn't fit their so-called perfect ideal. Gypsies, people with disabilities, gay people."

"I guess I wouldn't have exactly gone down well with them either," I say with a shiver. "I don't understand why some people get so hung up on our so-called differences. Why can't we just focus on what makes us the same?"

We go up some steps and into a room painted lime green. After the stark grey of the rest of the building the brightness feels dazzling. Long strings of small square cards hang like bunting from the ceiling. As we get closer I see that the cards are covered in handwriting.

"What are they?"

"Messages from people who've visited the museum. Do you want to write one?" Clementine nods towards a pile of blank cards on the side.

"Sure."

I take a card, then read the cluster hanging closest to me. *Politicians should be made to spend an hour a week in this place to get some perspective*, one of them says. *Love not hate*, says another. Others are in languages I don't understand but it doesn't matter because I know exactly what the sentiment will be. Clementine sits down on one of the giant beanbags in the middle of the room and starts writing. As I think about what I could write on my card I feel overwhelmed with emotion. There's so much hate in the world but there's so much love too. All I know for certain is which side I want to be on. Then I get one of those magical creative downloads Clementine talks about and an idea for a picture drops fully formed into my mind. I quickly sketch it out on the card. It's of my and Clementine's faces in side profile, joined together to form a double-faced head. As I shade in my skin and hair with the pencil I wish I had some colours to make it more impactful.

"What did you write?" Clementine asks, coming over.

"I didn't. I did a drawing."

"Oh, let's see." She looks over my shoulder at the card. "Is that — is it you and me?"

"Yes," I reply softly. So what if she thinks it's cheesy. This place has stripped all of the pretence from me. "I just wanted to do something that celebrates diversity instead of fearing it."

"I love it!"

"You do?"

"Yes. Could I — could I add something to it? Some words."

"Of course." I hand her the pencil and watch as she writes in bold capitals beneath the picture.

UNITY IN DIVERSITY

Four months later...

CLEMENTINE

The summer sunshine pours in through the long arched windows of the living room, causing the dust in the air to sparkle like glitter. I stand in the middle of the room, slowly turning, taking in the teal walls and the piles of books and the stacks of records and the squashy sofa, crammed with brightly coloured cushions. Then I have a sudden, freaky realization. I'm standing in the Brighton flat of my dreams. Only I'm not dreaming. This really is my new home – or Mum, Damon and my new home. And the best thing about it is, it's in Kemptown, and only a five-minute walk from Rudy's.

I hear Mum and Gina laughing in the kitchen and Rudy enters the room holding a paintbrush. Her hair's wrapped in her skull-and-crossbones turban and her jeans and T-shirt are flecked with paint.

"Your mum and her friend are talking about sex," she says with a shudder.

"Uh-oh." I pretend groan, but privately I don't care what Mum's talking about, as long as it makes her happy.

It's been four months since we got back from Berlin and

Gina and I sprung our surprise intervention on Mum – or friend-tervention, as Gina now calls it. I'd taken Mum to Kale and Hearty, under the guise of going for a mother–daughter hot chocolate. When Gina walked in I thought I might be sick with nerves, especially when Mum's first reaction was to burst into tears. But thankfully, they turned out to be happy tears. And thankfully, Gina was able to get through to Mum, and remind her of who she used to be, and give her the courage to finally leave Vincent. Of course, Vincent didn't go down without a fight, but then a tabloid newspaper revealed that he was having an affair with an assistant on his show and it finally gave Mum the ammunition she needed. Vincent put the house up for sale and agreed to give Mum half the proceeds. He even stopped threatening to file for sole custody of Damon.

"I've finished the mural," Rudy says with a grin.

"You have? Can I see it?"

"Of course."

Mum comes flying into the room. Like Rudy, she's also covered in flecks of paint. She and Gina are painting the kitchen hot pink.

"Aha, Rudy," she says, "could you come and give us a hand? I was wondering if you might do some kind of special effect around the kitchen window."

"Sure," Rudy replies. "As long as you stop with your old-lady sex talk."

Mum goes bright red and starts cracking up laughing and I feel another surge of joy course through me.

While Rudy and Mum head off to the kitchen I climb the narrow staircase at the end of the hall, leading to my attic bedroom.

Mum was worried that I'd feel claustrophobic up here after my much larger bedroom in Hove, but nothing could be further from the truth. The sloping ceilings make me feel snug and safe and if I stand on tiptoes, I can see the sea on the horizon between the rooftops opposite.

But I'm not interested in the sea right now. All I can look at is the wall by my bed. As happens so often with Rudy's work, my first reaction is to gasp. The painting is based on the picture she drew in the Jewish Museum. Rudy worked it up when we got back home and we entered it for the street art competition for Bare-Faced Chic. We didn't win in the end but we did come second and Sid got some proper prints of it made, which we've been selling in the café. But I love the version she's done on my bedroom wall even more. The colours are so vivid. And our faces look so powerful. I sit on the floor and gaze up at it. It's so strange to think that I started this year feeling so alone and hopeless but now I have the best best friend ever – and a picture symbolizing our friendship on my bedroom wall. It's almost impossible to take in how much things have changed. One thing is for sure: whatever might happen in the future, I'll always know that change can come calling when you least expect it, and make your bird of hope sing again.

RUDY

I get to Kale and Hearty right before it's due to close.

"Hey, Rudy!" Sid calls, from where he's cashing up behind the counter. "We had another great day with your prints. We totally sold out of the 'Rise' ones and there's only a couple of the 'Unity' pictures left."

"That's great," I reply, joining him behind the counter. "Have I got to the target yet?"

Sid nods and grins. Then he takes an envelope from the till and hands it to me.

"Thanks. Is Ty in the kitchen?"

"He certainly is."

I go through and find Tyler busy cleaning a stack of dishes at the sink.

"Hey, dude, what's up with the old-style washing-up?"

"The dishwasher broke," he says with a sigh, wiping his forehead with the back of his arm.

"How did it go at Clem's?"

"Great. I finished the mural."

"Cool."

"I've also got this." I come over and hold the envelope out to him.

"What is it?"

"Open it and see."

Tyler takes off his rubber gloves and opens the envelope. "It's a load of cash," he says, frowning.

"Not just any old load of cash," I say, shaking my head.

"What do you mean?"

"It's a mixing console fund… For you," I add.

"What – but – how – where did you get this?"

"Don't worry, I didn't rob a bank. I've been saving up the money from our prints. I want you to have it."

"Oh no," he holds the envelope back out to me. "I can't take your money."

"We want you to have it."

"We?"

"Me and Clementine. To be honest, I think she might want you to have it even more than I do." I look at him knowingly.

"She does?" He starts to blush, but it doesn't make me feel weird – well, only slightly.

"Yeah. She really likes you." I swear, if heaven really does exist, what I just did must have surely qualified me for a freedom pass. I hope you're watching, Jesus!

"Wow," Tyler says. He looks back inside the envelope. "But there's – there's enough here to…"

"Get a console? Yes, I know." I put my arm around his thin shoulders and give them a squeeze. "Me and Clem shouldn't be the only ones living our dreams. It's time you started too."

Tyler swallows hard. When he looks at me his eyes are extra shiny. "I really love you, Jedi sis."

"Yeah, well, you're not so bad yourself," I say gruffly. But deep inside it feels as if some kind of curse has finally been lifted, and the armour plating around my heart splits and falls away.

ACKNOWLEDGEMENTS

Many people compare writing a book to pregnancy and it's true that some "book births" are definitely easier than others. I wrote *Clementine and Rudy* during the winter of 2018/19, fuelled by hot chocolate and pumpkin spiced coffee, and the book just poured out of me. I am indebted to a number of people for making it such an enjoyable and inspired process. Firstly, my wonderful editor at Walker Books, Mara Bergman, for believing in my vision for the novel right from the start and for being so excited with the finished product. Thank you for always pushing me to do my best work as a writer, right down to the very last word and em-dash! Massive thanks as always to Jane Willis at United Agents for being such a lovely and supportive agent; the bumpy writing road is so much smoother with you beside me. Huge thanks also to translator extraordinaire Marie Hermet for encouraging the first seed of this novel during our urban art hunt on the streets of Paris – not to mention introducing me to the work of Miss.Tic. Thank you also to Celine Vial and Helene Wadowski at my French publishers, Flammarion, for taking me to Les Frigos for some incredible street art inspiration. And speaking of which, I'm so grateful to all of the talented street artists who have turned Brighton into such a vibrant outdoor art gallery and in doing so, inspired the character of Rudy – Jane Mutiny, Minty, Mazcan, A. Pozas and TrustyScribe, to name but a few. If you don't live in Brighton you can find them and their great work on Instagram.

Thank you to the Jewish Museum in Berlin and the world's largest and most powerful outdoor art gallery, the Berlin Wall, for the vital work you do in reminding the world of the importance and fragility of unity.

Thank you to Greta Thunberg and all of the young activists out there doing such vital work in making the world a better and more compassionate place and giving us all hope for the future.

Thank you to Extinction Rebellion for using art in such a powerful way – seeing your creations pop up around my home town while I was writing this book was a huge inspiration to me.

As well as being a celebration of poetry, art and activism, *Clementine and Rudy* is a celebration of friendship and I am lucky enough to have a fantastic circle of close friends who constantly support and inspire me. Tina McKenzie, Sara Starbuck, Linda Lloyd, Sammie Venn, Pearl Bates, Steve O'Toole – thank you for being my "friend family". And Jack Curham, Michael Curham, Anne Cumming, Bea, Luke, Alice, Katie Bird, Dan and John, thank you for being my family family. I love you.

Thank you to all of the friends I've made through my

writing workshops and coaching. The Harrow and Uxbridge Writers and the Snowdroppers and now my Rebel Writers Community – I'm so grateful to have gathered such a brilliant circle of creatives. (If you'd like to join us – and I'd love you to join us – you can find Rebel Writers on Facebook and Instagram.)

Big love and gratitude to all of the inspirational women I've been lucky enough to collaborate with over the past couple of years who have now become friends: Jessica Huie, Donna Hay, Kate Taylor, Sally Garozzo, thank you for all of the great work you are doing in the world.

Last but never least, colossal thanks to all of the school librarians and book bloggers and readers who have provided such vital support in helping raise awareness of my books. Special thanks to Mary Esther in Ireland and K-Ci in New Zealand for the international cheerleading. And to Nick Tomlinson, my fellow #TeamJaneMaraWalker author – hopefully one day we'll all be in the same room together. And to all of my readers and my publishers in Australia – I'm blown away by your support and dream of the day when I come and thank you personally.

SIOBHAN CURHAM is an award-winning author, editor and writing coach. Her books for young adults are *The Moonlight Dreamers*, *Tell It to the Moon*, *Don't Stop Thinking About Tomorrow* (nominated for the Carnegie Medal), *Dear Dylan* (winner of the Young Minds Book Award), *Finding Cherokee Brown*, *Shipwrecked*, *Dark of the Moon* and *True Face*. She was also editorial consultant on Zoe Sugg's international bestseller, *Girl Online*. Siobhan has lived in many different places but has finally found her spiritual home in Brighton, where she can mostly be found scouring the streets for art, the beach for hagstones and the cafés for coffee.

Connect with Siobhan online…
Website: siobhancurham.com
Instagram: @SiobhanCurham
Twitter: @SiobhanCurham
Facebook: Siobhan Curham Author